EVILUTION

Lisa Moore

authorHOUSE®

AuthorHouse™
1663 Liberty Drive
Bloomington, IN 47403
www.authorhouse.com
Phone: 1-800-839-8640

First published by AuthorHouse   12/27/2011

ISBN: 978-1-4685-0881-9 (sc)
ISBN: 978-1-4685-0880-2 (ebk)

Library of Congress Control Number: 2011961762

Printed in the United States of America

To Curtis
For your love and support
Max
My biggest fan
Mia
My fellow lover of books

Author: Charles Robert Darwin

Believing as I do that man in the distant future will be a far more perfect creature than he now is, it is an intolerable thought that he and all other sentient beings are doomed to complete annihilation after such long-continued slow progress

From Life and Letters.

Special thanks to

Ruth Harriet Jacobs
A mentor and friend

Colette Aufranc
Editor extraordinaire

My family and friends
For your enthusiastic support

CHAPTER 1

Hills College

She was beautiful to observe. Seeing her muscles flex and her sinews draw tight as her powerful legs propelled her forward in a frantic race for her life was exhilarating. As I chase her through the woods I marvel at her speed and agility even if her attempts are futile. She cannot elude me. I am toying with her, enjoying the chase. I can smell the scent of fear in her wake and hear her pulse growing more rapid as her eyes grow wide with terror. She senses I am pursuing her, a malevolent presence, unaware of what I am but knowing I mean her harm. She is right, for when I catch her I will rip her throat open and drain every drop of her precious blood.

I am in a heightened state of arousal, consumed in the moment. She is an easy target, out running in the woods alone. I have toyed with her long enough and now her efforts at eluding me are taking their toll. She is breathing heavily and panic has transfixed her gaze as she tries to find a hiding spot within the trees. She is spent, can run no further and resorts to trying to hide within the camouflage of the woods. What she does not understand is that I do not need to see her to find her. I smell her and hear the blood pounding through her veins. I spring on her as she tries to hide among small brush. I attack with blinding speed and sink my teeth into her smooth neck.

The torrent of blood threatens to shoot out the sides of my mouth as it explodes from her carotid artery, but I drink greedily and cleanly. I have had plenty of practice executing a kill like this. She is not the first to be sacrificed and she will not be the last.

Her body thrashes as she tries to break free but the attempt is weak. Shock sets in and she becomes compliant until at last she is dead and the final drops of her blood drain down my throat. My cells tingle with the influx of this crimson nectar. I feel a rush of energy as the blood of my prey courses through me. The intensity of power felt after a feed is in direct correlation to the type of blood consumed. The higher order the prey, the greater the rush. I am charged up from this latest kill and eager to feed more but the sun will be up in an hour. While these woods are off the beaten path and it is still very early, the sun's light just beginning to brighten the eastern sky, it is risky. There is always the off chance of an early riser or late night partier cutting through the woods going to or from campus nearby. It is time to go, I could easily deal with an intruder catching me on one of my nocturnal adventures, but I prefer to avoid complications.

My customary way of disposing of a kill like this is to dismember the remains and scatter them in the woods. Nature then becomes my ally as all manor of scavenger will feed on what is left of her, leaving little evidence behind. I rip apart her lifeless body with ease, snapping bone and tearing muscle and flesh. The bloodless tissue is still warm as I toss pieces of her throughout the woods far away from the kill site. I cross a small stream and rinse the fat and hair fragments from my hands.

As I finish cleaning myself by the stream I catch a familiar scent that peaks my attention. After a kill I have a harder time suppressing my desires to indulge in killing and feeding more. I get caught up in the frenzy of the hunt and the exhilaration of the blood, the feeling is so powerful it is hard not to want more. I smell potential prey heading towards me. I climb up into a large oak and become invisible in the thick foliage. A herd of deer are making their way through the woods just off a game path. They nervously forage in the underbrush periodically scenting the air, alert for danger. As I watch them move, in near silence below my perch in the oak, I find myself wondering if my last kill was a member of this herd. The beautiful doe I just fed from had a distinctly red shaded pelt and several young deer in this group have very similar coloring.

Caught up in contemplations of my latest prey's lineage, wondering if the young red doe below me would taste as sweet as her mother did, I was suddenly assaulted by another scent, a human female was approaching. This scent elicited a much more powerful reaction in me than the deer had. It was a fascinating mix of earthiness, mingled with soap and deodorant, but something else about her chemical fragrance made my already aroused state reach a new peak.

I could almost taste her, so potent was her pheromone laced aroma. Oh but to really taste her, how long has it been since I have drank straight from the source? This human's scent is intoxicating; it makes me hunger in a different way. Abandoning my original prey, I silently circle back around the deer herd and take position behind the base of a big white pine. From this vantage point I watch her approach. I watch her pulse throb in the graceful curve of her tanned neck and the beat of her heart sounds like a timpani in my head. I focused in on her every step, every breath, as she passed but a few feet away from my hiding spot and walked up the path through the woods toward the back of the campus that abutted this forest. I recognized this human; it was Professor Bean my new teacher getting an early start on the day.

I stayed hidden behind the trunk of the tree and silently climbed it once she was passed. From my higher vantage point I watched as she came upon the herd of deer ahead of her. At first she did not even see them, their camouflage hiding them in the woods. Suddenly she was near them, as they foraged just up ahead on the path. Miraculously they did not hear her approach as she stopped dead in her tracks and stared in awe at the 20 plus white tailed deer 15 feet in front of her, they simply continued to forage.

What the professor did next gave me an insight to her personality and brought a smile to my lips. She sat down right where she stood, in the middle of the path, and watched them. Twenty minutes passed when the breeze suddenly shifted, the tails of the deer stood up revealing how they got their name. The "alarm bell" having been sounded, the deer bounded out of sight in the blink of an eye.

Professor Bean seemed disappointed at the deer's rapid retreat, but when she looked at her watch and noticed she was late to class, she mumbled under her breath and raced up the path to campus. What Professor Bean didn't know was that she was not alone in the woods that early morning. I had followed that same deer herd and it was not her scent that drove them away but mine. What she also didn't know was that had she seen the smile on my lips at that moment, she would have been the one to run. However she could not have gotten away if I wanted to stop her. And finally, she didn't know I had heard her mutterings as she took off late to class. I was 100 yards away and perched high in the branches of an old white pine. She had a distinct New York accent, and I easily heard her mumbled "Crap! Their gonna leave!" as she ran off to campus, referring to students in her Evolutionary Biology class.

I knew the rule, students had to wait 30 minutes into a class before they could leave if a professor was late; she was cutting it close. I followed my new quarry. Out from the wooded path she burst into a group of undergrads as they made their way toward where she now fled. She apologized rapidly, never breaking stride. "Run Bean, run!" shouted one from the group, ala Robin Wright Penn's character from the movie Forest Gump. I watched her chuckle as she ran into the science annex where she apparently had her class. Leaping stealthily across the tree tops, staying in the deeply shadowed boughs, I followed the tree line behind the science annex. I could hear her strong voice coming from an open window on the second floor. Silent and well out of sight in the foliage, I sat atop my new perch in a majestic oak. My birds' eye view and exceptional hearing allowed me to eavesdrop on the class.

She arrived to class 29 minutes late just as her students were packing up to leave. She delivered an impromptu lecture on the evolution of the white tailed deer, focusing in on the evolution of their camouflage and their skills and adaptations for avoiding predation. I was captivated by her lesson, impressed with how she taught in the moment. Everything she taught was tied into the day's reality. She could bring her experience with the deer into the classroom and it was as if each student had been there with her. The rapport she had with her students was easy and confident. She exhibited a passion for biology without her seeming preachy or clichéd and brought alive, topics that would otherwise be buried in vocabulary and memorization. It was what I was so pleasantly surprised to find out about her when I started taking her class this week and one of the reasons why I will be tracking her every move for a while. Something about this woman intrigues me. How strange.

Winter comes early to upstate New York. Hills College is a moderately sized private college, located in bucolic Hills, New York. It is the third week of the fall semester and on a day like today, the campus looks beautiful. The surrounding hills and mountains are a riot of color and the early morning chill has the distinct smell of autumn with hints of winter to come. The peaceful campus is slow to wake.

Ever since the encounter in the woods two weeks ago I have been tracking Professor Bean's every move. I have found that she rarely drives anywhere and often walks through the woods as a short cut to campus. It has become my habit to follow her as she takes her morning walk from her residence to her office. It seems that each days trek is often a mini nature excursion. Today she almost walked right into a skunk as she made her way to the wooded path, the short cut she takes to school. Thankfully Mr. *Mephitis mephitis* was as afraid as she was and ambled off into the trees in the opposite direction of campus.

I broke off from following the professor to her office and went around the back of the science building to class. I entered the lecture hall, it was packed, every seat of the 150 seat, theater style room, filled with sleepy freshman and scattered upper classmen. Coffee cups, snack wrappers and the occasional piece of fruit lay strewn about like the freshly fallen leaves on campus. Just before 8:00, Professor Bean swept into the lecture hall; she brought the scent of crisp leaves, dirt and the faintest hint of skunk. I say swept in because when she moved the professor did so with an athlete or a dancer's grace, confident and sure.

The lingering scent of skunk tickled my nose. I rather liked the smell of skunk, the very earthy nature of it. I took a deep breath trying to inhale its natural aroma. It calmed me. It seemed I was a bit anxious for class to start, or more specifically to see Professor Bean again. My choice to enroll at this college this semester is proving more interesting than I had anticipated and not for the academic stimulation but for stimulation of a different sort, one that has eluded me for some time now.

As she unpacked her chocolate brown, aged leather backpack, she addressed the class. "Good morning! I am pleased to see that after three weeks I still have your interest." It was no small feat to have an 8:00am lecture hall filled by mostly freshmen. Every semester she expected attendance to drop but most semesters she had a packed house three days a week for her introductory science class titled Bio 108—Mysteries, Myths and Monsters. On the first day, the professor said it was her favorite class because it allowed for such freedom to explore new topics. She also mentioned that she taught Anatomy and Physiology and an Adaptations and Evolution class, the latter of which I surreptitiously observed. Her enthusiasm as she introduced the class as an exploration of myth, mysteries and monsters, their possible realities and the supporting scientific evidence, instantly hooked her student's interest.

The first week of class was spent relating some marine myths. Professor Bean talked about mermaids and sea serpents, their deep history in human's stories and the possible explanations for these myths, like the manatee for the mermaid and the giant squid for the sea serpent. She regaled the class with stories of her graduate work aboard the research vessel the SS Duke, which she nicknamed the SS Puke due to the fact that three out of the five grad students aboard were seasick for the first four weeks of the eight week trip. She showed slides of her research, many filled with beautiful and rare photos of elusive sea life.

By the end of the first week, I left class feeling like I had been aboard that ship and swam in that blue green water with the manta ray. It also made me think of some new and interesting hunting opportunities in my future, possibly spring break. It was Professor Bean's ability to weave details into her stories, like color, texture and smell that captivated her students, specifically me. She seemed to have extra sensory perception and an uncanny way of explaining her experience so that you felt it too.

Continuing on the theme of mysteries of the deep, week two was focused on the Loch Ness monster and the history behind maritime sayings like "red sun at night sailors delight, red sun in the morning sailor take warning". All in all, the first two weeks were enjoyable. I found the class and the teacher to be more informative and colorful than I could have hoped for. It is difficult to find new perspective in some ways when you have lived as full a life as I have. I sometimes feel like I have seen it all before. But this woman, this mortal young woman with her thirty something years of experience, somehow has been able to captivate me. She has shown me the world through a different set of eyes, and hers, by the way, are the most intriguing shade of brown with green speckles and hints of gold flecks. Of course to the normal eye, I imagine they just look brown, since most mortals lack the keen eyesight that a creature such as I possess.

This week we have discussed the myth of Big Foot and the Yeti. As I sat reminiscing about the last two weeks, I wasn't even paying attention and had failed to realize that the professor had started her lecture. I was only drawn out of my reverie when she withdrew a very large plaster cast of what appeared to be a foot print left by a Yeti. She explained how in her last semester of grad school, she went on an expedition to the Himalayas with her mentor and two other Grad students. She was just finishing up another story involving her "brilliant, eccentric, hippie, mentor", Dr. Vincent Derezinski. One of many we have heard now. He really seems like quite a character from the way she talks about him, yet she always maintains an overlying sense of admiration and affection for him when retelling adventures they have shared.

Apparently they made this cast when they were following up on reports of a Yeti seen by local villagers. They tracked the creature through densely packed woods, its foot prints obscured by the excited villagers and the dogs used to track the scent, until they found one un-obscured print at the base of a tree. This led to a rocky outcropping where they lost the trail. The class seemed to deflate as she talked about the trail going cold and not having found any more conclusive evidence. It was as if the class had been hanging on her every word, experiencing the thrill of exploration and the excitement of discovery until just around the next bend the trail went cold, eliciting dejected feelings of coming up empty.

As class wound down Professor Bean made an announcement to remember on the way out of class to leave the essays that were due today in the basket on her desk. A student, likely the rare upperclassmen, asked Professor Bean if she personally believed in the Yeti or Big Foot. Her answer, like everything I have seen about this woman so far, left me smiling; although this time my smile was not likely to scare anyone since I was not currently consumed by the hunt.

Professor Bean said "I like to believe in the possibilities of the unknown, the mysterious and the difficult to explain. I am also not so egocentric as to think that we know all there is to know. Remember the story of the Japanese fishing vessel I told you? Their radar showed what they thought was a large school of tuna. When they hauled up the steel mesh nets they used, they were shredded like tissue paper. There was never an explanation as to what did that. And what about the story of the Coelacanth, an ancient fish thought to be extinct since the end of the Cretaceous period over 65 million years ago, caught in fishing net off the coast of South Africa in 1938? For millions of years those creatures went unnoticed, living among us in obscurity. You see, Mr . . . ?" "Stevens", replied the student. "Mr. Stevens, some things have adapted extraordinary means of self preservation, like the ability to use camouflage or the ability to exist in extreme and remote locations, we can't possibly know of all the earth's creatures. Some things just don't want to get caught!" The Professor didn't know how right she was.

As I got ready to leave class, enjoying the strange way I felt after being near her, Professor Bean made one final class announcement. It was her weekly teaser. Every Friday she would let us know the topic for the next week's discussion so we were able to research the most recent information on the subject matter. What she said stopped me from my banal exercises and had I needed to breathe I might have inhaled sharply. I was expecting this; it was the reason I signed up for this class in the first place. Actually it was why I settled on Hills College, of all places, for my latest life chapter.

It has been many years since I lived in this part of the world. I was researching colleges and their various class offerings and it was this class title that drew me in. I always like to keep up with the latest concepts humans have of creatures like me, "the cold ones", "the undead"; vampires. These names show the level of ignorance humans have towards individuals like me. I am not cold exactly, my body maintains a constant temperature of 95 degrees, and the status of my death is complicated. I died as a human, the end result of my transition to a vampire. Now my cells function in the presence of an appropriate blood supply, yet I am not technically alive.

"Next week we will discuss the myth of the vampire, one of my favorite topics in this course. Studying this topic has brought me to some interesting places. I look forward to our discussion next week. Have a nice weekend." It was peculiar really; the reason for me taking this class, the reason for me coming to this small part of the globe, and suddenly, instead of looking forward to hear about her ideas on vampires, I was now terrified how she might feel about them, about me.

How did it happen that I have become inexplicably drawn to this woman? The sudden realization she might be repulsed by the idea of vampires or worse yet one of those who feel they, we, need to be hunted and destroyed left me with an ache where my heart continues to beat out of reflex rather than need. What is it about this woman that makes me feel?

CHAPTER 2

My Beginning

I was born in 1887 to a young couple in Franklin NY, a small town 7 miles south west of Hills College. Franklin was a rural farming community where the population of domestic farm animals out numbered the town's people three to one. My parents, Alexander VanderCreek and Elizabeth Gates VanderCreek were friends since birth. Growing up in a small farming community with a record high of 18 students in their school, every kid was friends with every other kid out of necessity. There just weren't that many of them. But it seemed Alexander and Elizabeth's destinies were intertwined.

They met on the day of their birth April 13, 1869 in the small delivery room in Dr. Monroe's office. A child's birth was an occasional event in the small rural community but it was quite another thing for two women to give birth the same day at the same time. Dr. Monroe had to set up the two beds side by side in the small delivery room. He needed to work quickly to help both women with their deliveries. Alexander arrived at 2:34 pm, crying up a storm; Elizabeth came 7 minutes later. When Elizabeth entered the world, she gave a short cry as if to say, "I am here" and then quickly quieted. At the moment of Elizabeth's birth, Alexander finally settled down and fell soundly asleep against his mother's breast. It was as if Elizabeth's mere presence could calm Alexander. The tired mothers joked "she has a soothing effect on him; they must have already decided to be best friends".

The two young families spent much time together. The young mothers enjoyed each others company and tended their children while their husbands worked. The two families would often eat supper together at one home or the other. The women cooked meals together and helped each other with household chores. When Elizabeth and Alexander were just 14, Alexander declared that Elizabeth would be his wife. Elizabeth just smiled and said "of course I will", as if she had known this fact forever. Three years later the two married. Nearly one year after their marriage, they had me, Maximillian Alexander VanderCreek. My beginning would be the end for Alexander and Elizabeth.

Something happened during the delivery and as a result Elizabeth bled heavily and continued to do so. Alexander was brought in to see his wife and child and wept at the sight of his beautiful Elizabeth, pale as the sheets that she lay upon. Somehow she looked more beautiful, almost angelic, as she gazed lovingly down at her infant son. She cooed into his tiny ear loving words, welcoming him into the world. "You look like a Maximillian. No, something grander, Maximillian Alexander" she said. Alexander kissed Elizabeth's pale forehead and marveled at the site of his newborn son. He watched her cradling their child, until her exhaustion overcame her and she fell asleep. Knowing Elizabeth was too weak to tend to the infant, Alexander asked the midwife, a young woman from town who had lost her husband and child in a fire the year before, if she would take care of Maximillian until Elizabeth was well. She agreed to watch the child and cared for Maximillian with love and tenderness.

Elizabeth died on April 13, 1887 it was their 18th birthday and one week after having me. Alexander was inconsolable. Elizabeth was the calming center of his universe. Her death left him with a hole in his heart. His best friend since birth, his wife, his lover, his reason for being, now lay dead in their bed, drained of her life's blood. The two shared a birthday 7 minutes apart, their entire life was intertwined. Each milestone in life was a shared experience. When they crawled, when they walked, when they talked, even when they lost their first tooth, all these happened within days of the other. Consumed by grief, Alexander lay down in bed, cradled his dead wife against his chest and quietly slit his wrists. Alexander's last breath would come 7 minutes after Elizabeth's. Like everything else they shared in life they would share death. As he held Elizabeth and lay there dying, his last words were a whispered "I'm sorry" to the son he would never get to know.

My father visited me the day before their deaths. He took me to see my mother. At barely one week old I know I can not remember them. The only memories I have of them are someone else's caught on film. Two photographs, one from the day of their wedding, and one from that last visit, with me in my mother's arms and my father helping her hold me. As old as the pictures are, you can still see the life and the emotion caught on film. My mother was beautiful, even in her dying hours. A smile, peaceful on her lips, as she gazed down at the infant in her arms. This, in sharp contrast to the anguish in my fathers face as he looked at his Elizabeth. Sensing her death? I think that is why he brought me to see her, the family, together for one last brief moment. I only know of this because of the kind woman who took me in and raised me as her own child, Genevieve Tully, my mother as far as I knew for those 18 years, told me on my 18th birthday the true story of my beginning and as a gift gave me the two pictures and a letter from my father.

The letter, read and re-read so many times, I have committed to memory was as follows.

April 10, 1887

Dear Maximillian,

    When I look into your small, peaceful face I see your mother's beauty, the graceful line of her lips and honey kissed skin mirrored in yours. Your hair is dark like mine; however your nose is as yet a mystery, the tiny button not yet resembling mine or your mother's. But it is your eyes that look at me with a remarkable clarity for only 4 days old; deep, soul penetrating eyes, which cause me to overflow with both joy and grief. Joy for your pure beauty and the awe I feel at your miraculous creation and grief because I know I will abandon them to follow your mother. When you look at me with those searching eyes, an exact copy of your mother's unique grey blue almost lavender color, I am haunted at the knowledge that your mother's days to look at me with those exquisite eyes are coming to an end. I feel her life slowly slipping away with the trickle of blood that continues to escape her pale figure. It physically drains my will to live as I sit each day by her side unable to help her. She has slept nearly three days and had awakened asking for you. I will bring you to see her today. I sense the time is near. She loves you as do I. I am sorry you will never have memories of your parents' love, but know that you are loved. The look of total devotion on your mother's face right after you were born as she stared down at you breaks my heart, knowing she will not be able to watch you grow into the exceptional man you are destined to become. Forgive me, my son, for leaving you but I have never been without your mother for more than the few hours each night we slept in our own houses as children. Our lives have been linked since birth and I know I can not continue to live without her. I can feel my heart break a little more each day. As your mother moves closer to death, my own death draws near. I can not let her go into the afterlife alone. When the time comes and your mother takes her last breath, so too shall I. I will hasten my sure demise and we will be together always. I am leaving you with a kind woman who has lost her family in a tragedy. She has love to give and a hole in her heart. Perhaps you two will help fill the others void. While it seems that our life no longer has a future, yours just begins. Out of tragedy, good will come, of that I am sure. Be a man who follows the path of goodness my son and one day our souls shall be together again. We love you Maximillian.

Your mother and father,
Alexander and Elizabeth VanderCreek

I loved Genevieve, the only mother I knew for the past 18 years. As she filled in some of the gaps in the story of my beginning and answered what questions she could, I was suddenly plunged into a sensation of overwhelming guilt for the death of the parents I never knew. It was strange; I was not sad for the time I missed with them as I grew to manhood, Genevieve was a wonderful mother and we had a very happy life together. My grief came from the knowledge of how they died from exsanguinations.

It is a bitter irony that both my parents would die drained of their life's blood. I feel as guilty for those deaths just as if I drew the blood from them myself. I know my mother died as a result of hemorrhage from childbirth. Medicine was not as advanced 122 years ago especially in such a rural setting. Possibly today in a hospital she would have lived. But I killed her by being born. My father, on the other hand, could never live without his Elizabeth, or she without him to be sure. As she lay dying the week before her last breath, Alexander was visibly dying a little each day along with her. Genevieve said "even had he not opened his veins that day, he would have died of a broken heart soon after." It wasn't until after I completed my transition that I would understand why the blood loss so affected me.

CHAPTER 3

The "Library"

Bloody Mary Sundays at the Library Pub, a local drinking establishment named for its' library decor, seemed to be a favorite respite for the professor. She sat at a small table in the front window of the bar, half buried by a stack of papers and bathed in the light of another beautiful fall afternoon, unaware of my figure across the alley watching her every move. I loved to observe her from afar, watching as her teeth tore the flesh from the chicken wing held between her two graceful fingers, the rhythmic movement of her throat as she swallowed was intoxicating. I watched each sip she took from her "Bloody Mary", leaving a drop of red on her lips, deftly attended to by a quick flick of her tongue. In the early days after my transition, this practice of following a beautiful woman and fixating on her delicious looking neck would have been dangerous. I am ashamed to say that my willpower in the beginning was tested and I failed. But now it was merely my uncontrolled fascination of this creature that sat before me unaware, instead of my desire to feed, that draws me to follow her every move.

I had decided after class on Friday that I would approach her. Simply following her and observing were no longer satisfying. I needed to talk to her, to get to know her. More importantly, I felt compelled to let her know me, to see me, possibly even accept me for the strange creature I was. I was treading into dangerous and unknown territory. I had lived a relatively solitary life since my mother Genevieve died. Of course, there have been times when I indulged in the pleasures of the flesh. However, these encounters left me unsatisfied and unfulfilled. The feelings that have been stirring in me ever since that first day in her class and that incredible morning in the woods are completely alien to me. I had better be careful to not let whatever is going on in me, endanger my well kept secrets, at least not yet.

As I walked into the bar, the sounds of Coldplay filled the background and scattered conversations of the few patrons mingled with the music. I saw the professor by the bar, her hand running over the tight crop of hair on the bartender's head. "Very patriotic" she said, commenting on his choice of red, white and blue stripes he recently added to his hair. "Always a patriot, Jellybean" he said. By their familiar banter, it was obvious they were good friends. However, that simple gesture made me tense. I didn't like her hands on another man. Was it jealousy or something stimulating my predatory nature that had me struggling to keep from leaping over the bar to snap the bartender's neck in my hands like one snaps a pencil?

"Paul, I told you not to call me that around my students. I don't want them calling me that." She said his name, with what I thought was more like sisterly affection than with longing. Paul would not die here today. I brought my emotions under control and walked up to the bar to order a drink. "I'll have a Bloody Mary and a fresh one for the professor" I said to Paul, keeping my tone as neutral as I could. The professor turned to protest the drink and I introduced myself. "Professor Bean, my name is Maximillian VanderCreek," I said as I extended my hand to her. "I am in your Bio 108 lecture." The professor extended her hand, my urge was to bow and kiss her hand befitting the lady she was. However that gesture in this day and age is considered forward. I shook her hand instead, taking care to handle her as delicately as one might handle a butterfly, so fragile I might break her. The Professor returned a firm handshake; I could feel her pulse quicken slightly when I held her hand for a second longer than necessary.

"Call me Lily" she returned. "Thank you for the drink, although I'm not in the habit of accepting them from students". "Then thank you for honoring me by accepting it." I responded. That first touch of her skin, her scent, and the way her pulse can be seen beating in the graceful curve of her neck, is something I will remember forever. I can't explain it but somehow she made me feel so alive! Quite a feat since technically I haven't been so for almost one hundred years.

"Ok" she said "but I will only accept it if you join me for a while. I have been grading those essays for the past two hours and I could use a break. Care for some wings?" she said as she gestured over to her table. Paul delivered our drinks with a scowl as he heard me say, "I would love to join you for a drink, Lily", her name like a delicious morsel on my tongue, "but the wings are all yours." "Vegetarian?" she asked. I smiled at the name and said "yes". I am a vegetarian of sorts. "More for me" she said. "I am definitely a carnivore! I don't know how you live without it." I let this line of conversation drop. Maybe one day I would trust this woman to the truth of my dietary habits, but today I would keep the conversation light.

We sat and talked for an hour, nursing our drinks. Alcohol has no effect on creatures like me; I would only have to purge later whatever I consumed here. I have, over the years, learned to be rather convincing in my consumption of food and drink. Most are fairly tolerable to swallow and bring back up in private. There are two things I will not ingest. Meat, when cooked becomes repulsive for me to eat, and also carbonated beverages. The constant popping of the bubbles in my stomach creates a sensation like hundreds of squirming worms in my gut. While neither would harm me or give me any sustenance, I have come to avoid their unpleasantness entirely. The only thing I need to sustain me is blood which I will need to procure soon.

The conversation was light; she shared with me the fact that Hills was where she completed both her undergraduate and graduate degrees. She told me of how it was the same class she was now teaching me, that changed the path of her life completely. Her teacher Dr. Derezinski inspired her to a career in Evolutionary science. He later became her mentor and the two worked together for several years on many exciting adventures. She expressed how she was enjoying the various opportunities working at the college afforded her. She talked of an upcoming trip she was planning as a winter break research opportunity. She was still looking for a few graduate students to work with her on her thesis: "The genetic explanation supporting the mythology of vampires"

This last sentence broke me from the trance she had me in. She misunderstood my reaction and instantly started to defend her ideas saying, "If you're going to take my class, it is best to have an open mind and not jump to any conclusions." I replied that "I definitely had an open mind and was simply intrigued by her choice of thesis topic". Stunned would be a more accurate term. My level of desire to learn more about this woman, once a mere curiosity, now burned inside me with an all consuming heat.

I used the break in conversation to make my departure. I needed to think about what I was doing. The path I was now barreling down was becoming more curious every moment. Lily remarked that she had better pack up and head home to feed her dog and finish grading her papers. She prided herself on a rapid turn around of student work. "I look forward to reading your essay Maximillian. What topic did you choose?" "I chose to discuss the myth of the dragon and my theory as to why there is a lack of fossil evidence to support their existence." "Excellent! I love the myth of the dragon. I look forward to your take on it. See you in class tomorrow."

I would see her sooner. My evening routine of late has me perched in her neighbor's maple tree, watching her read or work at her desk. I know I am invading her privacy, I have been a gentleman and only observed her while decent, but I can not help myself. Every cell in my body responds to her. It is like each cell vibrates with energy when she is near me. I must confess that I like this unique effect she has on me. In all my days of roaming this earth, no creature has caused the sensations I experience when I am near her. It is beyond a physical attraction; it is as if each cell in my body has a mind of its own and they all want her.

CHAPTER 4

In the Maple Tree

I have always felt at one with the natural world. As a child before transitioning, I would spend many hours up in my "tree house" in a large maple at the edge of my property. There was no house per se; it was just that the branches made sectioning off parts of the tree possible. For example, there were two branches that forked off one larger branch. They were my recliner. I could lay back with the seat of my pants at the base of the fork and the fork supported my back. I would lay there and watch insects moving around the tree. Some times I would sit so still for so long that a bird or a squirrel would come up the tree and not realize I was there. I loved being part of the natural world, immersed in it, not just skimming the surface of it as most people do today. Within my living "house" I had a place to lie down, a place to store my things thanks to some crisscrossing branches forming a nice shelf, and there was even an extra "seat" formed by a thick branch sloping up at an angle, if a friend should come to play.

Being in this maple, in this town so near to my place of birth was like coming home again. Long forgotten or suppressed emotions swam in my head. Something was happening to me. Something drew me to this place at this time. I could feel it with every cell of my strange being. Then, suddenly, a light was turned on in the upper floor of Lily's house. I watch through the raised blinds as she greets her dog "Pumpkin", rubbing under her chin and behind her ears. The fury beast bounces with excitement at the return of her mistress. With tail waging wildly it beats a loud drum as it bangs off the trash can or table leg. She pads quickly to the corner of the room where Lily just went, temporarily out of my site line. Lily walks back in with a bowl of food. Pumpkin follows at her heel. Lily stoops down and places the bowl for the dog who rushes in hungrily. The angle, at which the dog eats, brings us eye level to each other. The distance to the dog is too far for her to see me clearly, but she hesitates, eyes locked onto mine, a slow whine escaping her muzzle. I utter a slow shhh. I say to the dog, "It's alright girl, I mean you or your mistress no harm. Eat your dinner." I hear Lily say to the dog, "What's gotten into you Pumpkin? It's not like you to wait a blink to eat what's in front of you." Then the dog lowered her head and ate. It must not have been with her usual enthusiasm because Lily remarked to the dog that she hoped she wasn't getting sick. The worry that crossed her face as she looked down at her dog made me feel guilty. If I was not observing them, the dog would have behaved normally and Lily would have no cause for concern. Lily gave the dog one last pat on the head and then busied herself with making her own meal.

I watched as she prepared some pasta with a fresh marinara sauce. I could smell the garlic and tomatoes cooking in the pan. Apparently Lily liked a lot of garlic. Garlic along with a few other spices like curry and cinnamon, linger in the blood, subtly affecting the flavor. The spices can do no harm to me. It is a matter of preference that a vampire may choose to avoid spice laden blood like I choose to avoid feeding on humans. Well, when I say I choose to avoid feeding on humans that is mostly correct. I have taken to volunteering at the closest local Red Cross where ever I reside at the time. I help out with arranging local blood drives. I take a few bags of blood. It only takes a suggestion and firm eye contact to manipulate the right person in to giving me the blood. You see, I need to consume human blood to maintain my human form. Without the human blood, my form starts to degrade into a more feral form. Likewise, if I consume other blood from other sources like one of my favorites; wolf, I take on certain qualities of that animal. This is one of the reasons I have had a connection to the dog. It senses me, but I do not think it trusts me. It is a long and complex story; the reality of being a vampire, the bulk of which I will explain later.

Back to Lily, while she eats. She appears to me to always be working. Even at the bar she had papers at her side and graded as she relaxed. Now while eating she reads. A small stack of papers remained beside her plate, the last of the essays. Lily, instead of picking up the top page, scanned the names on each page, until near the end she found the one she was looking for. As she pulled it from the stack, the paper turned and I could just make out the title typed in bold across the top, "The Myth of the Dragon". My cells tingled with excitement. Had our encounter at the bar earlier today intrigued her? Had I left a good impression on her? What did it mean that she actively searched out my paper to read so soon after we had talked? Possibly it meant nothing, but it felt like it meant something. This woman makes me feel more like a school boy than the more than century old being that I am.

I watched as her eyes scanned my work. Her expressions changing with each new line she would read. Her emotions ranged from seemingly amused to contemplative, even pensive. From her facial expressions, it seemed she was enjoying my paper. It is not fair really. I have an advantage over the rest of the students. For one, I have been going to school on and off for over 100 years, so skills like writing have become very easy for me. But most students would never get the chance to speak to someone who actually had seen a dragon like I have.

Approximately 70 years ago when my travels had taken me to a very old village in England, I ran into a fellow vampire. It is tricky meeting another vampire. One never knows how they will react. Since a vampire is really the top predator on the food chain, we usually do not feel threatened by anything, anything other than another vampire. Only a vampire could seriously harm another vampire and, if I were to make one feel threatened in any way, it could spell trouble for me. Luckily for me Han was a very old and wise vampire. He certainly was not fearful of me. On the contrary it was I who was scared. I was a relatively new vampire still trying to make my way. I was still struggling with the need for blood and understanding how my new self worked. That is for another time, the story of Han and I and how he changed my life. We spent nearly 20 years together traveling the globe. For a vampire that is but a brief moment in time when time lasts as long as it can for my kind.

During our time together Han told me of his life in Medieval England and how he once captured a dragon. He was going to drain it but instead decided to study the creature first. It was his recounting of his studies on the beast that I used to write my paper. Because I believed what I was writing was factual, it was easy to write the paper and make my premise seem plausible, because it was all true, at least according to my source. Han was very old. He never did give me an exact age but he would talk of travels as far back as the 1200's so I can only guess he was ancient indeed.

As Lily finished reading, a smile spread across her lips revealing the slightly crooked front teeth that give her smile character. She wrote something on the paper I could not see from this angle. I would have to wait until the morning class to see what she wrote. But from her expression, I could tell at least she liked it. I wondered if she believed it. She certainly seemed to have the capacity to believe in the fantastic, "mythical", creatures of the world. I looked forward to her comments on the subject.

I watched her for a short time more and decided that I had better get some sustenance. I was out of my stores of human blood until next weeks blood drive. I wanted to be alert in class tomorrow and it has been days since I last fed. I sprang silently down from my perch and was a shadow in the woods in seconds. I decided to go deep into the Adirondack Mountains and try and find a black bear or bobcat. I had coyote last week but I am partial to the larger game. It adds a little more fun to the hunt when you are hunting a top predator.

CHAPTER 5

Catch a Bear, Save a Life

As mentioned earlier, I have an affinity for the natural world. Running through the woods of the Mohawk Valley, even at the fast speeds I travel, I notice everything. As I navigate my way around Raquette Lake, I can hear the nocturnal movements of the many creatures inhabiting this land. I observe signs of beaver at the base of a tree as I pass, and smell the myriad scents left behind by the inhabitants of this niche. I follow the scent left by a bear. It is old however and I hope it leads to a worthy opponent. I meander my way through the woods tracking bear scent. I must be cautious as his path has me move closer to a part of the woods favored by hikers. I travel too fast for any hiker to recognize who or what I am. It is not the fear of getting caught that worries me. It is that lingering fear of when consumed by the hunt I might come across a human and my predatory nature may overcome my desire to live among the humans and not feed off of them.

As I continue hunting I note the changes in the vegetation as I climb towards the high peaks, and then I smell them. The bear is much closer now and his path has joined that of two humans. They leave their own lingering scent mixed with the smell of wine and marijuana. The female is in estrus, I can smell her fertility as a potent trail of pheromones are left in her wake, announcing to her partner's subconscious that she is primed for mating. The male also leaves his own scent trail, a mix of perspiration, his own hormone laced musk and the faint smell of blood. Perhaps with the drinking and partying, he may have stumbled and gotten a small cut. The bear is following their scents and as I follow, the combined smells inundating me are adding fuel to my fire. I know the humans are in danger, the bear seems to be tracking them, but then again so am I.

This is a test of my reserve, my will power. Humans are easier for me to avoid hunting when I am in full control of my more feral, predatory instincts. However when I go hunting especially for top game, my body responds in a way that brings out my most primal instincts and behaviors. I usually like to let those instincts go when I hunt so that they don't build up and affect my resolve to not feed on humans. So now here I am fully engaged in the hunt, my primal nature expressing itself to the fullest, teeth barred, venom dripping from my elongated canines, eyes void of any trace of humanity. Instinct urges me forward toward my prey. But what am I hunting?

I can hear the sounds of my quarry, the bear's soft pant and snuffling sound his muzzle makes as he tracks the two humans is closer than the sounds of the humans themselves. It seems they have decided to stop and engage in some primal instincts of their own. I can hear faint splashing, the sounds of a babbling creek, and the moans of pleasure escaping the female's lips as her partner whispers a litany of words in her ear expressing his ardor. The sound of the bear as his paws quicken their muted thump across the pine strewn forest floor, hastens my advance. And then I am upon them.

The bear erupts out of the forest with a roaring growl. Standing up on his hind legs, the large male black bear is easily over 7 feet tall and likely over 400 pounds. As he approaches the hikers, fear freezing them in their intimate embrace, I see the woman and for a second am reminded of Lily. This woman is obviously not her, yet something in the color of her hair or the tone of her skin gives me for a fleeting moment the connection to humanity that means the most to me. That instant thought of Lily sets me on a course of action. In a blur of motion, I run up behind the bear, my fingers arching upward as I prepared to strike a blow to the soft spot just below his last rib. As my claw like fingers sliced into the bear's flesh, he let out an ear splitting roar. The woman screamed as she and the male stumbled back towards the opposite side of the creak. Unfortunately for the woman in her hasty retreat, she failed to navigate the slippery creek stones and slipped, landing with a loud thud as her skull crashed into the side of a particularly large protruding stone. The fresh flow of blood overwhelmed my senses. As I drew my hand back for another swipe at the bear, he caught me with his mammoth front paw and sent me crashing down to the creek bed.

As I prepared to rally on my attack of the bear, he turned with a ferocious roar and ran off into the woods. My foray into the creek helped to snap me out of my frenzied state. I saw the woman slumped against a stone in the creek, blood trickling down the side of her face mingling with the creek water and snaking its way down stream. The man was staring, likely in shock, from the edge of the opposite bank. I walked over to the woman and examined her injuries. They were superficial lacerations to the scalp. Head injuries bleed profusely even from the smallest cuts. The wine and accelerated heart rate would exacerbate this. She likely suffered a concussion, but the alternative was far worse.

I lifted the woman easily and moved towards the man on the opposite bank. He seemed to be trying to understand what just happened and grasp the realities of what he witnessed. I spoke to him, my voice hypnotic; I asked him if he had a car. He told me he had one parked a few miles away just off of the main trail. I reached around his waist and drew him to me; he just stared at me transfixed by my eyes and voice. I told him to close his eyes and, as he did, I took off towards his car. When we arrived moments later, the woman was starting to come to. I lay her in the back seat of the vehicle and told the man to take her to the town hospital. I then quickly planted a story of how the two were saved from the bear by a hunter who shot the bear and made it run off. I hoped my suggestion was enough to convince the man and also hoped that the crack to the woman's skull would be enough for her not to remember what happened. Either way, I wasn't that worried anyone would believe the two. High on marijuana and wine, plus the trauma of the attack and my "suggested" story of the hunter, all made enough mess of the facts that my identity was safe.

I went back into the woods and tracked the bear to a den just south of the creek. The bear was cornered in its den nursing its injuries. I was hungry. I quickly disposed of the bear. No longer in the mood for the fight and not wanting to torture the poor creature any further, I fed until I was satiated and then I sat in the den to contemplate what to do with the carcass. I didn't want anyone finding the carcass and drawing attention to the story the two hikers would have. As I sat and formulated my plan for disposal of the bear, it dawned on me that not only did I refrain from hurting those humans but I likely saved their lives. Again I thought of Lily. I buried the bear deep in the woods 10 miles from where I encountered the two humans. All the while I worked, I thought of Lily, her smiling face at the dinner table as she read my paper like an apparition before me.

I am not sure when it exactly happened, possibly the moment I stepped into her class on that first day or in the woods after that, or possibly before I even decided to enroll at Hills, but at some point I became connected to Lillian Bean. Could it be destiny, or the cosmic will of the universe, or some other force that had caused our lives to cross paths? The only thing that I know for certain is that somehow I am inexplicably drawn to her. Thoughts of her consume my every moment. Emotions that I have never had for any other creature make me feel both thrilled and confused. In all my years of existing, even in my early human childhood, I do not recall ever feeling this way. It is unsettling for me to have all of these new and often conflicting emotions running through my head. It is as if my body is at a constant state of high alert with every cell working in a coordinated manner to reach some unknown outcome. I am used to being in control, of my emotions, of other creatures. These feelings leave me with the sense that I am losing control. Historically when I lose control, bad things happen.

I arrived home well after 4 am. I showered off the remaining evidence of the evening's adventure, burnt my ruined clothes in the fire place and got dressed. I would still have a few hours until class and with everything that has gone on I sort of forgot that Lily was going to start her lecture on the legend of the vampire today. There were too many thoughts swirling through my crowded mind. I decided to go out to the barn and meditate. Vampires, when well fed, don't actually require much sleep. After feeding on human blood a vampire is in peak form. Every cell of his body is infused with all it needs for survival. Only when a vampire is in a weakened state, hungry or injured, does he require sleep. When sleeping, all the bodily functions shut down. It would appear as if you were looking at a corpse. All the cells in the body work in a coordinated effort at repair. After the repairs are complete the vampire will wake.

It takes much practice to interrupt this process making a sleeping vampire vulnerable. It is possible to be caught off guard and bested by a much weaker adversary. My friend Han once told me that many vampires used coffins as a safe resting place. It was thought that few people would open a closed coffin. This was especially true during time of widespread disease. A closed coffin often meant that the deceased died of disease. Today it is unnecessary to use a coffin when technology enables us to have a safe haven in our own home. I sleep in a bed, about an hour a day works for me though I have gone months without sleeping.

Out in the barn with the sounds of the resident barn owls and remaining crickets and insects providing nature's sound track, I sat on the barn floor inhaling the natural fragrance of my surroundings. This is a working farm. I have paid to maintain my old family farm since I re-obtained it 32 years ago. Around that time, I had a sudden urge to reconnect with my history. I was bouncing around Europe at the time. I had no agenda, no direction. One day while traveling the English country side, I came across a woman at a small farm house. It was like being transported back in time to a day in my early human youth. I remembered my mother Genevieve bringing me a plate of fresh made cookies and glass of milk. We sat in the cool barn atop a soft layer of hay while we ate and talked about school and everyday things. As I sit here now, I can almost smell the cookies and the bath powder my mother always used. Something about the woman or the barn made me feel an urgent need to get back my mother's home.

I arranged for the anonymous purchase through a real estate company in New York. In my early years after transitioning, I took more than just blood from my victims. What ever I needed I took or persuaded someone to give me. As I gained control over my new self and reconnected with my humanity, I obtained what I needed through more conventional means. Through sound investments and the time to wait out trends in the stock market, I have acquired significant wealth. I have procured many homes and property over the years of my existence and have places set up all over the world. Castles in England, a tropical paradise in St. Lucia, a barn in upstate New York, procuring land is something that I enjoy. It also provides me with easy retreats when I need to start a new chapter in my life. But that day with the barn was different. It was as if all of a sudden, in that instant, something happened to change my destiny and I was compelled to act on the sudden urge to get back this special place in which I now meditate. As I sit here now thinking of this bit of my history, it dawns on me that Lily is about 32 years old. Could there be some kind of connection or just coincidence?

CHAPTER 6

Intro to Vampires 101

Humans are creatures of habit. I have made a point to study human behavior at every opportunity. In my experiences, I have found that in a large lecture hall like this one, students will search for a seat on the first day of class and more often than not will sit in the same location for the duration of that semester. I have taken to this same practice, but today I was in the mood for some clarification of Lily's feelings about me. A simple test would do. Today I will sit two rows back and 10 seats to the left of my normal seat. The individual who had been occupying this seat for the past weeks was obviously unhappy to see me in "his" spot, but one look into my eyes and the suggestion he take the empty seat two rows down had him moving quickly to his new location. The power of suggestion is a potent and extremely useful ability. I don't, as a rule, manipulate people for sport but the look on that freshman's face made me laugh. It was just what I needed to distract me until class began.

My simple test was to see if Lily would glance in the area where I typically sat when she came in. I wanted to know if she would be looking for me. I also wanted to know if she did not see me, would she be visibly disappointed. I know how I feel about her, my obsession growing steadier each day, but did she feel the same connection to me? I thought she might. However, I was also aware of how much I wanted it to be true so I couldn't objectively judge. I sat anxiously watching the door, the ticking of the clock at the back of the lecture hall like a gong ringing in my ears. As the clock struck 8:25, the lecture hall door opened and I smelled her now familiar scent before I even saw her. Earth and deodorant, soap and perfume, a delicious mingling of aromas that make up her scent preceded her into the lecture hall. As had been the case each class, Lily entered the room with a flurry of excitement. A look of pleasant anticipation molded her perfect features.

The moment of my test arrived. I sat anxiously waiting for her reaction or lack thereof and was rewarded with my answer immediately. Lily looked directly at my previously occupied seat and for a split second registered disappointment on her lips. As her eyes continued to scan the lecture hall, I willed her to look in my direction. When her eyes found mine, I knew in that instant that my future was about to change forever. As our eyes locked, I was sure she felt a connection to me and the smile that lit her face sent my mind reeling. In that split second, I knew we would somehow be together. I returned a smile in her direction and, as if she had found what she was looking for, her smile widened and she prepared to begin her lecture.

"Good morning. Welcome to a new week of exploring the myths and mysteries of the natural world. Before we begin, I want you all to know I graded your essays. Some of you will see from my notes that your writing needs work. For those of you that I have written "see me" on your papers, please find a time during my office hours to meet with me so that I may discuss your writing with you. This may be out of concern for your effort or lack of effort and in some cases it is because I was intrigued by your topic and would like to discuss your ideas further. At the end of class please come and retrieve your paper. They will be in alphabetical piles over on this desk, last names beginning with A through G here, H through N in this pile and O through Z over here." I remembered her face as I sat in the maple tree and watched her reading my paper. Was it "Please see me" that she wrote across the top margin of my paper? It was going to be a long hour and a half as I waited to see those words.

"Ok. As you know today we start on one of my favorite topics: the myth of the vampire. I would like to start out getting an idea of what you all think about when you think of vampires. Raise your hand if you would like to tell the class your ideas of what a vampire might be like." As hands began to rise Lily wrote on the board the title "Vampire myths". The first girl chosen declared "evil blood suckers". I instantly disliked her. Lily simply wrote each person's ideas on the board without comment. "Burn up in the presence of sunlight" another girl mentioned, "Aversion to garlic and silver", "Wooden stake in the heart to kill them", "Crosses and holy water will defend against them". On and on the list grew with the typical Bram Stoker ideas. I had to stop myself from laughing out loud at some of the more ridiculous notions.

I decided to raise my hand, and when Lily saw me she called me by name. "Mr. VanderCreek?" My name on her lips was like music. I replied "misunderstood". Lily paused, hand halfway to the board and turned with a sly smile. "Excuse me Mr. Vander Creek what do you mean?" I answered that the first thing I thought of when I thought of vampires was that they were misunderstood. She chuckled, the sound like an aphrodisiac for my soul. "Very interesting Mr. VanderCreek, in all my years teaching this class that is the first time I have heard anyone say that." She added my comment to the board as a number of heads turned in my direction with questioning looks on their faces. The process continued for a few minutes longer and when no more hands were raised she turned and faced the group. "Very good ladies and gentleman, on the left side of the board are your ideas about vampires, now I would like to give you my take on the myth."

"I have had the opportunity over the last 10 years or so to travel around the world in my search to study vampire lore. I have gone to churches and libraries in Rome, England, and of course Transylvania to see what was written in the historical archives on the subject. I have traveled to remote villages in Africa, parts of Europe and Asia to talk to villagers who have said they have seen vampires in their villages. I have talked to mothers who tell of children being abducted by vampires and never seen again." The "myth", she said making quotation marks in the air with her fingers, "can be found across every demographic. From the wealthy Europeans to the secluded and uneducated villagers in the most remote areas of Africa, each separate culture has their own take on the subject. Many different cultures have their own list of vampire traits. Some of those traits are similar to the list we have compiled and others directly contradict traits we have listed. The one trait that all the cultures I have talked to have in common, is about how vampires feed on blood. It is this common thread that has been the focus of my research on the topic."

"Let me give you my hypothesis on the subject." Here was the moment of truth. Lily was about to share with us her ideas about vampires. It felt as if every cell in my body was frozen in anticipation of her next words. What she said next made me swell with emotion. "Actually I tend to side with Mr. VanderCreek on the topic of vampires. I too feel that they are a misunderstood creature. First of all, since people from all walks of life have had some type of "vampire experience" it makes me wonder how such a diverse population of individuals, each with such similar descriptions, could all be wrong. Every one can not be dismissed as a hoax. This has led me to look at the similarities in the stories I have learned. As I said, a common thread seems to be ingestion of blood. Why the blood? It is my current theory that there is a genetic component to Vampirism, and whatever causes an individual to become a vampire, a genetic mutation perhaps, might also necessitate the need for blood. Is it possible that some component of blood, a protein or other factor or even the cells themselves need to be replenished regularly in an affected individual? Could these vampires have a cellular structure different from ours which would have them crave blood for survival? Since I have yet to have my own vampire experience, I can only base my hypotheses on the accounts of others. Let us now deconstruct some possible explanations of some of the traits of a vampire that seem to exist across various cultures."

My thoughts flickered from amazement, to awe, to fear and fascination. This woman, whose incredible insights into my world, held the potential to unlock the possibility of me connecting to another soul on this earth. With the exception of Genevieve and Han, I have had a very solitary existence up to now. I suddenly want that connection very much. Lily continued with her lecture. "First let's talk about the aversion to sunlight. Is it possible for a vampire to be exposed to light without harm?" Inwardly I screamed a resounding yes! "Wouldn't it make sense for vampires to live under the veil of darkness, because people see less in the dark? It would be easier hiding one's abilities in a darkened setting, people don't trust what they see, blame the darkness for not being sure what they see."

It is true, in broad daylight it is harder to hide, that is why I have in the past, cultivated a slightly foreboding and uninviting outward persona. I do not typically let people see me, when they do they often instinctively want to look away and subconsciously fear me. However, outwardly I would not yet express my thoughts on this, since I was too intrigued to know Lily's thoughts on this rhetorical question. "Could it be vampires walk among us every day hiding in plain sight?" Again, I wanted to scream yes! And again, I held my tongue. "It makes sense that vampires would satisfy their need for blood away from prying eyes, the night is a thieves ally. And this need for blood does not seem to be limited to human blood, for many cultures that I have researched talk of livestock, and local game left exsanguinated. The only evidence of trauma being puncture wounds at the site of major arteries. What about the aversion to garlic, how many of you have eaten a particularly spicy meal, laden with garlic or curry, and later sweat out those spices? Could it be a matter of personal preference that a vampire would avoid blood tainted by the flavor of those spices?"

Her insight into the true nature of vampires was astounding. I hoped with all my being to one day enlighten her about how right she was in many of her hypotheses. As Lily was about to discuss her theories behind another supposed vampire trait, she glanced at the clock and realized, lecture time was up. She said she wanted the class to try to come up with possible explanations to the remaining traits on our list and that we would continue to discuss the topic in greater detail at Wednesday's lecture. She reminded us to pick up our papers on the way out and to make office appointments as needed.

I was shocked to realize the hour and a half had passed, being so enthralled by the discussion it seemed like only a few minutes had passed. I was disappointed to have the lecture end so abruptly but then I remembered the paper. I waited eagerly behind three students in the O to Z line and, when it was my turn, I rifled through the small stack of papers on the pile. In green ink across the top of my paper it said "Excellent job! Please see me to discuss your insights further." Next to the simple sentence that made my entire body hum with excitement was my grade of an A+. I expected to receive the grade; I knew I was an excellent writer. My many years of experience enabled me to hone my skills, but it was her desire to hear more of my ideas on the subject that gave me a sense of pride mixed with the excitement of the opportunity to be alone with her again.

As I was preparing to leave the lecture hall, Lily was packing up her backpack. She paused to call me over. "Mr. VanderCreek, do you have a moment?" I wanted to say, "For you I have eternity"; instead I walked casually over to where she stood. "I really enjoyed your paper Mr. VanderCreek." Call me Max, I insisted. "Well Max, I look forward to discussing your theories further if you have time." I inwardly chuckled since a vampire certainly has an abundance of time. To Lily I said "I will stop by your office today and set up an appointment." The next thing she said gave me such a thrill I had difficulty maintaining my previous casual air. "If you're not busy now, I have a few hours between classes. We could head over to the dining hall and grab a cup of coffee if you would like." "I would like nothing better", I said. And off we walked to the dining hall. I could feel my body hum with excitement as I fell into step beside her, trying hard to maintain a cool exterior.

CHAPTER 7

An Interesting Breakfast

For Lily, coffee was joined by a tray piled with pancakes, sausage, two eggs, hash browns, toast, and a Boston cream donut. She certainly liked to eat! When she saw me looking at her tray, a sheepish grin spread across her face. "I'm famished" she replied, "Are you going to eat?" I told her "No, just coffee for me. I had a large meal before class." The taste of bear still lingered on my tongue. "That was a very interesting lecture", I started. "I look forward to hearing more on Wednesday."

"I could spend the entire eight weeks of class on the myth of the vampire" she said between bites of pancake and sausage. "It is a topic I am quite passionate about. My great grandfather from my mother's side, Augustine Angelone, was a scholar who devoted much of his career to the study of vampire lore. His work was passed down to my mother, who was the only one in the family to ever show an interest in the old stories. I think my mother always thought of her grandfather as a bit of an eccentric, but I do know she enjoyed the tales of his travels and definitely liked the diversion his stories provided. When my mother noticed the interest I had in the topic as a child, she found her grandfather's work and passed it down to me. It was his work that I followed. I visited some of the locations he mentioned in his research and it has gotten me to where I am today. As a matter of fact, over winter break I plan to go to New Zealand to follow another one of my great grandfather's trails. I plan on bringing a few students who are taking an independent study course with me. You should think about signing up for the course. It's obvious from your paper and your insight in class that it is a topic that interests you."

"New Zealand? That is a very beautiful place", I replied. The images that came to mind at the mention of New Zealand were anything but beautiful. I couldn't tell her of the time I spent there, not now. Perhaps one day I would be able to let this woman into my world, but if I did eventually tell her, I wanted to tell her the whole story. Now was not the time for a discussion such as that. Instead, I said I would look into the class. For myself I now knew where I would be spending winter break. As she continued to polish off her food and I took perfunctory sips of my coffee, she brought up the topic of my essay on dragons. I told her that, like her, I had a passion for the mysteries and myths of the natural world since I was a child. Here I had to fib a little to accommodate the difference between my actual age and the age at which my body stopped aging. I did not like lying to this woman and wanted to be as honest as I could up until the time I could tell her everything. Would I be able to do that? Would she be able to handle the truth? Time would tell. Until then I was definitely going to learn as much as I could about this woman. I also wanted to find out about her great grandfather.

Back to the topic of my essay, I said, "dragons and the entire medieval period were a topic I particularly enjoyed reading about as a boy. What boy doesn't dream about dragons? I used to pretend that I was a great warrior and that I had my own dragon that would accompany me into battle. So you see I have had many years to formulate a hypothesis about dragons. Like you, I feel with so much talk of dragons through the ages, there must be some basis to all the stories. So, starting with the assumption that dragons actually existed, I tried to tackle the fact that to date there is no fossil evidence of them."

Not that I could tell her, but it also helped to speak to someone who actually had seen one. But the story of Han, like so much else in my history would have to wait to be revealed another day. I continued "I always like to revert back to nature to try and explain things. I looked at some of the common traits of dragons that have been written over the ages. One common trait is their ability to spit fire. I tried to think about other organisms that are known to exist that might share a similar trait, one that may have evolved from the dragon. I know of no other organism that can spit fire but there are certainly venom spitting snakes that exist today and it is a theory that there were venom spitting dinosaurs. I then thought what if the dragon actually spit flammable venom? Many warriors of the medieval time used torches to destroy their enemy camps. I wondered, could it be possible that the dragons spit venom that caught fire from nearby torches? It would appear as if the dragon actually spit flame. As far as lack of fossil evidence, well, many museums have huge stock piles of fossils that have yet to be identified. It is possible that scientists have yet to correctly identify a fossil they have found or even misidentified a dinosaur fossil when it was actually a dragon."

As I finished up my brief explanation of my theories of the dragon, I noticed that Lily had stopped eating and was staring at me with a most peculiar look on her face. Taking that look as one of incredulity, I started to say that my ideas may seem far reaching but to remember it was she who said to have an open mind on the subject of the fantastical. Lily shook her head and said "No you misunderstood my silent stare as disbelief. Actually I was just trying to process what you said and I find your theories quite extraordinary. You are an extremely insightful young man, Max. My mother would say you're an "old soul". You seem more mature than your twenty plus years." "Twenty six actually," I replied. "Really, I would have guessed from the look of your skin you were younger, but your attitude is that of a much older person." She said.

My revelation of my age seemed to register a small smile in her eyes. With me being older than she previously thought, perhaps she might not feel our ages were too far apart to be involved with me. This is an ironic thought since I am nearly a century older then she. Or perhaps I am projecting my feelings for her, into her every look and action towards me. I used the opportunity to inquire about her age. Not usually a favorite topic of women, I tried to phrase my inquiry into her age so as not to offend her. I said, "Well you can't be much older, you look as if you are in your late 20's but with all of your experience and level of education my guess would be 31." "Thirty two actually and proud of it!" she declared. "I am not one of those women who are afraid of their age, at least not yet. I have accomplished quite a lot in my 32 years and I am proud of where I am today. I suppose if I were not so happy with my life's journey to date I might feel more sensitive, but in order to do great things one must live a long life. I am simply trying to do just that." "That is a very healthy attitude." I replied.

"Thank you Max for a most enjoyable breakfast. Now it seems I must leave the realm of myth and mystery and head to my faculty meeting before my next class. I look forward to your insights at our next class Wednesday." "I have enjoyed our talk", I replied. "I am going to look into registering for your independent study class. New Zealand over winter break sounds like an exciting option." We both stood and our eyes held each others for an extra beat, "see you Wednesday" I said. As I watched her retreating form leave the dining hall, a new swell of excitement filled me. My next stop would be the registrar's office and from there the library to do a little research on Augustine Angelone.

CHAPTER 8

Evidence of "Evilution"

I left the dining hall, reflecting on my breakfast with Lily. Walking across campus, caught up in my excitement from being near her and the majesty of my surroundings, I reveled at nature's beauty as the autumn sun blazed overhead in a sky so blue, it seemed painted. The crimson and golden hues of the deciduous trees that dominate the landscape were providing a breath taking finale before winter's curtain falls across nature's stage. All my years on this earth have not dampened my reverence for the natural world. It is my connection to it that sustains me through the countless, lonely hours.

My first stop was at the Registrar's office, where I quickly enrolled in the independent study class with Professor Bean. New Zealand again, it has been a long time. My last and only trip to New Zealand was in 1923. My mother Genevieve died in 1912, the year before I transitioned. After I transitioned, alone and confused, I roamed the globe. I was an immoral, gruesome creature, caught between humanity and death. Unaware of what had happened to me and unable to control my primal instincts for survival, I spent nearly ten years ravaging anything that lived, one village at a time.

Near the end of that hellacious journey, I found myself in New Zealand. There was a small thatched house nestled in the lush greenery of the New Zealand country side. I was first attracted to the site by the scent of grazing sheep. After slaughtering nearly half the herd, a young farmer came out to investigate the commotion. I can only imagine his last thoughts as he stared at the hideous scene before him. Me, raising my head from the bloody carcass still steaming in my hands, a total lack of humanity to my stare, canines elongated and dripping blood mingled with venom. A feral creature of nightmares, illuminated by the quarter moon, I struck with a blinding speed, my fangs sinking deep into his neck. My attack, so quick and thorough, snuffed out his final scream before it had a chance to leave his lips.

The blood thirsty frenzy continued inside the small little cottage. There I encountered the rest of the farmer's family. Huddled together in bed were the wife and two young boys. As I tore at the flesh of the woman's neck the two young boys tried valiantly to stop my attack. They screamed and pummeled me with their small fists as I drained the life from their mother. Their two small bodies crumpled easily under my grip and their screams quickly cut off, as my bite nearly severed their tiny necks.

The room fell silent for a moment. Suddenly, filled with the blood of this decent human family, my savage nature was momentarily quieted. Like a sleepwalker awaking from a dream, I looked around at my surroundings confused and disoriented. The pure human blood from this small family seemed to quiet the beast I had become. For the first time in nearly ten years I could think of something other than the raging hunger and pain that consumed me. I had fed off anything I could catch and in the process became an amalgam of the various beasts I had consumed. As the fog in my brain continued to dissipate my memories of the past ten years started to become clearer. Just then a small pink arm pushed through the thin covering on the bed. Amid the ravaged bodies of her mother and siblings a tiny infant girl looked up at me.

The crushing despair and guilt for the devastation I had caused, mixed with lingering confusion over what I had become, overwhelmed me. I cradled that infant in my arms. As I sat in the midst of ruin, the tiny little creature reached out her small hand and stroked my cheek with one chubby finger. As her hand continued to explore my face, gingerly reaching out to touch my fangs, I sat staring down upon those inquisitive eyes, marveling at the perfect features in miniature. That child, so pure in nature, incongruous to the horrific reality of the moment changed my life's path forever. It was in that moment, that I regained my humanity. The first, of what would be nearly a centuries worth of attempts at redemption, was my handling of the child. I swaddled her in the bloody bed sheet and brought her to a farmhouse nearby. After placing her at the doorstep and knocking to wake those slumbering within, I retreated to a darkened recess and watched her until she was safely inside.

Over the years that would follow I have thought back on that night with conflicting emotions. There is always remorse for the devastation that I wreaked; however over time I have redefined my thoughts. I now view that night as my rebirth, and the years after my transition leading up to it, like one long, violent incubation period. During my long existence I have learned to accept my "evilution" and carry the guilt for the atrocities I have committed. I started out life as a human, I then evolved into a pure form of the darkest evil, yet with the astounding encounter with the family in New Zealand, I evolved further, into a new being, one that has learned to control his darkest tendencies. Recent experiences in my life seem to suggest I am still evolving.

Engrossed in memories of my past in New Zealand I walked along absently. As my thoughts are brought back to the present I realize that I walked past my intended destination; the library, to research Augustine Angelone. I find myself behind the old oak, from which I watch Lily. It's funny how the subconscious mind works. Your most basic needs or desires are always in the front of your subconscious whether you realize those needs or not. I realize that I need Lily.

My current mood leaves me with little desire to go back to the library for research. Augustine Angelone will remain a mystery for another day. I chose instead to retreat into the woods making my way slowly off campus. Well away from town, I feel safe enough to head off into the deep woods at my more natural pace. I usually hesitate to travel at "vamp speed", my personal version of "warp speed", during the day for fear of being seen. But today my mood is melancholy and a good run almost always picks up my spirits. As I run through the woods, a blur, startling all manor of lesser beast as I pass through their niche, my thoughts are drawn back to Lily. I envision her magnificent features, her intriguing eyes, the fullness of her ruby lips giving way to a brilliant smile, revealing slightly imperfect yet sparkling white teeth. My pace slows as I near the site of the bear and hiker encounter. I stop at the stream. As I stand at the waters edge, listening to its melodic sound as the water rushes over rock, breathing in the scents of nature around me, I feel centered again.

The thoughts of my past colliding with my present trouble me. Yet I am compelled along a path unlike any I have taken in my long years on this earth. I feel like a passenger in my own body, moving forward with a sense of excitement mixed with trepidation at the thought of having no idea where this new journey will lead. My instincts tell me that both my and Lily's future are intertwined, but how still eludes me.

CHAPTER 9

An "Error" in the Genetic Code

Mother Nature has worked her magic on me once again. Here in the woods my senses are filled with the sights, sounds and smells of the natural world. For me, this place has become my sanctuary; a place where I can go to find inner peace. Here, away from the bustle of life in town, my mind can settle down and I can think. One would imagine, with all the time I have had for self reflection, that by now I would have the answers I seek. It seems however, that over the nearly century that I have been a vampire, my self reflections often leave me with more questions than answers. There have been some occasions where I have found the answers I seek. My many years with Han, along with my relentless efforts at researching what I have become, have given me some insight.

I was born human. For 26 years I lived a typical life for the time. I went to school, graduated, and ran the farm where I now live again. There was no indication during my human life that I was "different". Sure there was a strong affinity for nature and a very strong sense of being in tune with my bodies' natural rhythm, but many people boast those same qualities yet never become a vampire. I learned most of what I know about vampire physiology from Han, he has had centuries to figure out the strange creatures we are. The rest I have figured out with the help of modern technology, easy access to information, and a substantial fortune to support my research.

It is really quite remarkable how the internet has changed the world. A person could stay isolated from humanity but as long as he has internet access and a P.O. Box, he has access to all he needs. I have used the anonymity of the internet to my advantage. I have procured the knowledge and tools over many years that have helped me in my studies of Vampirism. I have spent nearly the last three decades learning everything I could about the structure of DNA and how it functions in living things. I have studied genetic inheritance and mutations in DNA structure in hundreds of organisms. I set up a genetics laboratory on a small island that I own off the coast of Sicily. I have spent much of the last decade there, engrossed in the wonders of the blueprints for life.

All living things have their own genetic code. A tree grows the way it does because each of its cells is "programmed" to develop a certain way. Stem cells develop to support the tree, root cells develop to obtain nutrients, and leaf cells develop to form leaves. These cells have the ability to trap the suns energy and turn it into fuel to live. What makes a tree become a tree and a human become a human is the specific code in each cell that tells the cell what to do. That code is in the DNA, the blue prints for life. In simple terms our DNA is like the blueprints that direct the cells to grow and develop to form all of our parts.

To understand how a vampire's body functions one must first understand the basics of the science of Genetics. Our DNA is made up of parts called genes. Genes are segments of chromosomes that control certain hereditary characteristics. These genes instruct the cell how to function. The genes are turned on or off in different cells allowing different cells to follow different commands and thus having different functions. Like heart cells are different from brain cells, they are different because they have different functions. Each cell responds to the commands turned on in the genes of that cell. A gene may be "turned on or off" in an individual. For example; if you have blue eyes it is because you received the gene for blue eyes from your parents. A mother with brown eyes could have the gene for blue eyes but in her body it would not be turned on. Instead, the gene for brown eyes is turned on. If she passed the gene for blue eyes to her offspring and it is turned on in her offspring then that child will have blue eyes.

It's astonishing to contemplate life on the sub-cellular level, to realize the power in one cell. In order to fit all of this information into the cell, the DNA is organized into structures called chromosomes. Each organism has its own specific number of chromosomes. Chromosomes contain many genes and other information that instruct the cell in its functions. When there is a change in the number of chromosomes, or the order of the genes on a specific chromosome, this changes the blueprints and will cause a change to the organism. This is what causes many genetic disorders. Depending on where the error occurs different disorders will occur. For example Down syndrome, a common genetic disorder in humans is caused when an extra copy of chromosome 21 is found in the cells. This extra genetic material causes a variety of changes in the individuals make up. By changing the blue print the outcome is changed.

Not all genetic mutations end up being harmful to an organism. Genetic mutations that help an organism survive, get passed on in reproduction. If this happens continuously over long periods of time, it can cause permanent changes in the genetic code. This is one way species evolve and why I believe vampires are a branch off of the evolutionary tree of man. To simplify, as a human I was born with 46 chromosomes. For 26 years my genes in my chromosomes behaved in a way like most human men. My cells all did their specific jobs and coordinated their efforts to have my body functioning "normally". Then something happened and I transitioned into a vampire. I will recount the story of my transition later. To this day I am still unsure as to what triggered the change in my genes, but something changed the commands and caused me to become a vampire.

The human genetic code is incredibly complex. Scientists are still unraveling its' mysteries. For example, many genes in the human genome do not seem to have a function and scientists have called them "junk DNA". In certain cases when cells are replicating sometimes there is a mistake during the process. A change in the order or number of genes can occur. In the case of Vampirism, two gene segments of "junk DNA" that are normally separate, fuse together causing an extra gene segment. This new gene combination causes changes in the way the cells function.

I have studied my own remarkable abilities since transitioning to a vampire. I have collected hundreds of species of organisms that have similar characteristics. I have compared my traits of keen eyesight, acute sense of smell, extreme speed and strength, venom production and the ability for cellular regeneration to other organisms with similar traits. I have compared the genetic structure of these organisms to my own genetic structure. While as a whole, our chromosome numbers may be different, the way they work is basically the same. My latest research focuses on my findings of similarities in the extra segments of "junk DNA" that I possess, with segments of DNA in other organisms with similar traits. While the mechanism that supports the transition is still a mystery to me, it is clear my exceptional abilities that I now possess as a vampire have been caused by a re-programming of my genes to function in different ways.

One of the most intriguing abilities I have as a result of the transition to vampire is the ability for cellular regeneration. If any one of my cells gets damaged or destroyed, the surrounding cells immediately engulf the dead cells and replicate replacements. A cut on my hand will appear to heal almost instantly. Any blood that was spilled will be quickly reabsorbed through the skin into the cells. My cells have the ability to replicate with astounding speed. They have replication rates similar to viral cells and certain cancer cells. For this reason vampires are virtually immortal, not dead but technically not alive in the same sense as typical humans. When the cells replicate they follow the same blueprint of the surrounding cells. It is also what causes a vampire to stop aging.

Incredible feats of strength and speed are possible due to the way my cells communicate with each other. All the cells of my body have built into their blueprints an incredible survival instinct. Each cell is working independently to maintain itself as an individual but at the same time is working communally as part of the larger entity. By working together, my cells can coordinate their actions and energies, combining their strength. This allows for a much more powerful muscular stroke, increasing strength and speed.

This cellular communication also accounts for my heightened sensory abilities. Exceptional hearing, eyesight and sense of smell are all part of being a vampire due to excellent intercellular communication. While my brain coordinates the actions of my cells to have my body function as a complete entity, it is the individual power of each cell and the drive for self preservation in each cell that keeps me going. This intercellular communication can be seen in many species. I believe, in humans, we see evidence of it in identical twins. For example when one twin feels pain an identical twin located across the country can feel its twin's pain. Since they originated from the same fertilized egg, they have the same cells. Even outside the body these same cells communicate.

By far the strangest trait I have obtained since transitioning is the ability to produce venom and the ability for my canine teeth to extend like a venomous snake. The venom is produced by my salivary glands. These have been modified by the changes in my DNA. The venom, similar in structure to venom produced by the cobra or jellyfish contains anticoagulants, heart rate stimulants and endorphin like chemicals. These cause my prey to have accelerated heart rate which speeds blood loss, while the anticoagulants keep the blood flowing and the endorphin like chemicals cause my prey to be compliant and non resistant.

When I feed off another organism I must drink their blood. My canines allow me to puncture major arteries and as I drink the blood, it is immediately drawn into my blood vessels through the membranes of my cells that line my esophagus and stomach. There is no digestion that occurs in my body. No waste of digestion gets produced. What little cellular waste that is produced is removed from my cells by the reverse process of how blood is brought into my cells. This waste leaves the surface of my skin cells. This waste is mostly urea and this tends to give a vampire a slightly white overtone to the skin. The lack of pink flush and slightly lower body temperature tend to give off a sense of coldness. My digestive physiology is very similar to another hematophagic mammal, the appropriately named Vampire bat. Hematophagy, the habit of certain animals of feeding on blood, is a common evolutionary adaptation for many small animals. It requires little effort and energy expenditure, and the blood is rich in proteins, lipids and other essential nutrients needed by the cells for survival.

Some physiological functions that my body needed to survive as a human are no longer necessary as a vampire. Since I get everything my cells need to survive from the blood I take in, I have no real need to breathe. I breathe, as a matter of reflex, the function built into the lung cells blueprint. But this vestigial function is not vital for my survival and thus I can exist indefinitely without taking a breath. In addition, my heart still beats as a vampire, a muscular pump, sending blood around my body. However, if my heart were to stop beating I would not "die". Without the circulatory pump of my heart, my cells would absorb all the available blood in my body through the cell membranes. As the available blood is used up my bodily functions would slow and eventually stop. My cells would enter a type of hibernation mode.

The process is similar to how viral cells can exist for years unchanged out side a cell. When they enter a host cell they take on the characteristics of that cell and behave like they are alive. Outside that host cell they are not alive but have the potential for life in the right environment. My cells would hibernate until a blood supply became available. If that blood supply comes in contact with any of my cells, they would absorb the blood through the cell membranes. That blood, the vital fuel source for all my cells, would re-activate the cells and allow them to resume functions. Many plants for example, during a drought, can shrivel up and appear to die. In reality they are in a state of suspended animation. When the drought condition ends and water becomes available it is absorbed into the plant cells through the cell membrane restoring "life" to the plant. Cells resume their functions and the plant resumes its' life cycle.

That would be the most extreme conditions for a vampire. As long as the cells are not completely destroyed, only burning them seems to do that, they will re-animate under the right conditions. This may support the myth of vampires rising from the dead, clawing their way out of a burial plot in a cemetery. If an individual vampire were somehow entombed and drained of their blood they would appear dead. If their corpse were buried in the earth, and over time, if their remains came in contact with the blood of any living creature, a worm, a mole, a rat, etc. their cells will use the blood from those organisms and start the reanimation process. When strong enough the vampire will dig his way out of the tomb and be free to seek blood from larger more sustaining prey.

I sit in these woods engrossed in my past, contemplating my strange biology, my body so still a wayward deer foal walks right up to me unaware of the danger she is in. In a blink my hand reaches out, faster than the foal can see she is caught in my vice like grip. I make quick work of her, her large eyes stare lifelessly up at me. My reaction to the deer was more instinctual than deliberate. As I finish draining the last of the foal's blood I come out of my trance like state of reflection. The night has descended and past, the first hint of light on the eastern horizon a faint orange glow. "Red sun in the morning, sailor take warning" flashes through my mind. My thoughts are drawn back to Lily as I recall the lecture on maritime sayings.

As the realization that I have been rooted to this spot in self reflection for almost 17 hours sets in I am compelled to move. I first must dispose of the foal. To avoid anyone finding animal carcasses drained of their blood with puncture wounds, I have gotten in the habit of covering my kills. For a small carcass like the foal it a matter of simply tearing it into pieces and scattering the remains in the woods, I know nature will do the rest. The scavengers of the forest will feast and in no time the evidence will be gone. Once that unpleasant yet effective job is completed, I rinse myself off in the icy stream and make my way back home just as the last bit of darkness is erased by the morning sunrise.

Once at home I change my clothes and having no classes to attend today I decide to forgo my daily morning Bean surveillance and instead go to my bed and sleep. It has been days since I have slept, too excited and caught up in my obsession with all things Lily. As I envision her smiling face I slowly drift off to my death like sleep.

CHAPTER 10

An Unusual Blood Run

I awoke strangely hungry. The satiation I felt from the foal was gone. Instead I felt slightly agitated like waking up disoriented from a strange dream. After several bags of AB+, my particular favorite, I felt the intense sense of power and energy that surges through me when I feed on human blood. The feeling of connectedness between all the cells of my being creates an almost audible hum. Instead of feeling revitalized however, I felt supercharged; like a kid who eats too much candy, the surge of energy a little too much to rein in causing him to run in circles.

Normally after feeding and sleeping I would awake refreshed. My cells would have made any repairs necessary and the blood would have alleviated my hunger. My sleep is usually a deep dreamless state of blackness, but today something is different. Remnants of a dream, like wisps of smoke swirl in my head. Fragments come to the front of my memory, vivid for a brief instant and then they evaporate. I glimpse Lily and myself in moments of shared joy, I see visions of green pastures and ancient lands, and then there is darkness, Lily's screams pierce the blackness.

What is most strange about my dream fragments is that they seem to span the past, present and future. The green pastures and ancient land is definitely familiar from my past. New Zealand and the ghosts that haunt me there are obviously fresh in my subconscious since I signed up for Lily's class over winter break. The images of Lily and I however are strange. Some I recognize from the night at the Library and breakfast at the dining hall, but others are random snip-its of us laughing or talking or behaving in ways that are much more intimate then we have been. And then there is the blackness, with a palpable sense of evil, coupled with the sound of Lily's scream, I am left with an intense sense of dread.

I try to shake off my strange feelings and attribute them to my trepidation at revisiting New Zealand. The trip is still awhile off and I shall have plenty of opportunity to second guess the decision to go. Instead I decide to take some of this strange energy and focus it on getting myself in order. I have been slacking on my general daily maintenance issues. The farm and house are in disrepair. I need to make some repairs before the winter sets in. I have also let my supply of human blood dwindle. After this mornings feed I am left with just three bags of O-. Today I will find a blood drive or I will take a withdrawal from the nearest blood bank.

Once again the Web has given me the information I seek while still allowing me to maintain my anonymity. There are web search engines for everything. Blood drives and blood banks are no exception. Thank the good folks over at American Legion post 259 in nearby Delhi for hosting a blood drive today for the Red Cross. It will be a nice drive, another opportunity to get out some of this strange energy. The trip from Hills to Delhi is about 65 miles of winding country road. I will take my bike out for a spin.

The weather this afternoon is as charged with energy as I feel I am. There is a sense that something is coming. The temperature is a little too warm for this time of year. The winds are gusty and unpredictable. The clouds in the sky look foreboding. A storm is definitely coming. That just makes the ride on my bike more fun. I get to really test my abilities in a storm on country roads especially at night. It will likely be dark by the time I get back. First stop is the local Quick mart for some gas and some ice.

As I pull into the Quick mart to gas up my 2009 crimson on black Indian motorcycle, three co-eds turn their attention to me and my bike. I give the ladies a nod and a smile and they quickly turn into giggly girls acting coy. One of the girls calls out to me that I "can take her for a spin anytime". I smile at her flirtation, finish gassing up and go inside to get some ice to put in my saddlebags. I have custom made saddlebags for my bike that are more like mini coolers. My Indian is my preferred mode of transport when I am procuring blood. A motorcycle offers many more options for making a hasty retreat. Speed, maneuverability, and off road access make the bike ideal. I have yet to encounter resistance or trouble when getting my blood supply, but it never hurts to be prepared.

Ready for the trip, I saddle up and take off out of town. Once I hit the open road towards Delhi I let loose with the gas and fly down the highway towards my destination. I love the sensation of the wind as it whips my clothes, the rush of speed as I barrel towards my destination and the roar from the bikes overly loud muffler. Moving at speeds topping 100 mph, I am a blur of color and sound as I pass pasture and grazing cows. The trip is over faster than I would like, I slow to cruising speeds as I near Delhi's town center. I follow small streets and side roads until I reach my destination.

American Legion post 259 is a single level wooden structure resembling an old train station terminal. The building is L shaped. Inside there is a bar/lounge area taking up the short arm of the L. It is dark, wood paneled and the decor is old 1970's style. The inside has the dank smell of old men, cigars, and stale beer. There are a few old timers sitting at the bar nursing their drinks and swapping stories. To the right is the long arm of the L shaped building. This is the buildings reception hall. Tables and chairs have been moved to the perimeter of the space and are piled with cookies and juice. Several donors sit with their white cotton and band-aid covered puncture wounds nursing juice and a cookie. One donor, a young girl, looks dreadfully pale as she sits and waits for an assistant to bring her some juice.

It is after 3:00pm and the blood drive is winding down. In past blood runs, as I like to call them, I have found that the best time to insert myself in a position of access to the blood is near the end of the blood drive. As the nurses are packing up the supplies and the blood is being packaged for transport I simply show up and start assisting in moving the materials. My dress, mannerisms and the confident way I interact with donors and staff are usually enough to allow me access to what I need. On the rare occasion I am questioned as to my identity and reason for being in the area, I rely on my ability to "charm" whomever necessary to obtain my supply of blood.

I make my way through the room picking up a juice box and cookies from a nearby table and bring it over to the pale young lady I passed as I entered. "First time donating?" I ask. She sheepishly extends one slightly trembling hand to accept the juice and cookie. "Do I look that bad?" She replies. I smile and tell her to have some juice. As she takes a few tentative sips she says "This is actually my third time giving blood. I usually plan ahead before donating, eat a big steak and forgo my morning workout, but I just happened to be in town today and saw the sign for the drive and thought I could spare a pint. Thanks for the juice. I'll be fine in a minute." "Well, take your time, eat that cookie and finish the juice, get up slowly, if you need a hand I'll be over there cleaning up." I didn't need to charm her for her to think I was working at the drive. I just had to show a level of confidence that I belonged there for her to assume I was one of the volunteers.

To continue the charade, I picked up empty juice boxes and cookie wrappers as I made my way closer to the now visible box coolers where the blood was being packaged for transport. As I cleaned up here and there, stopping occasionally to check on the handful of donors at the tables, I established the illusion that I was someone working at the drive. The transition into the medical area was going smoothly. I started to package up extra IV needles and empty blood bags, moving ever closer to my prize. Then out of the corner of my eye I see a middle aged nurse, tired and carrying too large a load of supplies. Just as the boxes topple from her grip I am at her side to catch them. She thanks me profusely and asks me to bring them over to the transport area. The boxes contain the packaging materials used in preparing the blood for transport.

With the boxes settled, the nurse, Susan Littlefield, RN, according to her name tag, looks up at me. "Thanks again for the assist. I didn't get your name." She said. The look in her eyes told me she was questioning my being there. "Jack, Jack Night." I tell her as I extend my hand to shake hers. When our hands touch and I draw her eyes to mine, the remarkable physiology of my nature works its' magic.

As the top predator on the planet, my body has so many built in mechanisms to manipulate my prey, most humans don't stand a chance. Pheromones get released as I encounter my prey, in this case, Nurse Littlefield. As the chemical messengers carried in the air are unknowingly inhaled they start to affect the dopamine receptors of Nurse Littlefield's brain causing a general feeling of wellbeing to wash over her. Eye contact, once established is another important tool in my body's arsenal. Once she makes eye contact she is drawn in. I have the perfect camouflage, a monster hiding behind the face of an angel. Every one of my features takes on the subtle contours necessary to form my mask, giving Nurse Littlefield a false sense of security in my presence. And when I touch her hand an almost palpable current is passed from me to her. The result leaves her slightly confused as the electrical impulse temporarily interrupts brain waves, leaving Nurse Littlefield open to suggestion. Even the melodic sound of my voice, as I fill in my suggested idea, works to set the trap deeper.

Nurse Littlefield, any questions or concerns she may have had about me erased from her mind, has now become my unwitting accomplice. After a few more minutes of packing up the blood into the box coolers Nurse Littlefield asks me to bring out the first full cooler to the waiting Red Cross truck out back. Since this is the exact suggestion I planted, I quickly make my way out of the back door of the American Legion Hall. Instead of heading to the Red Cross truck I simply put the box cooler on the back of my bike, secured by a bungee cord from my saddle bag, and I head off into the now approaching dusk.

A few miles away I pull off the road to a secluded tree line and transfer the blood into my saddlebag coolers. I toss the Red Cross cooler into the woods and prepare to resume my ride home. As I saddle up, a smile lines my lips. I am always happy and relieved when my blood run goes so smoothly. While packing my saddle bag I noticed that nearly half the blood I have taken is AB+. Another reason to smile, for me AB+ is like the fine wine of blood. Just thinking of the taste has my venom flowing like Pavlov's dog. I don't know why but lately my hunger seems to be insatiable. In less than 24 hours I have had the foal and 3 pints of AB+ from my last supply and yet I want more. I don't like to go hungry long and it is unusual for me to want more blood so soon after feeding. I resolve to finish off the O- I have left at home before dipping into my new supply.

Back on my bike, and back on the road, twilight descends as I make my way home. It seems the strange weather that was threatening earlier, has finally made its way over the region. The weather in upstate New York can change in an instant. One minute it could be 70 and clear and the next a snow squall can roll through, layering the area in white. I am riding straight into the storms path. Ominous dark clouds roil overhead and fat snowflakes pelt my helmet and face shield. I remove the helmet to see, it's only for show anyway. Fear of unwanted attention from a cop has me wear it, not fear of injury. For anyone else, a night like this on a motorcycle would spark a sense of dread or fear being stuck out in this kind of storm. For me, it ignites a sense of excitement. I push the bike to its limit, as I race through the heavily falling snow. The road is slick and winding and for a mere mortal this would be a deadly ride but for me it is a chance to seek the thrills my special nature allows me to seek. My vision and reflexes allow me to maneuver my bike like no man can. I make my way through deepening snow cover up to the crest of a hill and several miles of country highway stretch out in front of me. I make out lights and smoke up ahead, it seems someone has not fared as well as I in this storm.

I slow my pace as I near the wreck. The first thing that assaults my senses is the smell of blood. My predatory nature, already aroused by my interaction with Nurse Littlefield and my letting loose on the ride, is now significantly in play. I take a moment to regain my composure and decide to see if there is anyone who needs my assistance. After all, I helped those two hikers, at that time there was plenty of blood and opportunity to "fall off the wagon" so to speak, yet I followed the right path.

I parked my bike up past the wreck. As I passed I saw the likely cause of the accident. Not far from my bike lay a large buck, well over 250 pounds. It lay dead in a pool of its own blood creating an oddly beautiful, lace like pattern, in the freshly fallen snow. I could see the large gash in its neck, caused in the collision with the small SUV that hit it, the exit site of all that blood; what a waste.

The SUV rested on its roof, the drivers side door slammed up against the remains of the old Birch tree that stopped its forward progress. The smell of gasoline was pungent as was the metallic smell of fresh human blood. I managed to pull open the passenger side door, the jumbled contents of the vehicle strewn about the interior along with the upside down nature of the vehicle was slightly disorienting. Then I saw her. Even paler now then she was at the American Legion hall, a lot more than a pint of her blood spilled here, the young girl from the blood drive lay barely breathing. Even with my exceptional strength the job of extricating this girl from the wreck was difficult. I didn't want to hurt her further as I tried to untangle her from the mass of crumpled steel.

Just as I free her from the wreck the first wisps of smoke start to rise as the gasoline ignites and the car begins to go up in flames. As I lay the young lady down on the snow covered ground, I note the extent of her injuries. While not a doctor I have studied the human body long enough to know she will not survive her injuries. I kneel down to see if she is responsive. Her breathing comes in wet gurgling rasps, her eyes rolled up so that only the whites are visible. She has pretty green eyes that as I touch her arm come momentarily back into focus. Just then the wind howls, like the cry of a dying animal the shrieking gust swirls around us. This fans the flames of the wrecked car intensifying the heat causing the rear tire to burst. The gust fans a second flame, one rising in me. The smell of all the blood and the intensity of the fire, coupled with my pre existing predatory state of arousal, are more than I can take. When my hand touches her neck to feel her pulse, barely there but palpable to my heightened senses, I lose the last tendril of control over the predator within and, before I realize my actions, my elongated canines are sunk deep into her pale neck. I drain the little blood she had left to give.

As the last drop of blood is drawn into my cells I pull back from this young blood donor. I am sure when she decided at the last minute to donate blood today, that this was not what she intended. I feel guilty for my action, more because it seems so vulgar than for remorse for her death. I take no blame for her death, I hastened it surely but I also know that with me her pain and suffering ended. When I touched her arm and her eyes focused momentarily it was because she was released from pain. It took just one whiff of the pheromones emanating from me and the touch of my skin to hers allowing the electric charge I emit to interrupt her brain impulses, and she was free. Free from the pain she must have been enduring for nearly an hour. She was gone when I started helping nurse Littlefield pack the blood for transport. I remember looking up to see if she was ok, and she was gone. She had at least an hour head start on me. But the crudeness of draining her blood still bothers me. While I drink human blood, it has been a long time since I have drank straight from a body.

To cover my indiscretion with the blood donor, I fling her remains into the heart of the burning wreck. The force I throw her with causes her to be mangled back within the wreckage. As the flames lick her twisted form, she quickly becomes engulfed. The last view I have of her is her face, peaceful in death, then swallowed by orange. With my acute sense of hearing I can just make out the wail of a siren in the distance. Someone from one of the nearby farms must have seen the smoke or heard the crash and reported it. I review the scene before me to ensure I have left no trace of my presence behind. The falling snow is a small problem. I have left many footprints. Most prints closest to the wreck are quickly obscured by the fire. It is the prints to and from my bike and the wreck that may bring unwanted attention to an especially astute first responder. I prefer to avoid any contact with authority figures, especially just after having stolen blood from a blood drive and drank more from this poor crash victim. I know most people would have a difficult time accepting my behavior; I'm having a difficult time of it myself.

After a quick consideration of the positives and negatives of me sticking around, I decided to chance leaving. I hoped the people who respond to the wreck would sufficiently muddle the scene. That, coupled with the rapidly falling snow, settled my decision to make a hasty retreat.

CHAPTER 11

A Chance Encounter

The remainder of my return trip to my farm was uneventful. With the death of the donor, so died my desire for a fun ride. I drove fast and strait and reached home quickly. The fallen snow, now several inches of fluffy white, lines my drive. I pull my bike into the barn. After unpacking my stolen prize and storing it safely away I catch a glimpse of myself in my reflection in a window. It's a good thing I chose to leave the accident scene, I look a mess. I take off my clothes, stained in soot, smudged with blood and dirt, and in my customary way of covering my tracks, burn them.

After a brief shower I look at the clock and see the college library will still be open for several hours. I decide to finally sit down and see what I can find out about Augustine Angelone. As I make my way on campus it is clear that few students are willing to brave the cold snowy evening. The parking lot was nearly deserted and there are few tracks in the snow leading to and from the campus library. By the time I settle myself in front of one of the many computers that fill this area of the library; the clock shows 9:00pm. I have the library virtually to myself. Having passed only a handful of scattered dedicated students, doggedly working away at their various studies, I settle myself into a corner computer and begin.

I first tried to Google the name Augustine Angelone. There were a few hits, a landscaper in Michigan, a salon owner in California, lots of sites for Saint Augustine, none for the Augustine I was seeking. Next, I typed in Professor Lillian Bean's name to my search engine. She came up in several places. First I went to Hills University web site. Lily was listed in the faculty profile section. Through a little digging I came across several research papers along with a link to her Masters thesis, "An Exploration of the Genetic Similarities of Hematophagic Organisms with a Cross Comparison to the Human Genome". She was comparing the DNA from animals that drink blood for food like the bat, leech, and mosquito and cross comparing their DNA to human DNA. I have done similar work and am anxious to discuss the topic with her.

The more I find out about this woman the more I want to know. I need to learn more about what she knows, or thinks she knows about vampires. With some more intriguing reading provided by her various research paper submissions I finally came across Augustine Angelone's name in a footnote. All it said was his name along with date of birth and death and "The collected writings and research on vampire mythology—a private collection" as a reference. I would very much like to see that private collection. I guess I will just have to ask Lily about him. I will tell her I signed up for the New Zealand trip, and that I did a little research into her previous work. Maybe I'll ask her out for a drink to discuss the trip and see where the discussion leads.

After a few more futile attempts at finding anything further about Augustine Angelone I decided to call it a night. My trip was certainly not in vain as I learned quite a bit about Lily from her work. Since I was so near her house I thought a quick trip to the oak tree was warranted. I made my way through the fallen snow. The campus was tomb quiet under its white embrace. I was approaching the path through the woods that Lily frequents as her short cut home when I picked up her scent. As I came around the side of the science annex

Lily was just ahead at the approach to the path. I called out to her as she stood hesitating at the paths entrance.

She turned around at her name and I was rewarded with her beautiful smile, and a quickly returned "Hello Max". I asked her why she was on campus so late and she told me she just got finished watching Hills woman's basketball whip Delhi 98-62. She asked me where I was heading and I quickly improvised that I was heading to the bus stop to catch a bus back toward my farm. There is a bus stop on the end of the street where the path opens up to. I lied and told her my car battery was dead and I had to leave my car at the library. Her mood seemed to be instantly buoyed. She had seemed hesitant to take the path a moment ago.

"Great!" said Lily. "I was just contemplating this walk through the woods and snow alone and was not looking forward to it. It's pretty bright with the snow and the moon but there have been a few times lately that when I take this path at night I sometimes feel like something is following me or watching me. My research is probably just giving me the willies." And that was the opening I needed. Could she have sensed me on the occasions I followed her or was this more of the generic creepy feelings from the dark woods? As we walked the path I had her follow behind me. I cut a path through the snow pointing out the various pitfalls as we went along reminding her to stay in my foot steps because there could be hidden rocks or roots under the snow and I didn't want her to trip. Just as the words were leaving my lips Lily stepped slightly to the right of my path and yelped as she twisted her ankle in a hidden depression in the path. I turned in time to catch her gloved hand as she stumbled forward into my arms.

For a moment we stood there, my arms protectively wrapped around her, steadying her. I could feel her warmth radiate from her and her scent was intoxicating. I could have stood like that for eternity and been happy. She looked up at me with a sheepish grin and said "Nice save". I smiled down at her and asked if she could walk. She said she thought she was fine but the first step she took on her sore ankle registered a pained grimace on her face. "Oh wow, that really hurt. I have glass ankles and should have known better then to try this path tonight. It's just so convenient, it practically leads to my back door" she said.

The path let out onto a small cul-de-sac. At the end of that block a quick right turn took her to her house. "Well it's a good thing I am here to help" I said as I quickly swept her up in my arms and proceeded to carry her the rest of the way down the path. Her instant displeasure about being carried was evident. She fussed, squirmed and protested at the indignity. I told her to stop arguing and assured her I was not about to put her down until she was safely home. She resigned and agreed, then told me her address. It is a good thing she did, because I was absently going to her home anyway though I should have no reason to know where she lives. I almost gave myself away. This woman makes me throw caution to the wind.

After a last complaint, that she was too heavy to carry and that I should let her walk with my support, was met with a stern look, she acquiesced, and allowed me to carry her. As I strode off down the path I made my way effortlessly through the snow and trees. She was a mere feather in my arms. The second woman today I had cradled against me. This ending would be quite different, I was sure. As I made my way to her door she told me to bring her close to the mailbox. Hidden in a small crack in the shingle she pulled out a key. She handed me the key and I let us in. A vampire does not need to be invited in to cross a threshold of someone's home. There is no place that I can't go just by my being a vampire, churches included.

The small entrance way led to a mudroom. There I sat Lily on the narrow bench reserved for removing boots and winter gear. I helped her off with her coat and gingerly helped her off with her boots. Her right ankle was swollen and already had signs of purple around the outside. Lily informed me she had an old soccer injury to that ankle that predisposed her to easy sprains. After taking off my own soaking boots I helped her into the kitchen where we were met by the sound of a low guttural growl. From under the kitchen table Lily called to Pumpkin. "Pumpkin, what's gotten into you? Come girl its ok." With that Pumpkin, Lily's black lab, cautiously made its way out from under the table. Whining as it went, it slowly moved to its masters' side, eyes never leaving mine for a second. "I'm sorry Max she is usually very friendly. "It's ok" I said, "Animals usually have good instincts. Maybe she smells all the different farm smells on me and is wary. Its ok girl," I said as I extended my hand down for her to smell. "I won't hurt your master. Good girl." I continued. Pumpkin reluctantly and warily retreated back to her bed in the corner of the kitchen. I helped Lily get situated in a chair with some ice on her foot.

What Lily has yet to discern about me is all too clear to the dog. She senses the predator in me. Her response to me is part survival instinct, part defense mode. She is not comfortable with me around Lily. Dogs have an incredible ability to judge a persons character. From a glance at your posture, facial expressions and scent they can tell a person's intentions. Once Pumpkin gets past her natural survival instinct to flee me she will see my intentions for Lily are good.

"Can I get you anything else before I leave?" I ask. Lily's response was as I had hoped. "The bus runs on the hour after 9:30, its only 10:15 now. Sit a while, I can make us some tea if you would like. I can't have you standing outside in the snow for 45 minutes; you'll catch your death, as my mother would say." I was hoping for a chance to stay and talk to this intriguing woman. "I'll stay" I replied, "but only if you let me make the tea." I got up and grabbed a teapot from the hanging rack above the sink before she could argue. After filling it with water and setting it on the stove to boil, Lily told me where the mugs and tea were. I got the sugar bowl/honey dipper set she had on the counter next to the stove and placed that and the mugs and tea on the table. "Do you need cream?" she asked. "No the honey is enough for me, thanks." I replied as I took a seat next to her.

"How does your ankle feel?" I asked eager to start the conversation. "It's ok. I'll be fine by tomorrow. I have an old brace I can put on if it's still sore in the morning. But now I guess I have to catch the bus in the morning since the path is obviously out of the question." She replied. "Don't you have a car?" I ask. "Yes, but I hate to drive to school when I live so close, one more car in an already overcrowded lot. I usually take the path or the bus, both very convenient for me, besides my car doesn't do well in the snow. It's more of a warm weather car." She said. "What are you driving?" I inquire. "A 64 Mustang convertible. She and the dog are like my children. My father and I rebuilt that car from a rusted out shell when I was 10. I won't even take her out in the rain, but on a nice sunny day, I love to go for a ride with the top down. If given the opportunity I usually like to open her up. She rides very well and I'm a speed junkie."

I admire the way she is so comfortable in her own skin. Lily is a confident, intelligent and self assured woman, and I am falling deeply in love with her. "I'm a bit of a speed junkie myself. My vehicle of choice is a motorcycle. Right now I'm riding a 2009 Indian. Maybe when the weather clears up we can go for a ride together." I try to say this casually. "I would love a ride on your bike. I'm not comfortable enough driving a motorcycle to get a good speed thrill." She responded with a beaming smile, like an excited child anticipating Christmas. "I look forward to the next fair weather day!" I said enthusiastically. Lily was so easy to talk to. Around her I feel totally at ease. It is almost as if my body, sensing her presence, reflexively relaxes.

The whistle from the tea pot stops our friendly banter. Pumpkin, who finally seemed to have settled down and stop giving me the eye, leapt up at the sound, emitting a low guttural growl in my direction. "Shh, girl, it's ok. It's just the teapot." I say as reassuringly as I can. I remove the pot from the stove and pour us both tea. The delicate smell of jasmine instantly fills the small kitchen. Once seated again, I call Pumpkin to me. She hesitates and looks to Lily for encouragement. Lily smiles at Pumpkin and at me. The dog slowly ambles over and gives me a tentative sniff. I gently pat her back and start to slowly scratch her behind the ear. This seems to calm her and she lays down at my feet contented. "Well, that's good news." Lily says gesturing toward Pumpkin lying at my feet. "I was starting to wonder if we would be able to continue with this developing friendship. If you didn't pass Pumpkin's character assessment, I don't know."

To hear Lily describe us as having a developing friendship was like words from a dream. As soon as I thought this, an image from my dream of Lily and I embracing in this kitchen, flashed before my eyes. "I like spending time with you Lily. I hope we can become good friends." I said as I picked up my tea and took a slow sip. I smiled at Lily over my cup's rim. Here we were at a crossroads. It seemed, undoubtedly, that I was drawn to this woman and my greatest desire for her to return my favor seemed a possibility. I finished my tea and placed my mug in the sink. When I turned to face Lily she was gingerly trying to test out her ankle. "How does it feel?" I ask. "Much better, a few Advil and I'll be a new woman." She replied as she took a few tentative steps. It seemed she would be fine. I glanced at the clock and saw I had five minutes to "catch my bus". I would continue with the charade. When the bus leaves I will make my way back to my fully functioning car.

"Thank you for the tea Lily. I enjoyed being here with you tonight." I said as I made my way to the mud room to retrieve my coat and boots. "I'll see you in class tomorrow. Oh, I forgot to mention, I signed up for the New Zealand trip. Perhaps we can have coffee after class tomorrow and you can fill me in on the details of the trip?" I asked. "I have a meeting after class tomorrow, but could you come for dinner tomorrow night? Say around 6:00?" She returned. "I would like nothing better. Until tomorrow, good night." She surprised me as she leaned into me and gave my cheek a peck. "Thanks for saving me tonight." As she pulled back, her fingers reflexively touched her lips. She felt it. She must have. For when her lips touched my cheek it was as if a generator had been turned on. The area where our flesh touched hummed with energy. I have never felt anything like it. I was momentarily stunned, like a deer caught in a headlight. "My pleasure" was all I could manage to utter.

I slipped through the door into the cold dark night. I watched Lily close the door behind me and I made my way toward the bus stop. As I came up to the stop, the bus was just pulling up. I walked behind the bus and back up the cul-de-sac toward the path. As I made my way back up toward the library I found myself unconsciously touching my cheek. I don't understand what just happened. In all my years no one has ever caused a reaction like that in me. It also seemed that what ever passed from me to her was different than what normally happens when my skin touches another humans'. And did I just dream about her asking me over for dinner? I made my way back to my car, got in and it turned over immediately. I feel slightly guilty for the lie that led to our chance encounter this evening but what transpired tonight makes me think there are greater forces at work. Lily and I belong together. I can feel it and I'm almost certain she feels it too.

I drive back home and head straight to the barn. It is after midnight, but the thought of sleep is the furthest thing from my mind at the moment. I sit in the barn atop a cushion of hay. I lay back and stare up at the bats that roost in the rafters, their nocturnal activity in full swing. I am surrounded by the sounds of night in a barn. The rustle of bat wing, the call of the barn owl as it returns to its nest in the hay loft, alerting its young chick that it is dinner time. Even the rustle of the hay and its sweet sent as I lie down atop it all help to soothe me.

That simple kiss is all I can think about. My cheek still tingles at the thought of it, as if the cells themselves are remembering the exquisite sensation. In that instant, I felt pure joy and contentment. The internal drive that has been propelling me forward in my existence for the last 122 years seemed to have found what it has been searching for. A sense of completeness and peace enveloped me, much like the feelings that a human would feel at my touch.

I awake to the sound of my own voice crying out for Lily, the sounds of her screams still echo in my head. Her cry is so full of pain and anguish that even now as I lie here amidst the hay of my barn, knowing that it was just a dream, I can't shake the sense of dread it has left me with. From the look of the angle of light coming through the barn window I guess it is close to 5: 00am. I will go back to the house, clean up and head to class. My mood is lifted by a hot shower and thoughts of spending an evening with Lily.

CHAPTER 12

A Much Anticipated Day Unfolds

I arrive to class 10 minutes early and take my customary seat. To amuse myself as I wait for Lily to arrive, I observe the humans filing into the lecture hall. I guess at the cause for their outward demeanors. One young frat boy type comes in with clothes that looked slept in, hair strewn crazily atop his head, and dark shades covering his presumably bloodshot eyes. The stench of stale beer, vomit and tequila assault my senses as he stumbles to his seat two rows down. No special powers needed to discern the reason for his demeanor this morning, but the young blond woman who just entered the room catches my eye. She looks upset, almost frightened. Her eyes search pleadingly through the growing crowd seated before her. Her eyes lock on another young woman's who frowns with concern at the site of her friend. I know I should not eaves drop but I feel genuinely concerned for this woman. Her eyes register great pain as she sits next to her friend. Quickly, they bow their heads, foreheads practically touching, and the blond unleashes her story in a torrent of words. I listen in.

"Oh my God Jenny I had the scariest fucking night of my life! I'm still shaking." "What happened to you last night Diane? You left me sitting by the keg next to that total jack ass from ITK!" "I know Jen, and believe me I am so sorry I left. I should have stayed with you. I left with Chris and his friend Jason and some girl named Janice who I never met before last night. Anyway we went to Janice's house, she's a "townie", she grew up in Hills. The four of us were all just hanging out and Chris lights up a jay and everything was nice and mellow when all of a sudden, Janice jumps up and runs into her room. She comes out a few minutes later in a red silk robe and little else underneath, dangling a plastic baggie from her fingers. She smiles and winks toward Jason who seems to smile knowingly. Chris and I look at each other and he seems as clueless as me when Janice says "Its magical mushroom time!" I look back to Chris who seems to know what Janice means but doesn't seem too thrilled with what he knows. I, on the other hand, still clueless, say "Come again?" To which Janice just laughs and says "I hope so sweetie." Blondie, Diane, pauses to take a breath. Jenny waits expectantly for her friend to continue.

"Next thing I know Janice is fixing four piles of mushrooms on the table. I sit closer to Chris so he can explain to me that the mushrooms are psychedelic mushrooms and when you eat them they give you a trip like acid. I ask him, what does acid do? I only smoke pot so what the hell do I know. So he explains it to me and asks me if I'm cool with this, glancing over towards Jason. I think he is trying to impress Jason and I don't want to fuck anything up with that, plus I really like Chris, and like an ass I go against my gut and follow along. We all eat the mushrooms, which taste like shit; literally, they are grown on shit I come to learn. "How long until you start to feel something?" I ask. Janice, ever the expert tells me in about 30 minutes to an hour. Aside from wanting to puke from the shit after taste I had in my mouth, at first I didn't feel anything. Then everyone started to get a little giggly. Jason breaks out a deck of cards and says "Strip poker?" Now I am starting to get a little freaked. Janice has been sitting here this entire time nearly naked. I have seen her looking at me when she thought I wasn't looking. The look creeped me out. It was almost predatory.

Chris sees my discomfort and says "Ok we play, but just down to the draws, no full frontal!" As he says this he looks over at me with a pleading look and I caved again. Stupid decision number three for the night. It gets worse.

Janice and Jason are making new rules up as we go. If you don't want to take off your clothes you can take a truth or dare, all this bullshit. I realize Janice and him are looking to turn this night into something bizarre. By now the mushrooms are kicking in and everyone is partly dressed. Its Chris's turn and he picks a dare since he has only socks and boxers on. Jason says to Chris to make out with me in front of them. Now here I am tripping hard on the mushrooms, colors and sounds distort my perception, it feels like every one of my senses is on over drive. As Chris kisses me, I close my eyes and sort of melt into him. I felt better with my eyes closed and reassured by his warm strong body. The next thing that happened was so fucking bizarre I don't know if I will ever be able to show my face at ITK ever again." "What happened?" asked Jenny breathlessly. "We were kissing and it felt great and then I feel what I think is Chris rubbing my thigh. It felt nice so I thought ok, then I feel a hand stroking my hair and another hand groping my breast. I open my eyes and Janice has my tit cupped in her hand and one hand stroking Jason's knob while Jason is inching his hand up my thigh. I jumped up too fast for my trippy legs to adjust, and end up with Janice catching me and planting a lip lock on me. I push away from her in time to see Chris deliver a right hook to Jason's face sending him flying on his ass with blood gushing from what was left of his mangled nose. Janice starts freaking out at the site of the blood, it was beyond fucked up! Chris and I wound up walking back to ITK and passed out in his bed. I woke up around six feeling like utter shit, a hangover like I have never had, and left Chris asleep in bed. I left him a note to call me when he gets up if he wants to get together later and made my way up to campus through that cow path. Lucky for me some other lunatic took the path last night and I was able to follow in the tracks."

"Holy shit Diane! Jason is a tool and Janice sounds like a freak. Are you ok?" "Yea, I'll be ok. I'm lucky. I made many stupid decisions last night, things could have gone worse. It makes me feel a little better knowing Chris thought it was fucked up too and hit Jason. He probably broke his nose." "He fucking deserves it, the creep." chimed Jenny. "If she is not here in five minutes I am outta here, I feel like I could puke." finished Diane.

I glance up at the clock, the dramatic story having ended. I conclude that Diane will be ok, and possibly smarter for the experience. I notice it is ten after 8:00, so caught up in the drama of the co-eds that I lost track of time. Just as I start to feel concern for where Lily is, the lecture hall door opens. In hobbles Lily, leather backpack over both shoulders, ankle in some type of brace and walking with a cane. "Good morning! Sorry for the late start, as you can see I am a little slowed down today. May I say to anyone thinking of taking the cow path to town, from campus at night, in the snow, find another option!" Diane and Janice glanced at each other at the mention of the cow path as if to say, lunatic identified. As she finished unpacking her back pack, Lily looked over at me with a wide smile then sheepishly glanced at her foot and cane. I returned the smile and laughed good naturedly at her embarrassment.

Lily picked up her lecture on vampires were we left off on Monday. Much of the class was spent with discussions of supposed vampire traits and the possible genetic component that may explain that trait. Lily mentioned that she was currently involved in work on her Doctoral thesis on the very topic. She mentioned how she is following the work her great grandfather completed before his mysterious disappearance and presumed death seventy two years ago. She told the class the story of how she obtained his research and journals and how she retraced many of her great grandfather's steps during the course of her research. She mentioned that the internship to New Zealand, which I so recently signed up for, was following another lead of her great grandfathers. She hoped to interview a survivor of a purported vampire attack.

Those last words left me feeling uneasy. But before I could dwell on it Lily reminded the class that Friday was the half way point for the class. We would be taking our midterm exam on Monday. She set out the guidelines for the exam, an essay. We could pick any myth or mystery we wanted to research. One we have discussed, or a new one and explain, using scientific rational, our stance of belief or disbelief in that particular myth. "New topics tend to receive better grades, and your topic must be approved by me. Submit three possible topics with your stance outlined by Friday. We will be watching some video footage of various mythological sightings, trying to determine if they look real or contrived. While you watch the footage, I will look at your proposed topics and select one from your list. If you do not turn in a list on Friday, or if your topic choices are not appropriate, you will be assigned a topic from me. You will have the weekend to do your research and you may come to class with three 5x7 index cards outlining your essays. You will get the full hour and a half class on Monday to complete your essay in a blue book. Bring a blue or black ink pen for the test. If you forget your index cards, you're out of luck."

The class started packing up; a few grumbles could be heard about the displeasure of the test. A few students were excited at the ability to bring in a "cheat sheet" for the exam. I over heard one student bragging about his ability to write so small that he was confident he could put his entire essay on the three index cards. Lily faced the class again and reminded us that she had office hours later today and Thursday if anyone needed some help in getting their topics together. I made my way down toward Lily, the smelly frat boy was asking her some question or other. When he and his stench were finally gone, I stepped up to Lily as she was slinging her back pack over her shoulder.

"How does it feel?" I ask gesturing to her ankle. "Not so bad, the slushy snow this morning made me think a brace and the cane were a safe bet. Are you still free tonight?" She asked with a look of hope in her eyes. "Absolutely, if your still up for cooking on that foot. Would you rather I pick you up and we go out to eat? "No, don't worry I'll be fine. I'm just going to whip up a quick marinara and a salad with some garlic bread and tofu cutlets. I remember you mentioned you were a vegetarian. That sound ok?" "That sounds delicious" I lied, having no desire for food. "See you at six then. I'm off to my department meeting." She said as she made her way slowly to the door. "See you later." I replied as she shuffled off to her meeting.

I would take a run into town to buy a nice bottle of red wine and some flowers for our date. So much about tonight excited me, the possibility to talk to her more about her great grandfathers work, the chance to learn more about our pending trip to New Zealand, but most of all the chance to learn more about her feelings for me. The memory of her chaste kiss has me reflexively bring my hand up to my cheek. The unexpected effect she had on me has left me intrigued.

CHAPTER 13

A Date with Lily

After class I shot over to the library to complete my midterm topic proposal. The three topics I have chosen are Witches, Aliens and the Legend of Atlantis. We have not covered any of them yet so my chance at a good grade is better. From the library I head to town to get the wine and flowers. To kill some time until 6:00pm I do a little window shopping along Main Street. Main Street as the name implies, is the central shopping area for town. The street is lined with a variety of shops and eateries. As I continue down the street, I peer into the dusty window of the antique shop. I decide to browse. The first thing I notice as I open the door is the smell. The smells associated with old linens, musty attics, and the aged proprietor, mingle in the air. Combined they convey a sense of entering a bygone era.

As I make my way through the shop, passing between cluttered tables, and narrow, congested aisles, I stop to admire an old lace tablecloth that reminds me of Genevieve and a lifetime ago, or an old sepia print faded, yet still clearly showing the solemn faced young man in the photo. From the clothes, I would date the picture early 1940's. Suddenly I come across a necklace hanging from a mannequin. The mannequin is dressed in a 1930's dress. The necklace looks to be much older. The simple pendant is of pewter and it has a vague cross shape to it. Thicker at the middle the four arms quickly taper to sharp points. Embedded at the center is a ruby, deep crimson, polished like a marble. The chain is woven pewter strands. It is beautiful in its simplicity just like Lily.

I turn to find the shops proprietor observing me as I admire the necklace. "That ones a real beauty, one of a kind." said the old gentleman as he walked over towards me. "It is quite intriguing." I replied. "It belonged originally to my great, great grandmother. It's made of pewter and ruby. I was told she made it herself. My wife wore it till she died. It is called "Evening Star". The story is that the stone has extraordinary powers when it is worn by a worthy woman. My mother wore it till she died. I was her only child, and my father gave the stone to my wife when we got married. We never had children, so when my wife passed, I resorted to carrying it in my pocket every day. It looks nicer on the mannequin. It reminds me of my Lilly."

"How coincidental, that I should be admiring this necklace for a Lily of my own." I replied. "Is it for sale then?" I asked gently. "Well that depends." He replied. "This Lily, is she special?" He asked me. "Like the necklace, she is one of a kind, a simple understated beauty, strong, yet capable of connecting deeply. We have a destiny together, of that I am sure." The man looked at me with rheumy eyes. He seemed to be trying to look into my soul, to decide if I was worthy of this most personal memento of his life.

"What do you think Lilly?" He said, glancing at a photo on a side table. As if in answer an extinguished bulb in the chandelier above our heads flickered on. The old man must have taken this as his dead wife's answer and replied "I couldn't agree more." Well young man, I hope your Lily brings you as much riches as my Lilly brought to me." Looking around I knew the man referred to riches other than the monetary sort. "Sir, just having met her has changed me. If I am fortunate to have her as my companion on our life's journey, I will treasure every day with her." He smiled at me, a tear in his eye not permitted to fall. After purchasing the necklace for more than the man asked, I took my treasure home, wrapped in a satin lined antique silver jewelry box. A beautiful piece on its own, purchased to make the right presentation when the time comes.

As I drove home to get ready for this evening, I glance to see the silver box is safely nestled in the seat beside me. Some people may view purchasing a gift like this, for a woman, before even having a first official date as brazen. However, since I am unlike most people, and all evidence points towards Lily being extraordinary, it feels right. It is as if that necklace or the old man's Lilly herself, called me into that shop to obtain that treasure. I would not be giving it to Lily tonight. When the moment is right, I will know. Until then, I place the box inside a satin pouch and put it safely in my dresser.

I arrive at Lily's home promptly at 6:00pm, dressed in black denim jeans, a pale blue shirt, black leather boots and coat. Armed with flowers and wine I ring the bell. Lily answers, looking slightly flustered. "Come in she beckons as she steps back from the entrance way. As she moves aside to let me in a familiar male figure appears in the hall way. "Max, this is Paul and he was just leaving." Lily says as she practically glares at Paul. "Nice to meet you Max." he says as he reaches out to shake my hand. I think he was trying to come off as imposing, his grip attempting to be vice like in mine. He registered a momentary look of surprise when it was met with equal vigor from me. Paul is a big dude. Probably in another life he could have been a lineman. He is probably not used to too many people being a physical threat to him. "By Jellybean, you know where I am if you need me." He says over his shoulder as he walks past me, chest puffed out like a cock strutting its stuff. His cock of the walk act is all to save face. The reality, Paul knows from one hand shake, is that I will not be intimidated.

"Sorry about that. Paul is a good friend of mine since we were kids. He thinks it's his duty to "protect me from predatory males" as he puts it. He means well, he is like a big brother to me." Lily says, as she draws me into her home and closes the door on the chilly evening and Paul. "It's good to have friends to watch out for you. I can respect Paul for wanting to protect you, but are you sure Paul doesn't want to keep you for himself? I could understand his motivation." I try to say this without sounding jealous. "A long time ago we gave it a shot, but it was weird, like kissing your brother. It was short lived and Paul knows there is no chance for anything more than him being my friend." She says this all matter of fact, as she places the flowers I brought her, in a vase on the table.

"The flowers are beautiful Max, thank you. Shall I open the wine?" "Let me." I reply. "You should be resting your ankle." Lily brushes off my comment with a wave of her hand and an "I'm a lot tougher than you think." She opens the wine to breathe and proceeds to put out a small tray of crackers, olives and cheese. After pouring two glasses we take the wine and cheese plate to the living room where Lily has started a fire. It is a cozy setting and we settle in on opposite ends of the couch with our wine and silently watch the fire. The silence between us is comfortable; there is no need to fill every moment with words. After a few minutes of alternating between watching the fire and watching the way the fire made interesting shadows across Lily's profile, she broke the silence.

"I find the hypnotic power a fire has, very primal. No matter how long you sit and look, it is always changing. The colors, shape, and intensity are all in a constant stat of flux, powerful, yet beautiful, destructive, yet necessary for survival." "I agree completely. The way you describe it as "primal", I have always felt that. When I sit before a fire I imagine our early ancestors and the fear and awe they must have had to overcome for fire to become a tool for man and a huge step forward in his evolution." My comment made Lily turn and look directly into my eyes. "Max, I am finding we share many common views. The way you think and talk, I sometimes think you are setting me up, as a joke, to poke fun at me, but then I realize you're sincere in your responses. I guess I have never found someone near my age, interested in so much of the same things as me. I feel remarkably comfortable around you Max." As she finished she stared into the flickering flames, their reflection dancing off of her magnificent eyes that today were a dark brown.

"Lily" I started. "Wait." She interrupted. "Before you say anything I just want to say that I like you Max. I see this friendship growing and that makes me very happy. But right now I am your professor and I wouldn't want to put either of us in a bad position with the Dean. I just feel we should keep our friendship somewhat low profile for now. While it's not unheard of teachers dating students, after all we are adults; I just feel it may not be perceived well by everyone." With the last word she drew her eyes away from the fire and looked at me. "Lily, I won't deny that I have developing feelings for you. I understand your concerns and I also believe in discretion. However, I would gladly take the grade of an F, if it meant showing you have no favoritism towards me in class. I trust that you can maintain your professionalism in regards to my grades and you can trust I would never do anything to put you in a compromising position." She smiled at my response and sipped her wine.

After a few minutes we moved to the table for our meal. I ate with false gusto and remarked at her cooking prowess. The discomfort of food in my gut was worth it if it gave me the opportunity to be with Lily. So much of human interaction revolves around food that I have had to develop fine acting skills to blend in as a consumer of food. After we ate, we both cleared the table. The kitchen was small and it was difficult to avoid brushing past each other as we set to our task. When Lily asked me to hand her a glass, our hands touched as she retrieved it. The hum of energy that passed to my cheek when she kissed me repeated in my hand where our skin touched. In a shocked reaction Lily dropped the glass. Just inches away from shattering on the kitchen floor, I caught the glass, my hand a blur as I reacted.

"Wow, great catch" she said a little breathlessly, her fingers absently stroking her other hand. Like the kiss the night before, she felt more than just the brush of lip to cheek or hand to hand. This response was a palpable hum inside your cells and she felt it too. She gazed up at me, and as if seeing me clearly for the first time, she leaned in and kissed me. Tentative at first, her lips exploring mine, and than like a fire being stoked with gasoline she pulled me toward her and we were consumed in a deep passionate embrace. The gentleman in me should have pulled away. After all we just agreed to take things slowly, but a greater force seemed at work. I slipped my arms around her body and gingerly lifted her in my arms, our mouths urgently exploring each others. When I settled Lily down on the couch we both came up for air. It was enough to break the temporary urgency with which we coupled. I looked in her eyes and at that moment could see the love she had for me in their deep chocolate depth. "I love you Lily" The words out of my mouth before I could stop them, a pure and vulnerable response to the moment. Lily answered me by pulling me down on top of her. Our passion was fervent. Clothes hastily removed a tangle of fabric on the floor. When I finally entered her Lily let out a cry of pleasure in my ear, followed by a whispered "I love you", as she pulled me deeper inside her. We climaxed together in a breathless tangle of limbs.

As I lifted my torso to look into the eyes of the woman who has forever changed me I saw tears stream down her cheeks. I must have registered a look of fear as I started to pull away from Lily afraid I hurt her. She shook her head as she pulled me back into her warm embrace. "Why are you upset? Did I hurt you?" I asked against her cheek. "No" she said as she held me tighter. "I'm not upset; it's just that that was the most intense experience I have ever had. I don't know what just happened, but when our skin touched, it was like being charged up. I can't explain it, except to say it felt like an electric hum was passing between our skin. It was strange, wonderful, and very powerful. I am full of emotion. Max, when we're together I feel . . ." her voice trailed off unable to put words to the emotions she was experiencing. I could understand her inability to put into words what we just shared. I don't fully comprehend it myself. She is right, though; it was strange, wonderful and very, very powerful.

We lay together in front of the fire, Lily's warm body cradled in mine. As I sat stroking her hair and gently kissing her neck she looked up at me. "Well so much for taking things slowly." She said. I leaned in and tenderly kissed her lips. "I'm sorry Lily, but the forces of nature that have brought us together are more powerful than both of us." With that Lily nudged her body closer to mine and closed her eyes and slept. I watched her sleep cradled against me, memorizing every inch of her glorious body. As she lay dreaming next to me a peaceful smile on her lips I reflected on how my life has been irrevocably changed by this remarkable woman.

CHAPTER 14

A Dream Realized

During the night as the fire died, I picked up Lily's slumbering form and moved us into her bed. Once I settled us, she nudged her body closer to mine and slept peacefully. I spent the evening watching Lily, dreaming of the life we could share together. I would allow myself this blissful moment to dream. For in reality, if Lily and I were to share a life together, I would have to tell her the truth about me. I resolve to enjoy some time with Lily, before I think about burdening her with the truth of my biology.

Lily wakes to find me dressed in just my jeans at the stove in the kitchen. I hope the smell of the breakfast I prepared for her was pleasing. It has been so many years since I needed food for survival; I have lost touch with my ability to discern pleasure in the smell of prepared food. It is not that the smells of prepared foods are necessarily unpleasant to me; it is just that the scent that would stir my hunger is very different than the scent to stir a humans hunger.

"Umm, something smells delicious" She says as she comes up behind me at the stove. I plate the last blueberry pancake on top of the stack I have prepared for her. I place the pancakes on the table alongside a steaming pot of coffee, cut fruit, and some fried bacon. Lily has a well stocked fridge and as I have seen in the past she likes to eat. "I hope you don't mind, I took the liberty of making you breakfast." I said as she slowly moved her body up against mine. As her arms circled my neck she pulled my face towards hers and gently kissed my lips. "Do I mind? No! I love blueberry pancakes. It was sweet of you to make breakfast. Do you have to leave now?" She asked, her eyes surveying the table set for one, looked up at me with disappointment.

"No. I don't have classes today. My schedule is wide open." I offer. "Oh, it's just that the table is only set for one, so I thought you might have wanted to leave." Lily's reply, delivered with such uncharacteristic insecurity had me quickly reassure her with a tightening of my arms around her. "The table is only set for one because I do not usually have much of an appetite in the morning, not because I was looking to run off. Actually I was hoping we could spend some time together today. I know you have office hours from 1:00 to 4:00 today, but I don't know about the rest of your day." I said.

Lily responded by hugging me tighter, her cheek pressed up against my bare chest, inhaling my scent as she took a deep breath. She spoke into my chest, eyes averted, afraid to show the feelings she tried to explain. "Max, that rational voice in my head is screaming to me, to take a breath, slow down, don't show my emotions so quickly, but I can't seem to stop myself. I want you to know, it has been a long time since I have had a relationship. I am not one to be easily swept away by my emotions, not that there has been anyone to sweep me away, until now. I know I probably shouldn't say this to you, I will probably scare you away, but as you said yesterday, there are greater forces at work." She looked up at me then and continued, "The truth is Max, I love you. Together we fit. I don't want to play games, and be coy. I don't want to waste another minute pretending to like you only enough to keep you interested, and not scared off. I am willing to open up my heart to vulnerability because I know that if you will have me, I will be yours always."

I leaned down and kissed her cheek, brushing away a salty tear with my lips. I stared into Lily's eyes and observed the depth to which she opened her soul to me. Her look, coupled with her declaration that she would be mine always if I would have her, let loose a flood of emotion in me. My love for this woman, a feeling long dormant, as a vampire and only barely experienced as a young man, swelled to the surface. "Lily, you can't imagine what it means to me, to have found you. I certainly had not set out looking for a relationship. Other then a son's love for his mother and my affection for my friend Han, I have little experience with the bonds of love, yet when I first laid eyes on you I was drawn to you. To hear you profess your love for me, it's beyond what I ever dared to dream. Lily, for as long as you will have me; I will devote my every moment to ensuring your happiness." I swept my love into my arms and caressed her face with butterfly soft kisses all along her nose, her chin, forehead and eyelids. Lily lovingly took my face in her hands and wiped away one tear that had slid down my cheek. The last time I cried was when Genevieve died. This time the tear I shed was for joy. For in this one moment my world is perfect.

I carry Lily back to her bedroom. This time our passion is less urgent. We take time exploring one another's body. Gentle caresses and lingering kisses; stoke the flames of our passion until Lily takes me deep inside her. We rock in unison, our bodies moving together in perfect harmony. Our hunger for each other, like a primal need, grows, until as one, rhythmic waves of pleasure wash over us. Deeply content we lay together on the bed. Lily's rapid breaths slowly give way to a deeper, more restful rhythm. We lay like that for several minutes, in the comfortable stillness, our steady breathing the only sound in the room. Suddenly a new sound causes Lily to turn sheepishly towards me.

With a smile she declared, "I don't know about you, but I certainly worked up an appetite, as my stomach just loudly attested to. How about we go devour those pancakes?" I returned her smile, and after she threw on my shirt and I returned to my previous attire of jeans, we made our way back to the kitchen. After a quick shot in the microwave, Lily had the breakfast back on the table. She piled up a stack of the blueberry pancakes, loaded on a hefty portion of bacon and filled the remaining plate with fruit. After applying the perfect amount of butter and syrup, the monstrosity Lily was about to dive into was complete. She ate with gusto. After several large mouthfuls, Lily paused to say, "Don't tell me you haven't worked up an appetite yet. You will give me a complex." That remark caused me to laugh out loud. "Lily, after the experience we just shared, I am left completely satiated. There is not a thing I desire; I am full with your love." I said, not entirely joking. "More for me then, I don't know what it is lately, but for months I have been on an eating frenzy. I am always hungry. Maybe I picked up a tapeworm on one of my trips. I don't know but I love food. You sir, are an excellent cook." She said as she finished off her pancakes.

After Lily finished off the rest of the food, followed by a tepid cup of coffee, we cleaned up and got ready to leave. I drove her up to campus and before she got out she leaned in and kissed my cheek. After agreeing to meet here at 4:30pm to take her home, Lily climbed out of my car. "Don't forget your proposal is due tomorrow" She called as she lowered her head to see me. "Already finished teach." I replied. She shut the door with an approving nod and a kiss blown my way. I watched her retreating form until she disappeared from view around the side of the science building.

I drove home and took care of two important urges. First the necessity to purge the food I had consumed at Lily's. I didn't want to chance getting up in the middle of the night and waking her, the bedroom is attached to the bathroom. I could have gone off into the woods and taken care of things there, but if Lily woke to find me gone she would have wanted to know where I had been. So instead, I fought down the urge of my body to rid itself of the useless waste inside me. Once that business was attended to I could address my second requirement, which was the intense need for blood. I drained about 5 liters worth of blood from my storage of AB+, enough blood to fill a grown man. "Now I am truly satiated" I said, as I drained the last of my AB+ supply. The rest of my storage that I obtained from Delhi, a few bags each of A+ and B- along with 6 bags of O- is all I have left.

Having completed my assignment for Lily's class, I have no other pressing concerns except those related to general upkeep of a farm and home. The workers come every weekend to maintain the grounds and the farm. I try to be gone when they come. The less people who get to know me the fewer questions when I must inevitably leave. Since I do not seem to age, I can only stay in one area for a short time; I usually stay less than 10 years. The kind of life I am used to living is one of solitude. Making friends is dangerous. The lies, the deceit, and the fear of being found out along with the ever gnawing pang of fear that I might inadvertently hurt someone, has kept me isolated. I can pretend to fit in for a while, but moving on is always just around the corner.

I don't let myself dwell on those thoughts; instead I focus on the house. I decide the most pressing concern is to prepare it for winter. I take down all the screens from the windows and close up the panes. The gutters need to be oiled and the wood trim needs to be painted. My strength and agility turn several days' worth of work for a typical farmer into several hours work for me. All the time I worked, the incredible high I felt after being with Lily and my morning feed, sustained me. When I stepped back to admire my handy work, I saw that it was now 3:30. After a quick shower and a change of clothes I drive back up to campus to pick up Lily.

CHAPTER 15

I Learn About Lily

The next several weeks would fly by. Time for a vampire takes on a totally different meaning the older you get, but for now I am sailing through it riding the crest of time Lily and I spend together, like a surfer riding the perfect wave. Mid terms have come and gone and the students are preparing for finals and holiday break. Lily and I spent most of our time away from campus together at her home. I drive Lily to campus in the morning; we each go about our day, meeting for lunch or coffee when we are able. At the end of the day I drive us back to her house where we often spend the evening learning more about each other.

This evening Lily was telling me about her family. As I have said previously, Lily is truly an intriguing woman. She was born April 16, 1977, in Oceanside, New York, the older of two children, to John and Isabella Bean. Her younger brother Angelo was born three years later. As Lily speaks of her early childhood and her family, I get a sense of a happy middle class family living in suburbia. That is until she told me the story that marks the end of her childhood. Lily's father was a Vice Detective in New York City, his territory included Chinatown. As we sat before her fire enjoying the closeness we now shared, she told me the story of how her father died.

"It was a family ritual of sorts; we used to go in for dinner at least once a month. Every time we walked down those familiar wear worn stairs, met by the exotic smells that would envelope you as you opened the heavy glass door, I would start to salivate like Pavlov's dog. When we walked into Hop Lee the owner, Jimmy, would personally come out and greet our family. Jimmy was a young Chinese man, too thin for a man who owned his own restaurant. He was a chain smoker, with crooked, stained teeth, that always had a toothpick hanging from one corner of his smiling face. He would say a few quick words to the staff and a table would be set for us.

Our family was always sat at a large center table. We would be one of the few, or more often only, non Asian family in the restaurant. Our table was also the only one that ever had a tablecloth on it. I remember that we never ordered from a menu, in fact Jimmy used to order everything for us. I learned to eat snails and frog legs and they soon became my favorite foods of all time. Jimmy used to like me; I think he was amazed at my willingness to try anything and the gusto to which I could bring to eating. When he would tell us about the food he ordered, he would always add "and of course some snails for you, little lady". Jimmy would often come by our table to share a drink with my dad at the end of our meal. I didn't understand then why we got such preferential treatment when we went to Hop Lee for dinner. I remember feeling like my dad must be important, he certainly was shown a lot of respect from Jimmy and the staff, but it wasn't until I was older that I would understand. My father was a Vice detective, Jimmy was heroine thin and my father worked to keep Chinatown clean and safe. Jimmy, even though he was an addict, appreciated my dad for his role in the community.

My Dad started as a beat detective in Chinatown and used to eat at Hop Lee for lunch or dinner when he worked. He and Jimmy knew each other for a long time and had developed a sort of friendship. I was twelve years old; we were on one of our regular trips to Hop Lee. After dinner we would often walk down Canal Street where the street vendors would sell their wares. We would digest as we walked passed stalls with brightly colored silk dresses, jade jewelry, and tubs of little pet turtles. Everything was as it should be, me and my dad walking hand in hand, my mother and brother a short distance behind us. My brother always had to stop and check out the turtles and each time pleaded with my parents to buy one."

Lily pauses in her story and wipes away the tears that have started to stream down her cheeks. She takes a deep breath and pushes on with her recollection. I can see this is hard for her, but I also see that she needs to share this with me. This would be a defining moment in her life and it is part of what makes her who she is today.

"So, as my mother and brother are looking at turtles my father and I continue walking ahead. There is a point where the vendor stalls end and the restaurant workers receive their deliveries. As we came up to this area two men were hunched over the back of an open van. I could just make out the shape of a long black object sticking part way out of a box as we walked closer. My father must have seen it too, because his demeanor changed instantly, his hand that had previously held mine in a light clasp, clamped down like a vice. What happened next seemed to occur in slow motion though in reality lasted only seconds. It seemed the two men were drug dealers. They had been arguing so intently that when we approached they seemed startled. One of the men reached into the truck and pulled out the long black object. My father seeing this shoved me back hard and I skid backward into the side of the last vendors stall. The sound of the gun fire was like really loud fireworks. The man with the machine gun had fired on the man who had been arguing with him. My father, who always carried a gun, even off duty, had pulled his hand gun as he threw me towards safety. My father fired one shot, hitting the man with the machine gun right between his eyes. As I watched the thin line of blood spill from that third eye I was hit with the metallic smell of fresh blood and gun powder mingled with the aromas of china town, I rolled to my side and puked. There was a lot of screaming and people shouting in Chinese. I guess I was in shock, because for several long minutes I was paralyzed. As I looked around at the scene before me, the blue acrid smoke from the gun swirling upward, my head ringing from the gun shots, I saw my dad slump down with his back against the van. A red stain started to spread from his stomach and down the front of his pants. Even as I watched this happen my mind would not connect the dots. I remember wondering what kind of drink must have spilled on his clothes, and the look on his face, like he knew mom was going to be mad. My mother's screams echoed in my head and yet I still could not move.

I remember Jimmy coming running out and him carrying my brother and I back into the restaurant. I remember thinking he was strong for such a skinny guy to be running with me and my brother in his arms. It is weird what the mind focuses on during times of trauma. My father died three days later from gun shot wounds to the stomach. His funeral was attended by all of the city brass, as was expected when an officer died, but in addition to all of the police and service members, about half the population of Chinatown turned out to mourn my fathers passing. It took a lot of years in therapy for me to be able to come to grips with what I had witnessed. I haven't said that story out loud in a long time. I don't know why I even brought it up, other than I feel like you should know about my family. It certainly isn't the cheeriest of family tales."

I pulled Lily toward me and held her tight as she cried softly against my chest. "I can only imagine what it must have been like for you to have to live through such an ordeal. I know even retelling me the story was extremely painful for you. I have always felt that we are not defined by the events of our lives but by how we respond to them. For you and your family to overcome such trauma and successfully rebuild your lives shows incredible strength of character. Lily, that experience is part of what has made you into the strong, beautiful, woman that sits in my arms. Through the terrible pain and loss you were not only able to survive but thrive. It is a testament to the human spirit, that even living through such a dark and turbulent experience a young soul can heal. I think your father would be proud of the woman you are. I know I have never met another as extraordinary as you."

Lily was drained after the emotional outpouring that went with revealing the story of her father. We lay together on the couch, Lily tightly tucked in by my embrace. We didn't talk, and we didn't have to. As I held Lily against me, stroking her hair, I thought of her pain at the loss of her father and the frailty of man. I am nearly immortal and in love with a fragile, mortal human. The pain of loss is something I have not had to deal with for a long time. I have suffered my share of loss, but the years ease the pain, and I have had many years to accept it. But now I suddenly feel very human, for the fear I have of losing Lily, of something terrible happening to her, is palpable. I made a silent vow to be this fragile creature's protector. I know I would walk through the very fires of hell if it meant saving her from harm. I also know that I cannot protect her from everything, and that is the thought that circles through my head as I watch Lily finally give in to sleep.

Her sleep is deep but troubled, from her sleep talking and anguished pleas for help, I surmise she is reliving the tale of her father's death in her dream. After a while she finally quiets and her slumber is uninterrupted. I lay there all night holding Lily in my arms, and all night I dwelled on the seed of dread that had been planted in my gut. The dread of knowing that one day, Lily would die and I would be alone again.

CHAPTER 16

We Take a Little Trip

I got up early and left Lily sleeping peacefully on the couch. In the kitchen I quietly prepared a breakfast for her. I fed Pumpkin and let her out, she has finally settled down around me and I would even say she likes me. Feeding her helps, she loves food, very much like her mistress. One thing I have learned about Lily is that food is not just about the sustenance for her. She seems to enjoy food on an almost spiritual level. Certainly her mood can be altered by food as well as alter her food choices. About the only constant I have noticed, is that chocolate seems to work at improving almost every scenario. This morning I make her a batch of chocolate chip pancakes, with a cheese omelet and fruit plate. The smell of the coffee finally stirs her. It is Friday. One more week of classes and one week of finals and then the College is on winter break.

"Good morning, how do you feel?" I ask as she walks over and takes the steaming mug of coffee I offer. She inhales the steam deeply, kisses my chest, which is even with her lips, and replies "I kind of feel like I have a hangover, an emotional hangover. I also feel a little lighter, like a deep dark secret from my past has been revealed and you didn't run away or turn to dust." "One thing you have yet to learn about me Lily is that I don't scare easily." I chuckled as I said this but not just for levity but because I am usually the one doing the scaring.

"Wow! Chocolate, cheese and fruit, the perfect comfort food breakfast! Thank you Max and not just for the breakfast, your support last night means so much to me." "I will be here for you for eternity if you will let me." I responded. "Now eat, you have to go to campus and I need to go home to check on a few things." Lily, finished eating and took a quick shower, it took a great deal of effort not to join her in the shower but I knew the responsible thing to do was let her be on time for class. Besides I had plans for this weekend. "Do you have anything pressing this weekend?" I asked her through the thrum of the shower. As the water turned off she poked her head out from behind the curtain, "Actually, no. I have my lecture plans and review for the last week ready and my final is finished and printed. Did you have something in mind?" "I would love to take you camping, there is a spectacular spot near Racquet Lake, and they have these Yurts that are beautiful. I promise it will be an adventure you will love" I said enthusiastically. "I always wanted to try out a Yurt and the thought of escaping for a weekend sounds like just what the doctor ordered." "Excellent, throw a few things in a bag before we leave, I will take you to campus, swing by my farm and pick you up at 3:00. We will be in front of a cozy fire by 6:00." "You're not going to class?" She asked. I smiled a sly grin as I replied "I'm good friends with the professor, I think I can persuade her to give me a recap of the lecture, and I'm sure I can get the notes from someone." She seemed to be weighing the fact of me skipping class with the prospect of our weekend getaway. "Hmm" was her only response.

I felt much better on the drive up to campus, buoyed by the weekend getaway plan that was slowly evolving in my head. I wanted this weekend to be one of those events in your life that you talk about when you're old, memorable and defining. I dropped off Lily and instead of her customary quick peck good bye she kissed me, a sweet passionate kiss. "I'll see you at three." She said and she was jogging

98

happily off to class. I had a lot to do to get ready for this weekend. First I called the campsite that rents out the yurts. The man told me he had no available yurts left. I decided an in person request was in order and drove to my farm. After parking I took off through the woods at the back of my property. From there, there is nearly unbroken forest between my home and the campsite.

I walked into the campground office to find the clerk to inquire about the rental. A man of about 40 came out from a back area. He looked like the stereotype of a park ranger. Ruddy, weather worn and sturdy, he came to the desk and introduced himself as Jack Miller, Park Ranger and general manager of everything, since he was the only full time employee during the winter months. I introduced myself and inquired about the yurt rental. He told me he had one left but it was reserved for a couple arriving tomorrow. He informed me he had a cabin available if I wanted. As I have mentioned earlier the power of persuasion is a gift I have, but infrequently use, this weekend however I want to be perfect. Within minutes Ranger Miller was apologizing for the mix up, he indeed had one yurt left, that couple arriving tomorrow were actually signed up for the cabin. I thanked him for "double checking" and gave him a generous tip. He tried to decline the money but a further nudge of his mind had him compliant.

I found the spot, it was indeed perfect; completely surrounded by woods on all sides save for the front, which faced a panoramic view of Racquet Lake in all its magnificent winter glory. I took a look at the accommodations and made a mental list of the provisions we would need. A quick dash out into the woods and I had enough firewood split and ready for three weeks worth of fires. After a quick chat with Ranger Miller, I head back to the farm. I feed on the remaining blood supply I have left from Delhi, shower, throw my things in a bag and head out to the grocery store. I get all the provisions I think we will need, stop by the liquor store for some wine and head over to Lily's. I pick up Pumpkin, some dog food, treats, and her bed and pack up my truck for the trip. Pumpkin decides to stretch out across the back seat and fall asleep.

I pull up to campus at five of three. I see Lily walking toward me. She is not alone. Her friend Paul is there. I can hear their conversation and a small guttural growl escapes my lips. Pumpkin picks up her head for a second but then goes back to sleep. I hear Paul questioning the idea of Lily and me going away for the weekend. It seems he has yet to accept that we are together. Lily turns from Paul and in an exasperated tone tells him she has to go. He calls to her back "Remember Jelly Bean I am just a phone call away if you need me." She does not turn around so Paul misses the look of annoyance on her face. As she sees me, her visage is morphed into a radiant smile and a look of love and longing. I come around to open the door for her and before she slips in I embrace her. I kiss her with a passion that has her slightly breathless as we release. She looks up at me with scolding eyes. I tell her "I know it is totally immature but something about that guy rubs me the wrong way. His persistent attempts at insinuating himself between us makes me feel very territorial." "Look, I'll talk to him again when we get back, he is a good person at heart and he thinks he is trying to protect me. Let's not worry about him. Let's just get away from here."

As I open the door for Lily to get in the car I see Paul staring at us with a look of contempt on his face. This is more than my predatory nature can take and the look I return to him hits its mark hard. The contemptuous look was quickly replaced by one of unease. I have an ability to portray in a look all the power and ferocity contained by my humanity, a glimpse of the feral beast I can be if challenged. My image morphs so quickly from calm to ferocious and back to calm that Paul isn't even sure what he saw. He only knows he is left with a feeling of unease and will think twice about interfering in my relationship with Lily. As I pull away from campus I can't help but smile as I glimpse Paul's retreating frame sulking away.

The drive to our camp site is leisurely. We enjoy the beauty of winter in the Adirondack region, even its starkness, in such contrast to the same area in spring or summer, is beautiful. The woods and mountains are blanketed in white, remnants of an earlier snow fall. As we drive into the campgrounds dusk dissolves all the hard edges, and its blue hue further distorts the view out over the lake. The effect creates a hazy dreamlike image of the surroundings. We walk up the two steps to our yurt. The key is under the doormat as I had suggested to Ranger Miller earlier. When Lily opened the door she inhaled sharply in surprise. I had suggested a few romantic touches to the Ranger as well, and it seemed he followed through to the letter.

CHAPTER 17

A Surprise for Lily

The interior of the yurt was a glow in a soft white light provided by dozens of tea-lite candles that seemed to dot every surface. A fire burning steadily in the fireplace at the yurt's center added to the effect. In addition to the candles, there were dozens of vases all filled with different varieties of lilies placed about the room. When we walked into the bedroom space I could see Ranger Miller had outdone himself. The bed had been turned down and at its center was a beautifully wrapped box, presumably chocolates, and lying across one pillow was a single white lily. The effect this all had on Lily was priceless. She quite literally flitted around the room looking at all of the flowers; as she came full circle, she threw her arms around my neck and said she forgave me for skipping class. "How did you do all this? It is so beautiful." She said doing a little twirl to take it all in. "I am a man of many talents, and you are by far, the most beautiful element in this picturesque setting."

Lily let Pumpkin out to do a little exploring while we unpacked my truck and settled in. As I was bringing in a bundle of firewood Pumpkin came back to the yurt. Two things hit me at once, one was Pumpkin's demeanor. She came slinking back to the yurt, tail between her legs, a pitiful whine escaping her muzzle. When she saw me she stopped dead in her tracks. It looked as if she were weighing her options, face what ever it was that spooked her in the woods or face me. I thought she finally started to like me, but in her state of elevated fear, it seemed I was only the lesser of the two evils, made tolerable due to the presence of Lily. The other thing, I felt, or more accurately, smelled. Just a hint of a scent but when it hit my ultra sensitive nose there was a split second of familiarity to it. My mind tried to process the information contained in that quickly fleeting scent. But it was gone, and I was unable to pinpoint how or when I had smelled that scent or something like it before. I was left with a lingering sense of deja-vu.

Before I could give it too much thought, Lily opened the door to the yurt and Pumpkin darted in as if she were fleeing her doom. "Pumpkin! What has gotten into you?" Lily asked the dog as she nearly knocked her mistress down with her efforts to get safely back inside with her. Lily looked at me with questioning eyes as I followed the dog in, my arms loaded with wood. "I don't know what happened. I was out getting the firewood when Pumpkin came back to the yurt. It looked as if she was scared of something, she wasn't exactly thrilled to see me, but I guess I rate higher than what ever spooked her. It's possible she saw a bear or moose, there are also some bob cats that can be pretty aggressive around here. Maybe we should keep her close to the yurt in the evening." I said.

I registered the look of unease that crept into Lily's eyes at the mention of the possibility of Pumpkin having run into such potentially large and dangerous animals. I gave Lily a reassuring hug and told her she was perfectly safe. I patted Pumpkin's head, to reassure her, but she looked as if she were reluctant to have me touch her. I took out a treat I had packed; she took it hesitantly and retreated to her bed by the fire. She lay there for a while, head cocked in the direction of the woods from which she retreated, until finally settling down and falling asleep.

After adding some wood to the fire, I set about fixing a plate of what I hoped was an enjoyable feast for Lily. Some aged cheeses, imported prociutto and salami, mixed olives and various other tidbits arranged with some sliced Italian bread and an excellent bottle of red wine, made for an impressive "farmer's meal". Lily eyed the spread appreciatively as she carried over two wine glasses. As I poured the wine I saw Lily give a worried glance Pumpkin's way. I carried the wine to Lily, handing her a glass. "Lily, I promise you that I will never let anything hurt you or Pumpkin. You are safe here with me." I said and gently kissed the worry from her lips. She looked at me then, her eyes searching the depths of my soul. She leaned in to kiss me, all the while keeping her penetrating gaze upon me. When she pulled back from that passionate kiss she smiled up at me and replied, "I know. When I am with you Max, I feel completely at ease, like together, we could face anything."

"Once again Max, you've out done yourself. This looks delicious", she said as we settled onto the couch with our wine and food set at the coffee table. "Lily, before we eat I have one more surprise for you. I found this at the antique shop in town and was drawn to it. Like you, it is elegant, beautiful, and seems to possess an inner strength and power." I handed Lily the antique silver jewelry box, wrapped in crimson paper, tied with a silver ribbon that I had hid beside the couch. "Max, you have done so much already, now a gift?" she said with a protesting look. "Lily, I hope to have an eternity with which to spoil you. And as I said I was drawn to this just as I have been drawn to you. Now are you going to open it?" With that, Lily gently took off the silver ribbon before tearing into the crimson wrapping paper. When she revealed the silver jewelry box she replied, "Oh Max! This is amazing." As she turned the box in her hands I noticed for the first time that it was designed with lilies intricately woven around a center crest on the lid of the box. In the center of the crest were two doves nestled in a nest. The silver work was quite remarkable. When I purchased the box it was an after thought, something to add to the presentation of the necklace. Looking at it now I see why Lily would think that the box itself was the gift.

I took the box from her hand and opened it, taking out the pewter and ruby necklace and laying it across Lily's hand. "The proprietor of the antique shop told me that this had once belonged to his wife Lilly." I proceeded to tell her the story the old gentleman had shared with me. When I told her the part about the flickering light in the shop, she nearly dropped the necklace. I finished the story with the part about the necklace having certain powers if worn by a worthy and powerful woman. "Now you know why I had to buy this for you. It's as if you were destined to wear it." "Max, I am at a loss for words. It's beautiful. But it's too much. I can't possibly accept such an extravagant gift." I took the necklace from her hands and moved behind her. I opened the clasp and slipped the necklace around her neck fastening the pewter clasp again. Still standing behind her I wrapped my arms around her, embracing her, kissing her neck and inhaling her scent. I made my way up from the nape of her glorious neck and stopped just behind her ear. Whispering, I said, "The necklace, like my heart, is yours, now and forever." Lily turned in my arms and lifted her face to mine. "I will take them both into my care, and know in return my heart and soul belong to you." We kissed again, long and passionately. With that kiss, the necklace, and our pledge to each other, a bond was sealed.

We made love amidst the candle glow; the scent of lilies surrounding us. Our passion was unhurried and tender. When we finally lay spent and contented, the fire was down to burning embers and the candles were reduced to pools of hardening wax. Laying there, our bare bodies pressed together, I could feel Lily's heart beat in my own chest, as if she truly gave her heart to me. "Why don't we change into some comfortable clothes and dig in to this neglected spread? I encouraged. Lily turned her face to mine, "Thank you Max, again. This is extraordinary." She said as her fingers stroked the smooth pewter cross and cool round ruby. "You are extraordinary!"

she finished as she broke from our embrace and gathered up our strewn clothes.

We changed into sweats and as Lily settled back down on the couch I put the rest of the firewood onto the embers and restarted the fire. While we shared the wine and various samplings from the plate I found myself thinking that I wish I didn't have to pretend to eat. I longed to tell Lily the truth about myself. I felt a pang of guilt for letting our relationship get so far without telling her the truth. I must have made a face as I was thinking this because Lily asked "Is something wrong?" Here was my opportunity, a chance to tell Lily everything, the truth of who and what I am. Instead I said, "Everything is wonderful, I was just thinking that we need more wood from the pile to keep this fire going for the night. I will be right back with some more." I kissed Lily on the head as I went outside, feeling like a coward for not being able to tell her the truth. The wood pile was out a short distance away from the yurt and out of view from the windows. As I made my way to the wood pile I decided to chance a quick dash into to the woods to purge. I knew I would only be able to purge the discomfort of the food from my gut, the discomfort my own cowardice caused would not be gotten rid of so easily. I needed to think about how and when I would tell Lily the truth. The longer I wait, the longer I live a lie with Lily, the greater the risk of her rejecting me for the lie. On the other hand, if she is not ready for the truth I could scare her off and lose her.

I made my way back to the yurt, first stopping at the wood pile for some more firewood. As my mind swirled and my conflicting emotions fought for attention I was hit by that same faint whiff of something I couldn't quite determine. Whether it was my guilt, or the scent, or a combination of both, I couldn't tell, but as I walked back into the yurt I was feeling slightly on edge. I called Pumpkin over to the door to see if she needed to go out once more for the night, but she just took one look at the open door and mewled softly and lay back down. I put the wood by the fire place and resumed my spot next to the woman I pledged my heart to. We sat by the fire, chatting some, but mostly content to sit and just be together. When Lily's yawning reminded me of her need for sleep, I led a sleepy Lily to our bed. We lay in bed together; Lily curled up beside me as I spooned up against her. She quickly fell off into a deep and restful sleep. I lay awake the entire night, watching her, mesmerized by the beauty of her magnificent features. The gnawing unease I had felt when I came in from the wood pile, slowly ebbed as I was soothed by Lily's closeness and the rhythmic beat of her heart.

CHAPTER 18

Sunrise Over Raquette Lake

At a little after 6:00am, Pumpkin nosed open the door to our bedroom. A slight whine escapes her muzzle as she licks Lily's face always keeping a watchful eye on me. Lily seems accustomed to this morning wake up and with her eyes still closed reaches out one hand to stroke Pumpkin's head. She rolls over and as she opens her eyes she is facing me. "Good morning. I would give you a morning kiss but not everyone is as tolerant of dog spit as I am." She says sleepily. I lean in and kiss her tenderly on the lips. "What's a little dog spit between friends?" I say as I shift up on to my elbow. As Lily laughs she pulls me back down to kiss her again. Pumpkin is growing impatient and breaks our embrace as she jumps up onto the bed between us. "Ok, I get it, you want out. It's your fault for not going out last night." With that Lily gets out of bed to take her out.

I watch as she looks through her bag for something to put on. She is breathtaking. As our relationship, both physical and otherwise, is still in its infancy, every day I see something new about her and everything about her makes me want to learn more. Standing in front of me, naked, as she searches for her clothes, she seems completely comfortable in her own skin. She has beautiful olive skin, with remnants of summer tan lines, smooth and silken over athletic muscles that define and contour her frame. After finally locating her elusive clothes, she dresses quickly to let out a very insistent Pumpkin. I follow them, grabbing my pants as I walk out.

When Lily opens the door Pumpkin darts out to do her business. Apparently nature's urges override her concerns from last night. The morning is just breaking, with the sun rising over the lake creating a red hue to the clouds. "Red sun in the morning, sailor take warning" I say as we walk out to the small porch along the yurt's left side. It is cold this morning and a heavy frost blankets the ground around our site. Lily shivers as we watch the sunrise over the lake. I pull her back against my chest and wrap my arms around her. "It sure is chilly this morning" she says as she snuggles back against my body. She turns her head as she realizes I am standing out on this very cold porch in sweat pants, with no shirt or shoes. "What are you, part Eskimo or polar bear?" She asks. I laugh out loud at that, a private joke, as I have drank polar bear. "The cold doesn't bother me" I say as I hug her tighter. We watched as the sun crept up over the horizon turning the red hued shadowy landscape, into a gloriously bright winter morning. Pumpkin came bounding back to the yurt and leapt quickly up the stairs and in through the door. Lily spun her body around in my arms and facing me put her head against my bare chest. She stayed there hugging me with her eyes closed and a serene look on her face. After a few minutes she gave me an extra squeeze and broke off from our embrace and we headed inside.

"So Max, what shall we do today?" she called over her shoulder as she fed Pumpkin and gave her fresh water. "I thought we could go for a hike, we could pack a lunch, I know a beautiful spot I would love to take you. There is even a place we could have lunch by a fire. I thought we could talk about the New Zealand trip. I am excited to learn about what you have planned for it." "That sounds like fun. Do you think the weather will hold out? This morning's sunrise, while beautiful, does make me wonder about the weather. It is not unusual to get some severe lake effect storms in this area." I reassure her that we won't travel too far from the yurt and suggest we get an early start. I remind her that if the weather gets bad we can always come back early. Lily agrees to the plan and we set about getting together our supplies. I put together the remains from last night's farmer's meal, some cheese, and meats and bread along with some fruit salad I had packed the day before. A bottle of wine, some water bottles and a blanket finished my pack. We got dressed in appropriate hiking attire and after careful consideration decided to leave Pumpkin behind. She was currently curled up asleep on our bed, and didn't seem to mind.

We headed out. I carried the pack with our gear and Lily slid a camera into her coat pocket and grabbed an apple on the way out the door. We proceeded out into a magnificent winter morning. The early clouds opened up to large patches of clear blue sky, the intermittent sun warmed us as we made our way through the woods around the lake. The spot that I wanted to take Lily to is near the stream where I had the bear encounter. About a quarter mile down stream from where I saved those hikers there is a bend in the stream. It cuts in close to a narrow clearing backed by a short cave. The cave mouth is large with trees on either side forming a canopy over the entrance; the cave itself only goes back a few hundred feet and ends in a slight downward slope. I have been to this spot many times; it is secluded and offers a serene place to meditate.

As we make our way through the woods our pace is leisurely. We make frequent stops to admire nature's beauty. Lily points out various plants and animal tracks and explains about each as we go. She has taken out the camera and is capturing on film the beauty of our surroundings. I stopped to admire a glistening web strung between two branches. The sunlight backlit the web making it appear to be adorned with hundreds of small diamonds glittering among the intricate web pattern. Lily snapped a photo of me as I was deep in observation of the miraculous creation. I looked up at her then as she brought the lens down. "I hope that shot comes out! The web was all sparkling and the light how it hit you, your skin looked like marble. It was beautiful." she remarked, slightly awed by what she saw. I smiled at her and she joined me in closer inspection of the web.

As we continued to move forward to our destination I felt a slight breeze picking up at our backs. We had been walking about an hour and Lily stopped to drink some water. We were stopped near a large rock that Lily sat upon as she drank her water. She looked like a woodland creature out of fairy tales. The earth surrounding her in deep brown hues, the rock a dark gray, mottled with lichens pale and dry from the harsh cold, and Lily rosy faced, clad in black jeans and red ski jacket, perched on the rock like a butterfly alights on a flower petal, the sun casting an ethereal glow around her. I took the camera from where she placed it near my pack and took a photo of the beauty that outshone everything else in my eyes. "I hope that shot comes out, because you are by far the most stunning of nature's creations." I said. Lily just smiled and after another pull from the water bottle resealed the cap and walked over to me ready to resume our hike.

We continued through the woods following a game trail as it meandered its way along parallel to the stream. The sounds of our boots crunching fallen leaves as we walked mingled with the sounds of the running water. The serenity of the forest enveloped us. We had been hiking now almost two hours and we were very close to our destination. As we neared the clearing by the cave I stopped to pick up fallen branches for our fire. Once again I am reminded of the frailty of humans. I find myself constantly doing a mental assessment to determine if I am neglecting Lily's needs. As long as I have blood inside me, my body temperature will remain constant regardless of my environment and I am sure the hike has kept Lily warm enough, but when we stop she could easily get cold and I want to be sure she is comfortable. It is very foreign to me, feeling the need to care for someone. I like caring for Lily.

We arrive at the site; the clearing is narrow, with the stream cutting in close to the cave mouth. The sun has just broken through a particularly large patch of clouds. The stream sparkles with reflected light and the view is spectacular. There are fresh deer prints in the soft soil by the streams edge, the only signs that some other creature has been this way. "Oh Max this is a special place, I can see what would draw you back here. Thank you for sharing this with me." We set up our blanket near the mouth of the cave. Lily looked into the cave, the back of which was shrouded in blackness. "How far back does it go do you think? She asked me. I told her it only goes back a few hundred feet and dips down in the back. As she squinted into the darkness I could tell she was uneasy that something might reside in there. I pulled a burning branch from the fire and walked into the cave illuminating the shadowed depths. There was nothing moving in the cave but there were remnants of bone fragments in the back, a sign that something used this cave in the past. Content that nothing would come out from the cave as we sat, Lily unpacked the rest of our provisions and set them out on the blanket for us. We would save the wine for later as it was still early. From the angle of the sun I guessed it was just after 10am. I placed some more wood on the fire and sat with Lily on the blanket.

As we sat nibbling on cheese and cured meats, amidst the peaceful surroundings I asked the question that I both anticipated and dreaded the response to. "So, tell me about the plans for the New Zealand trip." "The trip! I am getting very excited. I have been planning this for a year now. You know I have been researching the existence of vampires. Well my great grandfather Augustine Angelone was a scholar and had been involved in researching vampire lore. He kept detailed journals of his various expeditions. My mother gave me those journals when I was a young girl; I had a penchant for reading anything in the supernatural/vampire genre. I used to read those journals and dream of following in my great grandfathers footsteps. After I got to college and got involved with

Dr. Derensinski, I realized that I could make my dreams a reality. I started researching some of the locations my great grand father had mentioned and tried to follow his leads. None of the leads had taken me very far, after all his contacts date back almost a hundred years. I decided to focus on the last few trips he had taken before his death. He died at sea off the coast of Sicily; he had been following another one of his leads and was traveling by small boat along the Sicilian coast. He was presumed drowned; his boat was found capsized by a local fisherman. I haven't yet been able to bring myself to follow in his last journeys path, but his journal entry about his New Zealand trip was very extensive."

"New Zealand" I echoed the words. "He had names of purported witnesses and where they lived and various contacts with whom he was communicating. Last year I started to do some digging on the internet. I Googled some of the contact names and by chance came across the grandson of one of my great grand father's contacts. His grand father also kept detailed journals on his work. He sent me copies of the papers and I found the name of a town where a farmer and his family had been killed. The man listed it as a story of interest due to the grizzly nature of the killings. He made specific notes in the journal about the presence of puncture wounds and torn flesh around the victims' necks. The official explanation was animal attack. He noted there was one survivor, an infant. Next to the notation was a name Thomas. At first I thought with no last name I would never be able to track down this boy Thomas. As it turns out Thomas is the last name, and the survivor was a girl. Victoria Thomas aged nine months when she was left abandoned on the steps of a farmhouse near where the attack occurred, now aged 87 and living back on her families land in a small town located on Banks Peninsula called Little River. The official news report credits a Good Samaritan for finding the child amidst the carnage and taking her to the nearby farm. No other information was available. After a year of correspondence Victoria has agreed to see me. We will be going to interview her and several other old timers who were around at the time of the attack. One 96 year old witness claims he saw the attack, a boy of 9 at the time, he said he was playing in a nearby meadow when he heard the Thomas' sheep making horrible screams and snuck up thinking farmer Thomas must be slaughtering some for market. What he saw instead was something or someone attacking the sheep, ripping their throats. He said he ran home and was too afraid to tell his folks. It wasn't until the next day when they found the family killed that he said anything. They didn't take the rambled recollection of a scared 9 year old as fact and chalked up the killings to animal attack."

As Lily talked excitedly about the details of the trip I sat incredulous as her descriptions of the attack and the survivor started to sound all too familiar. I kept praying that in all of New Zealand it was just coincidence the details of a farm family being slaughtered so mirrored my own deadly rampage. But as the words "Little River" left her tongue I could only sit in stunned silence as the realization hit me. Victoria Thomas was the girl I left on the farm house steps the day I slaughtered her family and regained my humanity.

CHAPTER 19

My Past Catches Up to My Present

"Max are you ok? You look like you're in pain?" I was in pain, anguished at the thought of facing my gruesome past. The thought that the little girl was still alive, or that she would have any recollection of that brutal day so long ago never really entered my mind. So distant have I kept that memory. And a witness, what horrors had he seen, would he recognize me as the monster if he saw me again? What would Lily uncover from her investigations? If she learns the truth about the brutality that occurred on that farm so many years ago, could she ever see me the same way again? Every fiber of my being wanted to just run, as far and fast as I could, putting distance between me and the reality of the moment.

"Max, what's wrong?" Lily asked again as she took my hand in hers, a look of concern darkening her face. My brain swirled as I tried to process what all this meant. To Lily, I said "I'm fine. I think the cheese is disagreeing with me. If you will excuse me for a minute, I think I would feel better if I purged it from my system. I'll be right back." I got up and walked further down stream and behind a stand of trees. Indeed I did purge the food I had consumed, but I felt no better. Right now I just had to focus on getting through this weekend with out letting Lily see my true concerns.

I needed time to reflect on this turn of events, time to come up with a plan. But a plan for what? To tell Lily the truth? To find a way to keep my secrets hidden? I could disappear. Start a new chapter. But as I say the words in my head I know that leaving now is not an option. The thought of leaving Lily tears at my soul and a fresh wave of anguish washes over me. No, I will not run away, not from my past and not from the future I dream about with Lily. I have spent nearly a century trying to atone for my past transgressions. New Zealand was my rebirth. I will have to find a way to tell Lily the truth and if she rejects me, then I will leave.

I gather myself, and make my way back towards Lily. The wind has picked up since we set up our picnic; clouds are thickening and darkening overhead. Lily greats my return with a concerned smile. "You ok?" she asks. "Yes, much better, sorry for that." "Don't be silly, I just hope you feel ok, we have quite a walk back." "I'm fine really, and speaking of going back, the weather is turning, we should start heading back or we could get caught in a squall." "Ok. You sure you're ok?" I pull Lily into my arms her head resting on my chest. I breathe in her scent as I embrace her. "As long as I am with you Lily, everything is right in my world"

We pack up our few supplies and head back to our camp site. The walk is more difficult for Lily as the wind has picked up and turned icy. I take the lead and try and block most of the wind for her but I see she is tiring. After shifting my pack around to my front I pause in front of Lily. "Hop on!" I say, as I assume the piggy back position. Lily looks up at me with a look that says "are you serious?" "Come on, please?" I try to flash her my best pleading look, and with a giggle she hops on my back.

We make good time moving as one. An icy snow has started to fall and the wind pelts us. Lily hides her face from the onslaught. I chance moving faster, hoping the wind and snow keep her face hidden and eyes closed long enough so I can quickly get her back to the warmth and safety of the yurt. As the storm swirls around us

I once again catch the smell that spooked Pumpkin on the day we arrived at camp. The cold wet snow and wind pull the scent away again. I do not know what it is, but I am left with a lingering sense of unease. Something is out in these woods. My predatory nature senses that what ever it is, it is formidable.

I quicken my pace, aware how easily Lily could catch me moving at an unnaturally fast speed, but the combination of the worsening storm and the growing wariness I feel about keeping Lily out here in the woods with what ever it is that is out here with us, has me throw caution to the wind. We arrive back at the yurt in half the time it took us to hike out. As I stop to let Lily down she looks up in surprise at the yurt in front of us. "We are back already? I thought you were just putting me down to walk the rest of the way. How is that possible?" "Lily your so light I was able to move fairly quickly along the trail and I took a small short cut I hadn't noticed on the way out" I hated to lie, but it was miniscule in comparison to the real truth and Lily's safety was my only reason for chancing her seeing my ability.

We went inside the yurt and I quickly restarted the fire. Lily was cold and her hair glistened with melting snow. I grabbed a towel from the bathroom and proceeded to dry Lily's hair. When I had finished, her hair was a tussled mess, yet in my eyes she was never more radiant. As I stared down at her, my thoughts lingered on Victoria Thomas, the New Zealand trip, and the realization that in just two weeks, my newly perfect world was potentially about to be shattered. "You have that look again, like you might puke. Are you sure you're ok?" she asked, stroking my cheek with her chilled fingers. "I'm fine; I was just thinking of this storm, I hope it doesn't complicate our return trip home in the morning." My reply wasn't a complete lie. The storm was whipping up outside and it is not unheard of to have a foot or more of snow drop in a very short time with the lake effect in the region. "Stuck in a secluded cabin in the woods with the man I love, doesn't seem so awful to me." She said as she slid by me on the way to the bathroom. "How about we warm up in the shower? The hair style you have given me leaves a lot to be desired." "Why don't you start and I will join you in a few minutes. If we are going to be stuck here I want to bring in a lot more wood so we don't have to go out tonight in the middle of a storm in the dark." I replied. In addition to the New Zealand concerns, there was still a nagging sense of a presence in the woods that I needed to check out. It definitely had Pumpkin bothered and something about it made me uneasy. "Ok, I'm going to take a super hot shower, lately this winter weather has me cold to my core. The only way I can seem to warm up is if I cook myself for a while under the water. I'll try not to use up all the hot water, but don't be too long."

While Lily went into the shower I ducked out into the swirling snow storm. It was difficult to smell anything, the air so cold and wet, too turbulent to pin point any scent. I decided to take a quick run around the perimeter of the woods to see if I could sense what ever it was that had me on edge. I was just rounding the far side of the lake when I felt a sensation I had never felt before, a shooting pain in my right ankle, like I wrenched it, followed by a vivid feeling of fear. "Lily." I knew as I said her name she was in trouble. It was her pain and fear I was sensing. A wave of panic enveloped me. Lily was in trouble and I left her alone. I ran, fueled by my need to protect my love, and pushed to the limit my abilities of strength, power and speed. When I arrived back at the yurt I could hear Pumpkin inside. Her snarls and bark, so vicious, I could hardly conceive they were coming from the same dog I knew. I threw open the door, desperate to make sure Lily was safe. Pumpkin in her frenzied state lunged at me as I crossed the yurts threshold. As she sunk her teeth deep into my thigh, I tried to find a way to stop her attack without hurting her. I could feel her tearing the tissue of my quad and felt the wet, sticky sensation of blood running down my leg. I was finally able to grab her, and separate her from my thigh. I wrapped one hand around her muzzle, preventing her from biting me further. I spoke soothingly to the dog, looking her in the eyes as I spoke. She finally seemed to recognize me and stopped thrashing in my arms. When I released her from my restraining grip she darted to the open yurt door and emitted a long menacing growl, her hair raised on her back. As I closed the door, I finally registered Lily's screams coming from the bathroom. The fear in her voice pushed me forward and as I ripped open the bathroom door I found Lily, sprawled on the floor, soaked, with a towel partly covering her naked body, hands wrapped protectively around her right ankle. "Lily, what happened? Are you hurt?" "Oh Max, it's my ankle, I think it might be broken. I was in the shower, when just after you left, Pumpkin started going berserk. I could hear her barking and growling like she was the most vicious dog on the planet, not my sweet girl. I tried to jump out of the shower quickly to see what was wrong and I slipped and fell. I was screaming to Pumpkin trying to calm her, and then I was calling for you. Is she ok? What was she barking at?"

I picked Lily up off the bathroom floor and wrapped her in her towel. I brought her over to our bed and gingerly set her down. She winced as her right foot touched the mattress. Pumpkin had stopped barking and growling and now lay staring at the door to the yurt, a low whine occasionally escaping her muzzle. I stopped to assess the damage to Lily's ankle. It was swollen and purple and could very well be broken. "I think we should get this checked out. Let me help you dry off and dress, there is a hospital a few miles from here." "Max what happened? Why was Pumpkin acting so crazy?" "Something definitely scared her, but I have no idea what it was. When I was out getting the wood, I tried to take a look around to see if there were any tracks or signs that something had come close to the yurt, but with the storm I couldn't find any signs of an animal or anything else that might have spooked her. Then I heard you screaming and rushed in to see if you were ok." Just then Lily noticed my ripped and bloodied pant leg. "Oh my goodness, Max what happened to your leg?" I looked down at my pant leg and noticed for the first time the amount of blood that had soaked into my jeans before my body could repair the damaged muscle tissue. "Oh, it's nothing, a small scratch. I scared Pumpkin when I burst back into the yurt to help you; I guess she thought I was the thing that had spooked her. She didn't mean to hurt me. Once she realized it was me she calmed down. "She bit you? Max I'm so sorry, she has never acted like this! I didn't think she had an aggressive bone in her body." Lily was obviously troubled by Pumpkin's behavior. I quickly tried to sooth her. "Lily, Pumpkin was just doing what comes instinctually to her. She was trying to protect you. I don't fault her for that, in fact I am glad she showed the capacity to defend you."

I got together some clothes for Lily and when I returned to her side she was weeping quietly. "Oh Lily, is it that painful?" "No, actually, it feels a lot better. I'm just so worried about Pumpkin. She has been acting strange on and off for the past six months. I guess I'm afraid I'm losing her. She's ten and I have had her since she is eight weeks old. Pure bread Labs have a life expectancy of around 10 years. Maybe she is getting senile or sick. Her behavior has been erratic and biting you, I just don't know what to think." "Lily, I'm sure Pumpkin is fine. Something spooked her. With the storm raging outside, all the strange noises, in a place that is unfamiliar to her, her response is normal. And even though she is ten, she has plenty of spunk in her." I thought of the viciousness with which she attacked me earlier. "Look I'm sure she will be back to her old self once she gets home, and even if she is in her waning years, you don't want to spend the rest of the time you have with her focusing on her eventual demise. When we open our hearts to love another we risk the potential pain suffered at the loss of that love. I realized I was not only thinking about Lily's love for Pumpkin, but for my love of her as well. "I'm sure you would agree that the love, companionship and time you have shared together are worth the eventual pain of loss. However, if you spend your time worrying about losing what you have, you won't enjoy what you have before you lose it. Now let's get you dressed and have that ankle checked out."

Lily composed herself and said "Your right. I'm sorry for acting like a blubbering child. I can't dwell on the inevitable loss. I don't know what's wrong with me; I am usually much more level headed." "It's hard to be level headed in affairs of the heart" I said as I helped Lily on with her clothes. As I handed Lily her pants I noticed her ankle did indeed look better. Had I imagined the bruise being worse? Yet now when I looked at it, her bruise was lighter and had a faint tinge of brownish green, often seen in a bruise that has been healing for a few days. After Lily finished dressing she stood up to test her ankle. As she got up and gingerly took a few steps she declared it to be fine, just a bad twist. At her insistence we would forgo our trip to the hospital. With the storm continuing to rage outside, staying put seemed like a good idea.

We cuddled up on the couch by the fire with Pumpkin curled up asleep at Lily's feet. The excitement and emotion of the day has left Lily drained. We sat by the fire in quiet contemplation until Lily drifted off to sleep beside me on the couch. As I sat staring at the flickering flames listening to Lily's rhythmic breathing I tried to organize the flood of thoughts swirling through my head. One more week of classes, followed by finals week and then the college is on winter break. We leave for New Zealand on December 20th and are scheduled to meet with Victoria Thomas on the 22nd and the witness to my attack on her family on the 23rd. We will spend two weeks in New Zealand to research vampires and follow the leads of Augustine Angelone. I try to think of the possible outcomes of my past colliding with my present. Perhaps time and the effects of age have erased any memory of me from the mind of the witness, I don't have a concern that Victoria will remember me, she was only an infant not even a year old. But the witness was nine at the time, old enough to remember, hopefully now old enough to forget. Then there is the nagging feeling of unease about the presence in the woods. Lily mentioned Pumpkin has been acting strange for six months. I have only been in town close to Lily for the last four months. So, either Pumpkin is going senile, which I doubt, or possibly there is more to the presence in the woods than I first thought. Could something be tracking Lily as I had been? Or possibly tracking me? I find myself rooting for senility, sorry Pumpkin, but the alternative leaves too many questions. And then there is Lily. I have to tell her the truth. We have vowed our love to one another, I know I must face the risk of losing her and tell her the truth. What life could we possibly have together without the truth being told? I know the answer is none.

I cannot hide my true self from Lily much longer. She is smart and observant. She has noticed things already like my speed. Soon she will see that I do not age or injure, or any of the other traits she has been researching for years. It is not possible to hide being a vampire from such a compelled researcher as Lily. As I think of this I notice I still have on my bloody pants. I quietly get up and change in the bedroom. I hide my pants in the bottom of my bag. I hope Lily forgets about the bite, as I have not a scratch on my leg, which should be torn and bruised were I not able to heal so quickly. After putting on sweats I notice a change in light as it comes in through the yurt window. It is nearly dinner time and I am sure Lily will wake with an appetite. I prepared a quick marinara sauce, as I had seen Lily do on the occasion I watched her from her neighbor's tree, and put up some pasta to boil. I put a salad in a bowl and tossed it with a little vinegar and oil. I took out some Italian bread and gave it a quick toast and opened a bottle of red wine that we never drank on our earlier walk. I was determined to salvage the good feelings we had at the start of this trip. As I set the dinner on the table Lily begins to stir from her nap.

CHAPTER 20

A Moment of Bliss

I watch as Lily slowly awakens from her nap on the couch. Like a lioness waking from its noon time slumber, stretching her body the length of the couch, her muscles outlined beneath the thin fabric of her pants, she is slow to rise. "Wow! The last time I napped during the day was when I was an undergrad. I'm sorry for passing out on you like that but I have to say, I feel awesome. I guess I needed that." As Lily got up from the couch she made her way over to where I stood and a sudden and overwhelming desire to feel her flesh against mine over came me. I cupped her face in my hands and kissed her greedily. Standing in the kitchen, I undressed her while my mouth explored hers. As I moved my lips down her neck I could feel her pulse quicken with desire. My mouth explored the point where her slender neck reaches her collar bone. As Lily's passion grew she arched her body up toward mine, allowing me to cup her breast in my hand as my tongue circled her hard nipple. Lily, reaching around my waist, freed me from my restrictive pants. In one swift motion I picked her up off her feet, straddled her legs around my waist, and drew her onto me, plunging deep inside her warmth. Our passion was intense, Lily cried out in ecstasy as she pulled me deeper inside her until waves of pleasure rippled through us. As our intensity slowed my mouth continued to explore her breasts, neck and face ending in a deep, passionate kiss. As our lips parted and I looked into the face of the woman that has forever changed the course of my future, I resigned myself to enjoy every moment that I was lucky enough to have with this remarkable woman.

"I'm not sure what I have done in my life to deserve such a moment of bliss as this; but right now my world is perfect." I said, as I slowly lowered Lily till she was standing facing me. "Lily what ever happens in our future I want you to know that my love for you is eternal and pure. The passion we share, the look of love in your eyes a reflection of my own, this moment is real." I was overcome with emotions so foreign to me it was almost painful. I pulled Lily into my embrace, her warm flesh smooth against my cool skin. She felt incredibly warm against me, warmer than usual, not feverish but a degree or two higher than normal. "Are you ok? You feel hot." "Could that possibly have anything to do with you being on fire? Max that was the most intense sexual experience of my life, definitely capable of raising my body temp a degree or two. You on the other hand, how is it possible you are not even flushed? You're actually cool." I reflected her astute observation with "What is that saying, never let them see you sweat?" a reference to some type of product that I cannot recall. I quickly bring the subject back to Lily. "Well, don't let my apparent lack of sweat be seen as a lack of intensity. I have never felt with another soul, the way I feel with you. Every moment I share with you is like a gift. I feel complete with you Lily, like I belong with you. I have never felt that way with anyone, ever." "I love you Max, and as for our future, as long as we are together we can handle what ever is ahead of us." I hoped with every cell of my being that she was right.

We got dressed and ate the dinner I had set out some time ago. After dinner we sat by the fire playing scrabble. The game box looked at least 20 years old; left by some previous occupant, or possibly the park supplies it. We had and enjoyable evening, Pumpkin showed no signs of fear or worry. She even ventured outside the yurt, albeit staying within eyesight of the door, to do her business with no sign of concern. As the logs in the fire slowly burnt down so did Lily's energy. "How are you not tired?" She asked between yawns. "What makes you so sure I'm not tired? I ask. "I don't know, but you always seem so alert, not the least bit extended or worn out. It must be your youth." She said the last remark with a playful tone, but what really concerned me is that twice tonight she has seen me. With the intensity of our passion I should have been sweaty, any typical human would, and my lack of tiring, I never thought to mask it. My emotions are making me sloppy, and Lily is too observant to fool for long. I will have to tell Lily the truth soon, the sooner the better. And then it hits me. I will tell Lily the truth in New Zealand. After we meet with Victoria, I will tell her the truth and if the old woman seems up to it maybe I can seek redemption from her for the lives that I stole from her.

As we settle into bed Lily quickly falls asleep curled up under my arm. As I sit and watch her slumbering form, a new sense of relief envelops me. With the decision made when to tell Lily the truth I feel that soon my fate will be decided. What ever happens after my revelation is beyond my control. I will be at peace having experienced at least this moment of pure joy in my existence.

The storm has quieted and I go out on the porch to see what Mother Nature has left in her wake. The now clear night sky, so dark in this secluded area reveals some of the mysteries of space. The visible stars, so much more numerous in this region, far from all the light pollution of life, shine their ancient light down upon the earth. And the Milky Way, so distinct, creates an arc of white above the trees. The trees themselves are also coated in white as is the ground. The snow is windswept and forms beautifully carved drifts. The landscape has an overly bright quality that gives it an air of the surreal. This truly is a magical place, in these woods I could live peacefully. I venture out to the wood pile, everything is quiet.

No menacing scent lingers in the air, no footprints or tracks alluding to the presence of something or someone, I sense that I am alone. I purge the dinner eaten with false gusto earlier. I smile as I finish knowing that at the very least my charade as a consumer of food will be coming to an end soon. It is quite amazing the amount of time typical humans have to devote to eating. It is really an inefficient system. I look forward to not having to endure this discomfort.

I make my way back to the yurt. Lily is still curled up in a ball asleep on the bed. I let Pumpkin out and she quickly does her business and returns to her bed. Her demeanor is calm. It is early, not quite sunrise, but it looks like it will be a beautiful day. I crawl into bed beside Lily and enjoy the felling of her pressed against me. Her touch, the mere presence of her near me makes me feel whole. I lie next to her content to breath in her scent and feel the beat of her heart against my chest.

CHAPTER 21

Being a Vampire is "Totally Awesome"

Lily came into the kitchen dressed in my boxer shorts and a t-shirt. I had prepared her a breakfast of eggs, bacon, toast and coffee. She looked even more radiant this morning if that is possible. Sitting at the breakfast table, happily eating her meal while absently fingering the pewter and ruby charm hanging around her neck, Lily let out a contented sigh. "This was a spectacular weekend Max. I feel recharged and ready to face the last week of classes and finals week. I still have so much to do before we leave. I have to make arrangements for someone to watch Pumpkin while we are gone and put together some things for our trip, not to mention pick up a few gifts for Christmas and send them out to my mother and brother. It will be strange not seeing them for Christmas. My mother was disappointed when I told her of the timing of this trip; I have never missed a Christmas with my family. My brother on the other hand thinks my research is cool; his only comments were to bring him back something from New Zealand, and try not to get bitten by a vampire. But if I should get bitten, then come back and bite him. He thinks it would be "totally awesome" to be a vampire."

"What do you think?" I ask her. "What do you mean?" she says. "Do you think it would be "totally awesome" to be a vampire?" She laughed at

127

my youthful imitation as I said "totally awesome". "As a young girl I had more than my share of fantasies of becoming a vampire. Being bitten and turned by a gorgeous young vampire stud, living together for an eternity, all very glamorous in my dreams." "And now?" I couldn't stop myself from asking. The situation seemed like a perfect opportunity to gain insight into her true feelings of vampires. "Hmm, well first of all the only person I want nibbling on my neck is you, but now I think life as a vampire would be much like life is now, full of ups and downs, challenges to overcome. It is probably a lonely life though, and alone for eternity doesn't seem very glamorous. Outliving everyone you know or care about, I imagine that would be very difficult. And obviously I would have issues with killing people, but think of all the things you could learn and do with eternity, all the places you could travel. To have the world to explore, and the time to explore it with special vampire abilities, I bet it could be pretty cool at times. What about you?"

"Me?" I was trying to digest her response and never expected for her to turn the question to me. "Ha!" How do I answer that? "Well I think that if it is not a choice, one would have to just accept it. Like being born with a disability or as a twin or even as a boy or girl, we can't choose these things so it would just be who you were. Everyone, whether, a typical human, boy or girl, with or without a disability, you go about living the best life you can with the tools that you are given. At the same time, cool abilities, an eternity to explore the world, with the right partner it could be paradise." These types of conversations, "What if?" questions, I remember as a child. In school the teacher would always assign these as essay questions. "What would you do if you were President, if you could fly, if you met an alien?" All questions designed to make you think creatively, but one's response is seldom as it would be in reality. For example, ask a person what they would do if they met an alien, you get a lot of answers like ask them about the universe outside our world; ask them about how we can solve the earth's energy problems, all relatively benign reactions. In reality, humans would be more likely to shoot first and ask questions later if an alien being showed up. Fear is a big driving force of human actions. New things scare them and differences are not usually embraced. So while I am encouraged by Lily's response to my question, I don't have any grand delusions that when I tell her the truth it will turn out like the fairy tale fantasies of her youth. My only hope is that it doesn't seem to her more like a nightmare.

After breakfast we packed up the truck and decided to take one last walk amidst the serenity of the woods and lake. I remarked to Lily that it seemed her ankle was ok. "It's fine actually. It's weird, when I stepped out of the shower and slipped I definitely felt and heard a snap. I thought for sure at the time it was broken, but now it feels fine and there is hardly even a bruise. I have hurt this ankle so many times my ligaments and tendons are pretty loose. I guess one just snapped over a bone or something. It made a loud sound but I guess didn't cause any real damage. I consider myself lucky. How is your thigh by the way? I never got to take a look at it, how bad did Pumpkin get you? It seemed to bleed quite a bit." "Oh, she barely scratched me, I think some of the blood may have come from her mouth or something, my leg is fine." I quickly tried to steer the question away from me. I really didn't want to keep telling Lily lies. Soon the truth. Will it set me free or resign me to a life of solitude? Only time would tell.

After our short walk we piled into the truck and said goodbye to our beautiful hideaway. The drive back was smooth and uneventful. We talked about the class I missed on Friday while setting up this trip and about the class winding down this week. When I pulled up to Lily's house I helped her inside with her things. I told her that I had some things to do to get ready for the week and that I would pick her up in the morning on the way to campus. "Oh, I will miss sleeping with you tonight. I love having you beside me in bed." "I like having you beside me too." I confessed. We have been practically living together for the past two months and I have enjoyed the closeness. But I have some things to do, like feed, and I need some time away from Lily's too observant eyes. I only have to keep my secret for a short time longer, but it grows more difficult each day, she sees too much of me and it is only a matter of time before she starts to realize there is something different about me. "Ok. I will see you in the morning. Thank you again Max for such a wonderful weekend and the necklace and the jewelry box. It was a perfect weekend, one I will remember always." We kissed, long and sweet, and then I left my love until the morning.

I drove home to my farm and unpacked the rest of my things from my truck. After making sure everything was in order around the barn and house I decided that I would venture into the woods for a quick feed and come back and do a little research to find a nearby blood drive this week. I wanted to make sure that I fed well in the next two weeks. I knew I would not be able to take any human blood with me on the trip so it was important to be well fed and strong before we leave. It will be nearly two weeks, away without human blood, and while I can exist indefinitely on animal blood, I like to feed on human blood at least once a week just to be strong and satisfied. I am sure New Zealand will be a difficult trip, facing my demons from the past, and facing my past with Lily. I do not want to add to that by being weak or under fed.

My trip into the woods alone is liberating. As dusk falls the nocturnal creatures start to become active, I am filled with a childlike joy at being able to run and move at my extraordinary speed without fear of being caught by Lily. I go deep into the woods and travel into the upper regions of the Adirondacks. My pace is unhurried and I enjoy my time, free to behave as nature allows me. Climbing to the tops of the tallest pines I get a panoramic view of the valley and woods for miles. I feel a little like a kid being let out at recess. Free to break away from the constraints of the classroom for a brief time of pure play. Up in my perch I notice tracks that move deeper and higher into the mountains. Staying in the tree tops I leap from perch to perch as I move toward the tracks. I smell the distinct scent of wolf. A small pack is moving in the night, weaving its way through woods as it searches for food. As I continue to track them I finally catch up to where they have gathered. There is a strong alpha male nuzzling his alpha female lovingly. They are joined by four more females and two young males. Three young pups frolic nearby. When I feed on a pack animal like a wolf, I try not to destroy the pack dynamic by my choice of animal to kill. Killing the alpha male or female could allow a rival clan to come in and destroy this pack. The young pups would certainly be killed to put the females back into estrus. I decide on one of the young males. There are two, both strong and at an age where they will soon be forced to leave the pack to start their own. If the alpha male lets them stay too long one could take over as alpha and he would be killed or exiled.

I make my way closer to the wolves and am close enough to hear their whines and yelps as they communicate with one another. I give my best wolf call, trying to draw one of the adolescent males towards me. Both young males seem to be interested in my call and they break off from the group and follow my call into the woods. Leaping to the ground ahead of them I assume a four legged stance and howl to the two young wolves. They approach cautiously each moving to opposite sides of me. They are working together, sizing me up. When I stand on two legs, their demeanor changes instantly. Close enough to see me now; they have also picked up my scent, their mood changes from curious to combative. The two males start to circle me, snarling and showing their teeth. I let loose with my predatory self, as a guttural snarl leaves my own lips, my canines elongate and my venom begins to flow. The scene becomes frenetic as the two wolves move in simultaneously to attack. I am hit by the lunging form of the larger male as he leaps towards me. His canines rip into the flesh of my right buttock as I turn in time to deflect his partner's attack, a glancing blow to my shoulder all he manages. There is a flurry of growls and gnashing of teeth as I spar with the two. When the larger male makes a powerful leap his teeth latch on to my shoulder, missing his intended target my neck. I swivel my head and body enough to sink my canines into his powerful flank. As he howls in pain from the bite, he made the crucial mistake of letting go. I move swiftly and lunge, this time my teeth sink into his throat and puncture his carotid artery. The second male has taken a hard fall when I threw him off me as he attempted to maul my leg. I see him retreat, limping off in the woods. I drink greedily and the wolf's thrashing slowly ceases as the last of his blood is drained. Completely in the moment I let out a howl of satisfaction as the energy form the wolf's blood surges through my body. Still hyped up from the fight, I follow the tracks of the retreating male wolf. He hasn't made it very far. A few hundred yards from where I drained the first I find the second. He is alive but badly injured. When I threw him off me in his attack he suffered two broken legs. Coiled up in a defensive posture, his growls less menacing and more pleading, I put the animal out of his misery. I lift him by the scruff of hair on the back of his neck and tear at his throat, finding his artery and drinking until he is drained of life.

The pure savagery of the moment has ebbed. The power of the blood fills me and my body hums with energy. I make my way slowly to a stream and wade in. The icy water washes over me, pulling away the last vestiges of my feral nature, cleansing me of blood, dirt and fluids from my battle. My wounds suffered during the attack are already healed as I step out of the stream; my clothes on the other hand have no power of regeneration. I am left in dripping tatters, but I feel good, powerful and satiated. My trip home is swift. I arrive home under cover of darkness, enter my property and go into the barn. Once home I undress, and once again burn my ruined clothes in a fire. I head naked, into my house, shower and retreat to bed where I sleep for several hours. It has been days since I slept, the rejuvenating power of blood combines with the healing power of sleep and I awake refreshed. Sometimes being a vampire, is totally awesome. Last night was. I haven't let go like that in a long time and it felt great. For now, I get myself together and make my way to Lily's to pick her up for class.

CHAPTER 22

Passing of the Evening Star

The last week of classes thankfully, has flown by. I wish I could say I enjoyed them but as each day ticks off closer to New Zealand and confronting my past, I find it harder to concentrate on my present. Lily has been busy finishing up with her responsibilities for the semester which has kept her working on grades and such late into the evenings. I have not slept over at her place all week. I miss the closeness and warmth of her flesh, the feel of her body pressed against mine. I miss getting to watch her as she sleeps, being soothed by her rhythmic breaths. I miss her.

Yesterday I had to travel to Cortland, New York. Cortland State, home of the Red Dragons was holding a blood drive on campus. I was able to obtain 10 pints of AB+ with relative ease but it took me much longer than I would have liked. By the time I got back to the barn and stored my bounty and gave Lily a call it was after 9pm. She answered the phone and I could tell I had woken her. She wanted me to come by saying she would get a second wind, but I told her to rest up and I would come by early in the morning with breakfast. We were going to do some shopping in town or hit the nearest outlets. Between Christmas and the trip, we had several things to get.

I brought over breakfast of yogurt, fruit and muffins, along with coffee, a "prerequisite" to starting Lily's day. I let myself in and called out to her and Pumpkin, "Good morning ladies it's me Max". Pumpkin padded over and licked my hand in greeting. I gave her a scratch behind the ear and she shuffled back over to her bed. I went into Lily's room and found her curled up on the freshly made bed, dressed, and asleep. I sat down next to her and gently caressed the hair back from her face and she stirred. As she opened her beautiful eyes and rolled onto her back she pulled me towards her. My lips find hers and we kiss. "I missed you this week. I don't like sleeping without you. Mmm, you smell good. Will you stay over tonight? We can go to bed early, big test tomorrow!" She said, as I nuzzled her face. I realize my behavior mimics the wolf behavior I witnessed last night. As our skin touches and I am enveloped in her scent I feel very much like that alpha male. My actions express my emotions for my love and my protective nature towards her. Today something seems different. Her scent seems subtly changed, although it could be that we haven't been together in a week, and her closeness is intoxicating.

I lay beside her on the bed and as we face each other we talk. "Why were you asleep on top of the bed?" I ask. "Well I got up early this morning. I was starving, so around six, I ate an omelet, bowl of cereal and a banana. Then I finished all the grading stuff I could do before the final tomorrow and I came in to make the bed. I was just laying here waiting for you to come by and I guess I fell asleep." "Well I brought some fruit and yogurt and some muffins, you can have them later since you already ate. I also brought you some coffee." "Actually, I can definitely do breakfast part two. Come on, we will plan out our day while we eat." She replied, "While you eat" I clarified, "I had something before I came."

As we sat at the table and Lily ate breakfast part two, I suggested we start our shopping today locally. "Why don't we try our luck in town first? You should take a look in the old antique shop where I got your necklace. I thought there were a lot of interesting pieces there and you are certain to find something for your mother there. I thought we could go to the CVS on Main Street for the trial size stuff for our trip and some film and batteries." I know Lily wanted to stop by Paul's bar, he would be watching Pumpkin until Lily returns. I know it is immature and petty but the irony makes me smirk, he gets the dog and I get the girl. "If you want, we could stop by the Library for lunch, I know you want to discuss with Paul the plans for when he is watching Pumpkin." "I do need to talk to him but I'm not so sure putting the two of you in a room together is such a good idea." "I can behave if he does." I said, but I was thinking that it might be more fun if he didn't behave, I'd have an excuse to knock him down a peg or two. I know that would not make Lily very happy, but a man can dream. "Why don't we play it by ear? By the way, those muffins were yummy! Thanks for bringing them. I'm ready to go if you are." "Don't you want the coffee?" I ask, motioning to the untouched Styrofoam cup. "No, thanks, for some reason I am just not that into coffee lately." I said "Wow that might be a first, no morning coffee. Good, too much caffeine isn't good for you." She replied "You're my drug of choice Max, I just need to wake up next to you to have my fix and right now I am suffering serious withdrawal." "I miss you too." I said.

We took my car the short trip into town and found a spot on Main Street just in front of the CVS. We did a quick stop inside, got various travel size toiletries, batteries and film. Our next stop was a short walk down the street. Main Street in Hills is a mix of the old and new. New shops like CVS and Starbucks stand beside old-time, mom and pop establishments. Sandwiched between the Maple Tree Pub and Casual Set, the local beauty parlor, was The Antique Shop. Not a very unique name but as simple as the name is, there are many treasures to be found amidst its cluttered interior.

Walking into the shop with Lily, I felt the strangest sensation, it was as if a cool gust of air passed through me and swirled above the old proprietors head. "Oh my, yes! I do." He mumbled to himself, as he made his way down the antique obstacle course deftly stepping

135

around stacks of old art, tea services, and table lamps. He moved well for an old timer, but it appeared he talked to himself quite a lot. "I don't know, but you're right, powerful." He said to himself. When he made his way over to us he extended his hand to me. "Mr. VanderCreek, a pleasure to see you again." "Hello Mr. Adammo, it's nice to see you too sir. This is . . ." "Lily" he said finishing my sentence. "You were right Mr. VanderCreek; she is one of a kind. Pleased to meet you Lily, my name is Charles." He said, as he took Lily's hand in both of his. "My, my, you are special. You radiate a powerful energy Lily." Then seeming to talk to himself again he said, "Well if you're right then we should see in a moment my love."

"Lily, do you believe in fate? Because I believe it was fate that brought you and Mr. Vander Creek to my shop. There are powerful forces at work in nature and if you are open to accepting that fact then many wondrous things can happen." As he said this, he turned his gaze to Lily, eyes locked onto her necklace. I watched as his pupils contracted to pinpoints and rebounded to a light appropriate level in response to the ruby's fluctuating brilliance. I saw from the corner of my eye the stone, it appeared to grow extremely bright, radiant for a brief second and then reverted back to its rich ruby iridescence. "It is done, the Evening Star has been passed on; it has chosen her Lilly." With a look of exhilaration, he said this to himself, even though he used Lily's name, and then I understood. He was not talking to himself; he was talking to his Lilly.

I was just thinking that perhaps a trick of the light caused the supposed change in brilliance of Lily's necklace when just then the strange sensation of the cool gust of air stirred again, and then I saw it. Lily's necklace, the ruby had changed, it looked different. Instead of the deep, even, blood red color, the stone now sparkled along inner facets, like a diamond, or more like a fire ball caught inside the small ruby sphere.

"Lily, your necklace" I started, "The Evening Star" Charles chimed in. "It has been over 32 years that I have waited for this day. Lily the pendant has found you. It holds great power and can protect and guide you. Each woman, who it finds worthy, will unlock its potential. Once the Evening Star is lit, it is bound to you till your death. How the power will work for you Lily depends on your actions. Pay attention to the connection you have to it. Learn to read the subtle changes in its energy as you face the struggles of life. If you learn its subtle language, it will lead you down the right path."

"Oh my, it's radiant! It didn't look like that before, but what do you mean it found me? Lily asked. "And it's powerful and bound to me?" she continued, confusion in her eyes. "Come sit a moment so I can explain" said Charles as he led us toward the back of the room. We sat at a cluttered antique coffee table. This must be where Charles spends his time when not with customers. Set about the table was today's Hills Gazette, an empty cup of coffee, a dog eared book of crossword puzzles, and a worn deck of playing cards.

Charles began. "With great power comes great responsibility, and you are now in possession of a very powerful object. It is only fair that I tell you the history of the Evening Star as I have been told. The Evening Star was made by my great great grandmother Gwendolyn McAlister in 1853. The story passed down to me was that she was seventeen, and interested in crystals and gems and a practicing Wiccan. She and her mother often prayed to a Goddess called Inanna. She made the Evening Star pendant and cast a spell over it on the eve of her wedding. I have been told that the spell was a connection spell, one that would allow her to sense her true love anywhere in the world. The spell was designed to bind their souls for eternity, so they would find each other in the afterlife."

The small shop seemed to grow colder and Charles gave a small involuntary shudder as he continued. "She was about to marry Mr. Robert Smith, whom she loved dearly. When the spell was cast the stone was lit with an inner glow as it has now. It gave her the ability to sense her husband, to know his moods, to feel his presence even when he was away from her. As time went on their love produced a son and then a daughter. As Gwendolyn learned more about the stones power she would learn to use it to help her and her husband become prosperous and keep her family safe. When her husband Robert confided in his older brother Jonathon about the secret of his fortunate life, he had no idea how it would irrevocably change it. Jonathon was jealous of his younger brother's fortune. He hated being the subject of ridicule for not being able to marry before his younger brother. He had even suggested to Gwendolyn a few days before their wedding, that she should marry him instead of his brother. Gwendolyn rebuked his advances and this turned his jealousy to rage.

In 1864 Jonathon met in secret with the town council. He convinced them that Gwendolyn was a witch. The council decided as punishment for witchcraft, Gwendolyn should be cast out of town. The day before they were to announce their decision, the remains of Gwendolyn were found in the woods near her farm. She was found beaten and partially burned. There was no proof Jonathan or the council was responsible for her killing, and no one was ever charged for the crime. Sometime later, as Jonathon lay dying from consumption, he confessed his involvement to his brother and pleaded for absolution from his sins. Robert was despondent at his brother's betrayal. He went home, retrieved his pistol, wrote a letter to his children explaining the truth of their mother's death and his apologies for what he was about to do. He returned to his brother's bedside where he shot him before turning the gun on himself.

Gwendolyn's and Robert's daughter, Carolyn Smith had possession of the Evening Star after her mother's death until her own death in 1941. Carolyn Smith Gardner, my great grandmother, passed away from natural causes, she was 86 years old. Carolyn and Jack Gardner had a long and prosperous life. They had one child, a daughter Evelyn, born in 1881; she was 60 years old at the time of her mother's death when she took possession of the necklace. Evelyn Gardner Grey was my grandmother. She had nine children, 8 boys and one girl. Joan

Gray, my mother was born in 1909. She married my father James Adammo, in 1927 and they had me their only child in 1933.

My grandmother Evelyn died of a stroke in 1949. My mother had possession of the necklace for the shortest amount of time and had barely discerned its powers. In 1951 my mother was killed in a car accident. I was 18 years old. In 1955, I married the love of my life, Lilly Sweeney Adammo. As a wedding gift, my father gave me the necklace. He said he knew my mother would want Lilly to have it, he had never seen a woman make me so happy. Lilly and I were happy, and in 1978 after nearly 17 years of marriage and having long ago given up on the idea of being parents, Lilly at 44 years old, became pregnant. At that age a first pregnancy was risky. Everything seemed normal in the beginning but there were complications. At around 5 months into the pregnancy Lilly hemorrhaged, it was a tubal pregnancy, I lost them both. We enjoyed 17 years of absolute bliss. No two people on the planet had the type of bond we shared.

When she died, I knew the instant it happened, even before the doctors came out with the news. It was as if, at that moment, the place in my chest where I could almost feel Lilly's heart beat was suddenly empty. The vacuum left behind as her presence, her energy disappeared, nearly sucked me into an abyss. I withdrew from everyone I knew, and barely spoke to my father, until about a month after Lilly died. I was sitting on our bed; I had her favorite scarf in my hand. It still smelled like her, it came from the hospital bag that had held her clothes and other belongings when she was admitted to the emergency room. I hadn't been able to look at her things until then. The necklace was in there, and as soon as I touched it I felt her again. I kept that pendant in my pocket for 32 years.

While I lost Lilly's physical presence with her death in 1978, her spirit has remained connected to mine. Since the day I found her pendant I have felt Lilly with me. She continues to guide me and protect me through the power of the Evening Star. On the morning before Mr. VanderCreek came into the store, as I sat to read my

morning paper, I was pierced by a point from the Evening Star. I took
it from my pocket and hug it around the neck of that mannequin,
fully intending to return it to my pocket after I read my paper. I think
she made me prick myself that day. When I placed the necklace on
the mannequin I felt her positive essence. When Mr. VanderCreek
offered to purchase it, Lilly sent such a positive surge of energy as way
of telling me to accept his offer that she lit a bulb in the chandelier.
And now she is letting me know it is time to move on."

Lily and I sat, mouths agape, as Charles enthralled us with his
story. Lily was first to speak. "Charles, the history of this pendant
is rich with intrigue. However, knowing how this pendant has been
in your family for so long, I do not feel right keeping this treasure."
"Ah, but you miss the point my dear. The Evening Star has chosen
you. The special bond that you and Mr. VanderCreek share, it is the
power of that bond that has re-lit the Evening Star. If it were not
meant for you, you would not be in possession of it. Now, we have
been sitting here for nearly an hour, I must get up and stretch my
legs. Is there another reason you came in today? I am sure it was
not to listen to my ramblings, it is just that I felt it my duty to make
sure you understand the potential and power that you wear around
your neck."

Lily looked as if she were about to try again her attempt to
persuade Charles to take back the necklace. The look on her face was
a mingling of confusion and worry. "Lily was looking for a Christmas
gift for her mother" I interjected. Charles showed us the beautiful
lace tablecloth I had admired on my first visit, Lily remarked that
it was perfect, though I could tell she was preoccupied. Charles
wrapped the tablecloth in tissue and placed it gently in a bag. "I hope
your mother enjoys a bounty at many a holiday table with the ones
she loves." "Thank you Charles. You have taken us on an incredible
walk through history. I must admit it is a lot to absorb. I am honored
to keep the Evening Star Charles. It was given to me out of love, and
we have pledged our hearts to each other. So, if love is the source

of the power you say it contains, then it should be powerful indeed. Perhaps we can chat again sometime, you are a remarkable historian and story teller."

"Thank you Lily and you Mr. VanderCreek, your love for each other has allowed me to fulfill my responsibility, and pass on the Evening Star. You were right about another thing Mr. VanderCreek. Your destinies are entwined, your souls are now connected and not even death can break that bond. May the strength of your love give power to the Evening Star, and may it keep you safe and help you have a long and prosperous life." He left us by the door, and as he walked toward the back table I heard him whisper to his Lilly, "Good bye my love, until I am by your side again."

Lily and I left the antique shop, ushered out by that same strange cold air. The bright sunlight, in stark contrast to the dim light of the shops interior caused Lily to squint as her eyes adjusted. She took several cleansing breaths and turned up her face to the sun. "I need some chocolate." She said. "I think I am a little freaked out by Charles' story. A vigorous regimen of hugs, kisses and copious amounts of chocolate may take away some of the lingering sense of unease I have been left with." "Chocolate sounds like just what the doctor ordered" I agreed. We walked down the street to the Krispy Kreme donut shop and ordered several chocolate laden items.

Lily ate her fill of the sweet confections. I ate half of a chocolate donut, not a bad flavor, the texture not unpleasant. It would not be so bad on the way back out. We sat in silence as we ate at a small table in the corner of the shop. We were both deep in thought, processing what we had just learned. After eating three quarters of a third doughnut, Lily tossed the last piece onto the napkin and let out a long sigh. "Ok, so let me see if I understood the gist of Charles' story. I am now in possession of the Evening Star, which seems to be more than just a stunning piece of jewelry." She fingered the pendant and turned it in her hand as she admired the new look of the stone. "The pendant has gone through five generations of woman, four in

Charles' family and his wife. Three of those women died young, one brutally murdered by her brother in-law. The stone somehow picked me, through you, due to our powerful bond. The stone is now bound to me till death and will somehow connect our souls forever. It and I are somehow powerful and if I follow the direction the Evening Star leads, it will be the right path. That about sum it up?"

Lily left out a few things that I am sure her less sensitive ears missed. I heard Charles mention two things. First he mentioned that Lilly had told him it was time to move on. Second he whispered a goodbye to her, until he returned to her side. Together, I took it to mean that Charles feels he is not long for this earth. I believe, now that his "responsibility" has been fulfilled, he thinks he will join his Lilly in the after life. I must say that the cold draft I felt when I entered the shop, and again as we left seemed like a presence. It seemed as if Charles felt it too and responded to it as if it was his wife.

Lily seemed more than a little freaked out by the history of the Evening Star. I tried to persuade the scientist in her to look at this objectively. To Lily I answered, "Well, you have the basics but let me add a few thoughts I have. Yes, the stone has passed through five generations, and yes three of those women probably died prematurely. Gwendolyn was murdered for being a witch. I don't think that is a huge concern in today's world. Joan died in a car accident, a statistical possibility for anyone who uses a car, and Lilly died due to an anomaly during her pregnancy, also a statistical possibility for any woman that conceives a child. The other two women lived long and prosperous lives. Lily, the stone is not cursed or malevolent." She quickly chimed in "I didn't say it was." I replied, "You didn't have to, I could see the concern in your eyes as the history of the Evening Star unfolded." "Well it is a lot to process and you and I both saw the stone change, right? I don't know Max, how is this possible?"

"Charles said that the stone would guide you, if you listened to it, it would lead you down the right path. You also left out the part I found to be most important. Charles said it was the strength of our bond, our love for one another that allowed the light to pass to you. He said we would be connected for eternity. Anything bound by the power of love can't be that bad."

I watched Lily's brow furrow as she tried to organize the swirling thoughts in her mind. "Lily I have to confess to you, since the day I put that necklace around your neck and we devoted our hearts to each other, I have felt connected to you. It is as if your heart beat beside mine in my chest. The day you fell in the shower, I didn't hear you call, but I felt something. I felt your pain and fear. Don't you see Lily, I think Charles is right. The Evening Star has connected us. You just have to learn to listen to it. Once you accept this to be true, I am sure you will feel the connection."

I pull my love in close to me, reassuring her with my firm embrace. "Lily, I have known all along that you are special. So if the necklace truly picked you, it made a good decision, because you are a strong woman with an amazing heart. I know it is a lot to think about but you yourself have said in the past to keep an open mind. If you let go of your fear, suspend your disbelief, and focus on the love we share then perhaps you will feel it like I have. The connection is there." Even as I said this I was actually hoping she would continue in her state of disbelief for a little while longer. I was fearful, if she felt that connection, she would learn the truth about me, and I hope to keep that secret just a little longer.

"You know you always seem to say or do just the right thing to make me feel better. When you analyze the facts as you put them, talk about statistics and such, it seems plausible that the stone is not malevolent or cursed. It's just that witch craft, was never something I studied in detail, I have always been a bit leery about the subject. To think this came from a woman that died for being a Wiccan, well it seems that something associated with the death of a witch might be very powerful. It is all a little daunting. Either way Max, the Evening Star came from you, out of love, and when we pledged our hearts to each other I meant it and I know you did too. I will stay focused on our love and try and hear the "whispering" of the Evening Star. If such power exists, I hope that I will follow the right path." "So, you're ok?" I asked. "Max, I'm with you, and as I said before, together I think we can handle what ever life throws our way. Together, I'm way better than ok, together everything is perfect."

CHAPTER 23

Loose Ends Tied Up and Some New Truths Reveled

We left the Krispy Kreme, and made our way down Main Street. Paul's bar, The Library, was up on the other side of the street. Above his bar was a novelty/head shop called Odd Ball Gifts. Its' name was appropriate, for when you ascended the 99 numbered steps, each with Odd Ball factoids, you knew you were not entering a typical shop. The interior was divided into two sections. The front section did indeed have an impressive array of strange novelty items that the typical college student would find irresistible. Posters by the hundreds, representing every team, music group, and heart throb were all displayed in hanging protective sleeves, numbered for easy identification. There were walls of gag gifts with items such as fake poo and vomit, pepper gum, hand buzzers, exploding cigars, and the like. On one wall there was over fifty t-shirts identifying the various prints that could be made while you wait, under which were shelves of mugs and picture frames and various knick-knacks.

The back of the shop, accessible by passing through a beaded curtain, was the adult section. A sign posted on the counter by the entrance said, "Adult content section. All patrons must be 18yrs. or older beyond this point." Passed the "highly secure" bead barrier, was the head shop and sexually explicit material. Bongs, pipes, incense and candles, along with a horde of related drug paraphernalia dominated the left side of the back section. Vibrators, dildos, various sex toys and adult videos were on the right side. Lily and I stayed up in the front section of the store where Lily picked out a few items for her brother for Christmas. Along a back table there were several books for sale. The books included *Growing Pot For Dummies, The Encyclopedia of Marijuana, The Joy Of Sex,* a book on Zen principles, and several others with a new age feel. Lily picked up a small paperback book entitled, *Gems, Crystals and Stones: The Hidden Powers Within.* "Perhaps some light reading for the airplane." She said as she added two more books to her purchases. *Channeling Your Inner Wiccan,* and *Wiccan Gods and Goddesses,* seemed anything but light reading. "What? I'm trying to be objective like you said. I am a scientist remember? I have questions. If I read up on the topic, maybe I will be able to find some answers. Anyway, it will give us something to read on the plane. I figure they could be informative or funny or at the very least so dull as to put us to sleep. Any of those outcomes are worth the price. Don't you agree?" "I do" I said as I added a fourth book to the pile. "*The History of Witchcraft and the Supernatural* might be informative as well."

We took our items to the register, where a young co-ed stood, bored, waiting to ring up the next patron. "Hi Ginny", said Lily. "Professor Bean, how's it going? Hey, I got my index cards right here. Study, study, study! I am going to ace your final." "Glad to see it Ginny, I would expect nothing less. Ginny Grimes, this is Max VanderCreek. Its nice you two get a chance to meet before the trip." "You're going?" We said in unison, Ginny giving me a flirty smile. Lily answered for us, "Yes you are both signed up, there are two others as well, Bill Treetop and Andrew Jensen."

I had not given much thought to anyone else going on this trip. In my mind I only pictured going with Lily. These three will have to be doing something else when Lily and I interview Victoria. That is if Lily even planned on having me with her. It dawned on me that I would have to do a little research of my own. I had to discuss the trip itinerary with Lily. As if reading my mind Lily said to Ginny and I, "I e-mailed the itinerary and group info today, I figured I would give you a hard copy tonight." As she addressed me she clasped her hand in mine. The look on Ginny's face did not go unnoticed by Lily or me. Disappointment quickly turned to resentment, as Ginny looked between me and Lily. There was so much riding on this trip, it was too important to be distracted out of concern for how these three students might interfere with my plans. After I get a look at that itinerary I will be better prepared to plan how to keep those three in the dark.

In the mean time, I used my power of persuasion on Ginny. As I grabbed the bag of merchandise, I made sure to brush Ginny's hand with my finger. That along with direct eye contact had her receptive to my suggestion. "Ginny, this trip will be fun, I heard the local New Zealand men have a thing for American women. You will be quite busy sifting through the hordes in search of the man of your dreams." Ginny's eyes brightened and her demeanor towards Lily went from resentment to camaraderie. "Yeah, I should look on line at New Zealand dating services, just to see what's out there. I hope it's a hot bed of male studs. Too bad your attached Bean, we could have done some damage together. I guess there will be more for me then." This was said with absolutely no malice or ill will. Ginny was excited to "do some damage" and at least for now the issue of her interfering between Lily and I romantically is no longer a problem.

"Thanks." I said as I took the merchandise. "See you tomorrow, Ginny." Lily said as we walked hand in hand out of the store, down the 99 steps and up to the door to Paul's bar. Before we went into The Library, Lily turned and looked at me and said, "For a minute I thought there was going to be a problem with Ginny, she kind of gave me the evil eye when I held your hand, but then she did a complete one eighty and seemed ready to go on the prowl for a New Zealand hottie. Good redirect Max. Now if you can promise me you will be civil, I would really like some lunch. I will quickly go over the dog sitting responsibilities with Paul, and then I want to go home with you. This has been a productive, yet exhausting afternoon. The sooner we get back to my place the sooner we can cuddle up together. I need some serious lovin', and you are what the doctor ordered." "I will be a perfect gentleman." I said as I kissed the top of her head.

We walked into the Library, with its walls lined with faux books. The bar looked like the circulation desk at a real library. The college students love this place. They can tell their parents that they were at the Library all night, and they are not technically telling a lie. Although the only studying being done is researching the mating habits of their fellow co-eds and seeing how much booze it takes to get your beer goggles on. We grabbed two menus off of the bar and found an empty table in the back. Paul nodded a greeting toward Lily; his reaction to me was neutral. So, maybe the old dog can learn. It seems that Paul has finally dropped the arrogant attitude. Our last encounter was like a virtual neutering. Good dog.

The waitress came over and took our order. When she had left to get us our drinks Lily eyed the bar, empty at the moment, except for Paul cutting up the fruit for garnishes. "I'll be right back Max, while the bar area is quite I want to go over the details of dog sitting with Paul." She bent in and kissed me, one sweet chaste kiss on the lips. I realized the significance of her gesture. Once again I am reminded of my encounter with the wolves. With one small kiss the parameters were laid out. I was the alpha male, and Paul was a lucky member of the pack, as long as he stayed in line he would be able to continue to be in the pack, but step out of line or try to take over as alpha and he would be forced to leave the pack or fight to the death to be alpha male. Here I go dreaming again.

I admire my alpha female as she makes her way over to the bar. She is more beautiful to me with every new detail I learn about her. She has great legs. I find myself looking for lunch to be over quickly, the afternoon "lovin'" Lily mentioned has me working up a different appetite. "I listen in as Lily and Paul talk. "Hi Paul, how are you?" "I'm good Jelly Bean, you look . . . incredible, I hate to even say this, knowing the reason, but you look really happy, you're practically glowing. Well, I'm happy for you Lily, you and what's his name; I always want you to be happy, even if it's not with me." "Thanks Paul, I am happy. I love Max and if I am lucky I will get to spend the rest of my life with him. You know you're my best friend, God your like a brother, I hope that hasn't changed." "No problem there Jelly Bean, I'm a lifer when it comes to caring about you, I will forever be your friend. Now wipe the worried look off your face, I love Pumpkin. I have watched her before, you forget? Let me see if I remember: Out in the AM by 7:00, fed breakfast by 8:00, let out in yard or take for a walk for an hour, and then she pretty much sleeps around till dinner. Dinner is at 6:00pm followed by an evening walk and its back to sleeping. One late night quick pit stop outside and she sleeps till morning. She has an enviable schedule."

"Well it sounds like you have it down. Not too many treats, and easy on the bar food scrapes. If she pukes you'll be stuck cleaning it up. I really appreciate this. She's too old and used to her freedom to be kenneled. I e-mailed you all the emergency numbers, her vet, the animal hospital, my cell, and the number of the hotel where I'm staying. Give me a call if there is any problem. I'll bring her by Friday night if that's ok." Friday's fine, she can hang out behind the bar with me or sleep in my office. It's all good Jelly Bean, she'll be fine." Paul stepped out from around the bar and gave her a hug. It was quick and followed by a hasty glance my way. That's right dog, respect your rank and mine, I thought.

Lily came back over to the table looking relieved that everything was taken care of. "Now I am almost ready for the trip, I just can't get too excited about it till everything is done. The only thing left I have to do is grade my exams after the tests, put the grades in, and I am ready for New Zealand." As she sat down the food came. "And now I am ready to eat", she added. And eat she did, her dinner and the half of mine I was "too full to finish". Maybe she does have a tapeworm, or a parasite. After our meal we settled the check and walked back to my car. I opened the door for Lily and as I turned to let her in I noticed the Antique Shop was closed. The red closed sign in the window and lack of lights inside struck me as ominous. I quickly helped Lily into the car. I don't know why, but I definitely did not want her to see that closed sign.

"If it's ok with you Lily, can we go back to my place first? I have to pick up some things to be ready for tomorrow. You haven't seen my place yet, what do you say?" "I would love to see your place Max." "Excellent!" I had hoped to get an opportunity to bring Lily to my home. I made sure to remove any evidence of my alternate life style, even going so far as to put food and drinks in my refrigerator and pantry. I have an old horizontal cooler in my barn. I store my personal supplies in there. Blood lasts about a week as I store it. I have eight bags left from my Cortland haul. I am trying to ration my supply until we go away. I will have to go at least two weeks without human blood, not a big deal really, but I feel the need to be at my peak for this trip. I want to be prepared for any eventuality.

We take the short drive out of town and out toward my farm. I am excited to bring Lily to this very special place of mine. It is not like I can bring her home to meet my family, so this is the next closest thing. This place holds my early history. The peace I get from sitting atop a pile of hay in the barn is unparalleled. I want to share this part of myself with her. If she can get a sense of the human I was, perhaps when she finally learns the truth, she will see that I am very much that person still. Albeit virtually immortal, with a black stain on my soul for the horrors I committed in my past. But I have spent nearly a century trying to atone for my sins against humanity. And given time I believe Lily will be able to accept me for who and what I am. Could

I be that "gorgeous, young vampire stud" of her youthful fantasies? I seem to have swept her off her feet. The thought of "turning her" however, is too unpleasant to contemplate.

It is possible to "turn a human", force a change in them to become a vampire. But it is not something I have ever done nor is it anything I would want to do. To turn a human, a vampire must first drink from them till they are nearly drained of their blood. It is extremely difficult to stop feeding once you start, especially from a human, the blood is so powerful. It's a very primal process; you are forced to overcome the natural drive in every cell of your body to obtain more human blood. If you can stop, the human must be very near death, and if they do die, then they can not be turned. If the vampire fails to drain enough blood however, the human's immune system may fight off the invading foreign cells. This would also be excruciating and still potentially fatal for the human. As the vampire drains a human's blood and it enters the vampire's system it becomes part of him. His DNA is infused with each new cell. He then must open his own vein and force the nearly dead person to drink from him. The human must drink to the point the vampire is nearly desiccated. The vampire must then break away from the feed and drink from another blood source to regain his strength. I have heard that some vampires bring two people to a transition, one to turn and one for food.

The changed blood that enters the human will slowly infect every cell of their body, injecting the mutant DNA into each cell. As each cell is infected it will change. A cell by cell restructuring will occur, changing the human cells into vampire cells. This is very much like how a human born with the genetic mutation for Vampirism changes, except the process is triggered by his own cells as a result of the genetic mutation. However a human without the mutation is near death twice, once being drained, and again as the transition takes effect. The process is grueling and torturous. I wouldn't wish the pain on my worst enemy, let alone the woman I loved. Once the transition is complete they will have to feed. They will crave human blood as anyone does who transitions. And then the real challenges present themselves.

I quickly dispel the images these dismal thoughts have given me. My mood is slower to brighten. We are almost to my farm when Lily asks, "Are you ok, Max? A very sorrowful feeling just washed over me, and I think it was your feeling. I know that sounds strange, but it was as if, for a fraction of a second, I could feel your emotions and sense something troubling you." Inwardly I was shocked by this revelation. Lily was connecting to me. She was using the power of the Evening Star. This would mean that soon she would sense things about me that will reveal me. I would have to be careful now to control my emotions. To Lily I said, "I'm fine, perhaps a little melancholy. I was just thinking that I have no family for you to meet, just the old family home. I wish my mother Genevieve was alive to meet you, she would have liked you instantly."

My remark to Lily was not entirely a lie, I did feel those things, just not at the moment Lily felt my emotions. "I'm sorry Max that was insensitive of me. It must be especially hard not having any family, around the holidays or to mark important occasions." "If by important occasions you mean meeting the woman I love, then yes it is hard not to have someone to share my joy with. But perhaps, had I not experienced these losses, I would not be the man I am now, capable and honored to be loved by you."

As we pulled up to my farm, I had to admit it did look picturesque. My mood was naturally lifted as it always is coming home. A white blanket covered the fields. The old barn, a dappled red, sitting back from the quaint white house welcomed us as I pulled my truck up the drive. Lily beamed a wide smile as she took in the scene. "Oh Max, it's beautiful, so peaceful and serene." And suddenly I felt very peaceful and serene. It felt like coming home, but for the first time in nearly a century, I was coming home with someone I loved, who loved me too. Could this be our home? I wondered, and then stopped my wonderings short, lest Lily connect to me and read me again.

CHAPTER 24

A Glimpse Into My Past

I take Lily into my home. The quick tour of the simple house begins as we walk in the front door which opens to a large mud room. We take off our coats and shoes and enter the main residence. There is a large bright kitchen with massive windows along the back wall giving a spectacular view of the fields and woods that lay beyond them. To the left is a large family room with an impressive fireplace. Up the center hallway is a small guest bedroom. There is a bathroom and a narrow winding staircase that we take up to my master suite. This room has been converted from the original plans. The second floor was originally divided into two large rooms. Now it is an open floor plan with one expansive room and four large wooden pillars required for structural support. The back wall is almost entirely glass. Floor to ceiling windows and a sliding glass door leading to a deck give a panoramic view of the farm and surrounding woods. In the back left corner of the room is my bed, to the right of the stairs is the master bath. The remainder of the space is occupied with books and music and a few mementos of my life. Most of my older possessions are kept in storage or in one of my other dwellings around the world.

Twilight has fallen over the woods that back my farm. The setting sun casts a waning glow across the snow covered fields. Dark shadows have begun to fill the gaps between trees, muddling the lines of distinction. Lily walks over to a wall lined with books and CD's. As she peruses the titles I watch her expressions. "You have an impressive collection of literature and music. It's like a mini library. Your tastes seem to sample works from the last century. Some of these books are first editions. How has someone as young as you, managed to amass such a collection?" "Well, Lily in my past, I have been known to go after the things I want quite tenaciously. And being an orphan, I was left with a considerable sum of money when my birth parents died, and when Genevieve died, I got the farm. I knew at an early age that land offered me the sense of permanence I needed. When I came of age I took the money left me and invested it. Some wise investments helped to expand my portfolio and today, well let's just say I have sufficient enough wealth so as not to be required to work. I have spent the last several years traveling the globe and exploring what life has to offer. I have a passion for learning. I have taken many interesting courses. It is very liberating taking a college course for the sheer pleasure of it, not being bogged down worrying about a grade. When I am not traveling or taking classes I study on my own."

I watched as Lily pulled out and admired several old books from my collection. "I particularly enjoy reading works of literature that have been influential in past history. Reading is a passion of mine and I have been fortunate over the years, as I travel, to obtain many treasured books. You would be surprised at the treasures that can be found. Besides old book stores and antiques shops, I often visit estate sales, where entire libraries can be purchased. As for music, that is another passion of mine. I enjoy all types as my collection can attest. Again, my unconventional lifestyle has afforded me the opportunity to study music from around the world. I have learned to play various instruments and enjoy the challenge of learning to play a new piece. Perhaps one day I will play something for you."

I was feeling melancholy. I was also saying and feeling too much. It is hard to hide over a centuries worth of life experience in the body of a twenty six year old. I have been fortunate to possess enough resources and limitless time, and have used both in the pursuit of knowledge of the arts, science and history, and anything else that strikes my interest at the time. But this was dangerous. Lily was starting to sense our connection. Once she has learned to tap into that bond she will see me, all of me. I am torn between wanting to open myself up to her and her learning the truth. Something is preventing me from telling her everything at this time. For some reason I feel the need to tell her in New Zealand. Only a few days now and if she accepts me, I will have her lifetime to share with her.

"Wow Max, I suddenly realize that I know very little about you. For the past few months I guess I have done most of the talking." "Lily, in time you will learn more about me, perhaps more than you'll want to know. That's part of the excitement of a new romance such as ours, everything is so new. Every day I feel as if I learn more about you, and everyday I want to learn more still. And now I want to show you my favorite place." I took her hand and led her out to the barn. I grabbed a blanket along the way and inside the barn, spread the blanket atop a pile of hay. "This is my favorite place. Lying back on a soft mound of hay, inhaling the earthy aroma of the barn amidst the sounds of the barn owls, bats and various other inhabitants I am at peace. There is something very centering about this place. I imagine it has something to do with my mother. This is where we would sit and talk. Here, we would share our deepest thoughts and solve life's problems often with a hug and a plate of homemade cookies."

We lay back on the blanket staring up at the barn rafters. Lily inhales deeply and sighs contentedly. "I can see why this is your favorite place. Laying here with the smells, the sounds, and the hay beneath you, it's like being wrapped in a hug. This place exudes such a powerful feeling of hominess, it's very serene." We stayed like that for a while, lying next to each other atop the sweetly scented hay, a comfortable silence between us. We watched as the bats nocturnal activity began. It was slowly getting dark outside. The interior of the barn was being swallowed in shadows as the last sun's rays gave way to darkness. In the dimming light, I rolled to face my love and embraced her as we kissed.

We made love atop the hay pile. It was sweet and tender. As our bodies touched, the now familiar hum of electricity enveloped us. As Lily neared climax, I was suddenly struck with mental flashes, like a black and white slide show. Each image as it flickered in and out of my mind was tied to powerful emotions. This was both extremely pleasurable and frightening. Pleasurable, due to the magnitude and intensity of the feelings I sensed in Lily combined with my own, and frightening because I knew our connection through the Evening Star was growing stronger. As we lay back against the hay, I searched Lily's face for a sign that she may have experienced a similar cascade of images and emotions from me but nothing in her face suggested she suddenly knew my secret.

"Max, that was indescribable. Each time we make love, I think we have reached a level of passion and connectedness that is unparalleled and then, well . . . and then this. It was like I could feel your heart beat in sync with mine. I could actually feel it beating in my chest. And the raw emotions, the absolute love and passion you have for me, I could feel that too. But Max, I also felt fear, what are you afraid of?"

"I guess Charles was right. It seems the Evening Star has given us a much deeper connection. I must admit its power is daunting. I felt your emotions as well and perhaps the fear you felt was my concern of one day losing you, like everyone else in my life who I ever loved." It was the truth, not all of it, but I do fear the pain of one day losing Lily. As much as I want to protect her from all harm, one day she will die, by old age or something else, I know I will have to face that future.

Lily took my face in her hands and kissed me gently on the lips. As she stared into the depths of my eyes she said, "Max, you and I both understand the pain of loss. Unlike you, however, I have been fortunate to have family to support me. I can only imagine how difficult it must be for you to feel so alone. I want you to know, you are no longer alone." I hoped with every cell of my being that after Lily learned the truth she would still feel the same way.

It was getting late. We dressed and went back into my home. I got together some clothes and things I would need for tomorrow and we headed out to Lily's house. On the ride back I tried to keep my thoughts and emotions under control. It seemed Lily was as yet unable to fully read me, but since I got those flashes of her thoughts, I fear she too will soon see my own. At the wrong time that could be devastating. From the corner of my eye I noticed the look of empathy etched on Lily's face as she said, "Max, thank you for sharing a special part of you tonight. Your home is rich with history, it was almost palpable. I feel closer to you somehow, having glimpsed a bit of your past. I think this trip is going to give us a chance to become even closer. I can't explain it, maybe it is the Evening Star, but I feel like we are on the verge of something big."

Lily's eyes twinkled with excitement as she talked animatedly about our trip. She was excited to further her research and hoped that what ever we learned in New Zealand was not just another "dead end". She had no idea just how "big" the thing she was on the verge of learning was. Further her research? I think learning that the man you love is a vampire is pretty "big" on a number of levels. As far as her research goes, she gets absolute proof of the existence of vampires. If she doesn't run off petrified of me or try to kill me somehow, she will be able to learn the truth about vampires, satisfying years of research and questions. As far as her emotional side goes, I hope the love we share now is strong enough to let her except me, to continue loving me. I don't know what I would do if I lose her now. I am so deeply connected to her, the thought of losing that connection is like cutting off ones limb, or more like cutting out ones own heart. I push the thoughts quickly from my mind. The overpowering emotions I am feeling as I think these thoughts could easily be felt by Lily.

It's ironic that the Evening Star, a gift from me to Lily, which Charles seems to think somehow chose us, could potentially break us apart. I guess keeping secretes in any relationship is potentially destructive. But sometimes a secret must be revealed at just the right time, and under just the right circumstances. I have felt since the beginning of our relationship, that one day I would tell this woman my truth. The first time I saw her I think my body knew the importance of my discovery, before my brain sensed the special nature of her. The cellular response was like nothing I have ever experienced with another creature. But I failed to understand how the effects of being emotionally tied to this woman would impact my ability to reveal the truth to her. And now as events have unfolded and the connections to my past have crept into the equation it has made an exceedingly difficult task, with the possibility of a potentially disastrous outcome, into a nearly impossible task with a disastrous outcome likely.

Thankfully a diversion from these troubling thoughts presented itself. As we were driving toward town a large white column of smoke could be seen rising in the distance. Lily rolled down the windows and inhaled deeply, "Oh my god! Could you please pull over to Rudy's? I am absolutely salivating at the aroma. The smell alone must make the local's cholesterol go up. I know you do not partake in the delicacy of charred flesh, but I suddenly must have some Rudy's barbeque."

Rudy's Barbecue was a local staple. Apparently the food was excellent, at a great price. The huge parking lot was always packed, and tonight was no different. I pulled in and Lily jumped out at the curb. "Do you want anything? I think they have salads. Other than that this place is strictly for carnivores." "No, thanks, I'm not really hungry right now. You get yourself your meat fix to go, and I'll circle around a few times and pick you up back here." She gave me a quick peck and was out the door. I drove around the massive parking lot several times while I waited for Lily to walk out to the curb. On my fourth pass she walked out with a bag of food and a smile from ear to ear.

I pulled over to let her in and as she got in the car she carried the scent of barbeque with her. Lily sat contentedly eating her pulled pork barbequed sandwich and cucumber salad as we drove to her home. "I'm sorry to eat in front of you. But I have to say the only non meat food they had was a sad looking salad." "Its ok, I'm really not hungry." "You eat like a bird." She said. More like a bat was what I thought.

We got back to Lily's around 9:00pm. It had been a long day. Lily took care of Pumpkin who was eager to go out and do her business, "Sorry, girl. You were cooped up inside here all day and it is way past your dinner time." The dog looked at Lily as if to say "and how will you make it up to me?" In response, Lily added some barbeque chicken to the dog's food. A special purchase she got at Rudy's for Pumpkin. She must have felt guilty then, at how late we were getting back.

Owning a pet is a little like having a child; one more individual to care and provide for. Pumpkin seemed to forgive Lily with the first bite of food. She ate ravenously and licked her chops clean when she was through. Pumpkin seemed so content she almost looked like she was smiling. All was forgiven.

We agreed to retire early so we would be rested up for tomorrow. We curled up in Lily's bed and within minutes she was fast asleep. We lay together with her small frame pressed up against me, radiating heat. Her breaths were deep and rhythmic and looking at her peaceful face it was like watching an angel. I sat and stroked her hair as I watched over her sleeping form.

As I sat entranced by my sleeping beauty, it occurred to me that I had spent a considerable amount of time contemplating scenarios in which Lily would not react favorably to my revealing the truth to her. I had spent relatively no time thinking about if she responded favorably. I certainly did not want to get my hopes up, but as I sat gazing down at the miraculous creation sleeping in my arms I suddenly knew exactly what I would do if Lily accepts me. I decided one more trip to Charles' antique shop was in order.

CHAPTER 25

Final Exam Day

Lily and I got to campus early. I left her at her office and spent the next half hour before class planning the rest of my day. After the final exam, Lily would be grading papers and getting in her grades. We decided to meet for dinner at her place at 8:00pm. I told her I would have something prepared since she would be working straight through the day. That left me with the day to myself after the exam. We are leaving for New Zealand on Saturday. I was almost packed and finished most of what I needed to do before we leave. Today I want to accomplish two things. I need to feed and stop by Charles' antique shop, not necessarily in that order. I hope Charles is ok. Leaving his shop last week, I was stricken by a persuasive feeling of sorrow. Seeing him close up shop, right after we left, felt foreboding. I will stop by there today after my final, perhaps I may find one more treasure among his collection of artifacts of days past.

I make my way over to the lecture hall for my final. There are several students already there nervously milling about. Several smokers anxiously puff away, others review index cards of notes, and several sit in a circle on the grass throwing out questions to each other to practice their response. I glance over to see one solitary girl sitting on the wall. She has on head phones and her foot incessantly moves to an unheard rhythm; it is Ginny Grimes. I walk over to her and as she pulls the head phones out of her ears I can hear the sound of loud rock rhythms accompanied by a vocalist, who's style is to scream each word with a guttural howl. The speed at which he speaks/screams blends words into a mash of angst ridden howling. The music is technically good, although not my preferred choice and I do not know the group.

"Hey Ginny, who are you listening to?" She took off her headphones as she said "Hi Max, Vexed, they're a new group out of Massachusetts, pretty hot on the college circuit. So you ready?" "For the test? Yeah. I'm not worried, I'm prepared." She replied with a smirk, "Doesn't hurt to date the professor, as long as you don't have a fight before she gives you your grade." "Now Ginny, don't talk that way, besides I'm not taking this class for a grade. So it doesn't matter what I get, I just decided to take it because the content interests me. Meeting Lily was a very fortunate accident."

I don't really believe meeting Lily was an accident. It seems our paths have been destined to cross for some time. But I was certainly not about to go into that with Ginny. I was simply trying to be cordial, seeing as we were going to be spending the next two weeks working together. Her tendency to exhibit acrimony towards Lily, especially with issues concerning us as a couple, was beginning to irritate me. As if sensing my feeling she said, "Hey relax, I'm just screwing with you. I don't care what you and "Jelly bean" do, you're both consenting adults." "Don't call her that!" I said a little too defensively. "Ok, take it easy, I heard that bartender at the Library call her that once, she seemed pissed. I would never say it to her face." "Don't say it at all." I corrected. "Alright!, it's just that I'm a little bummed, I think Bill and Andrew are a couple, so that sort of leaves me as odd man out on this trip."

It finally dawned on me. I must say my understanding of women and their emotional needs is limited at best, since I have shielded myself from human interaction for the better part of my life. But it seemed that Ginny was just a young girl looking for a good time over winter break. Her options have just shrunk down to zero and she feels left out. I get it, nothing more sinister than jealousy, of wanting what the rest of us seem to have. It's the perennial conflict. People always want what the next guy has. The proverbial saying of the grass is always greener in your neighbor's yard. I figured I could help Ginny.

As destiny seemed to be at play, Ginny put her hand on my shoulder as she hopped down from the wall. I managed to grab her hand as her body slid into place next to me on the walk. "Ginny, don't' worry about the test, and don't worry about the trip. You're going to do great on the test and the trip will be an exciting adventure. You will have fun and be a positive part of the experience" As my gaze locked with hers and she listened to my voice I could see her pupils dilate as she was drawn into my influence. My influencing Ginny a second time bothered me a bit. I really don't like manipulating people. It's wrong and deceitful, even if intentions are good. It is the main reason why I chose solitude for so long. Avoidance was so much easier than the lies and deceit that breed like a virus.

It has been my usual custom, something I learned during my time with Han, to adopt an uninviting persona; one that is just cordial enough to get by in necessary social interactions but ominous enough to preclude any interest in socializing. Basically I give a glimpse of the predator, not too much, but enough to leave the lingering sense of unease. It prevents people from getting close if they are innately afraid of you. But now I have let down that shield and have started several social interactions, first Lily, then by default Paul, and now Ginny. The more social interactions I have with a person, the longer they know me, the greater chance of them seeing clues to my different nature. I am living dangerously right now, I feel almost reckless, so unaccustomed to having any long term or repeated relationship with any typical human since my transition.

"Let's go ace this test!" Ginny said excitedly as I let go of her hand and we walked into the lecture hall joining the several other students that had started to go in ahead of us. I moved to my customary seat and Ginny, smiling happily, moved to hers. Lily entered the room at the bottom of the lecture hall and as usual I was rewarded with a glorious smile as her eyes found mine. The lecture hall was rapidly filling up as the clock approached 8:00am. Lily instructed the class to take out the index cards allowed for this exam, and a pen, and remove all other items and place them under the seat. She reminded everyone of their responsibility for academic integrity, and that cheating would result in a zero and notification to the dean. At 8:00am on the dot, she passed out the exams, informed everyone that there was to be no more talking from this point on, and she wished us luck. Lily wrote the test start time on the board and the test end time underneath that. We had an hour and a half to complete the exam.

I took my time completing the exam. I finished the multiple choice and true false section fairly quickly. There were several humorous questions, photos and captions in the exam. A slight giggle could be heard intermittently as people came upon them. The second part of the test was short answer. I found the questions thought provoking and several required us to choose a side of a particular debatable topic and give our argument and support for which ever side we chose. The last question was an essay. In 500 words or less give a detailed argument supporting or refuting any one myth, monster or mystery we discussed in class. Several other directions outlined the parameters of the essay.

I was done with the entire exam in 40 minutes. I took 15 more minutes rechecking my work and stood up at five minutes to nine and walked up to Lily with my exam. Several astonished faces turned my way, unable to conceive how I could be finished. Lily looked a little surprised to see me done so soon. As I handed her my exam I said, "Good test, factual, analytical, humorous, it had it all. See you later." I added a barely audible I love you, and left the lecture hall. I would see Lily at her house later, now I will visit Charles' shop in town and afterwards address my need to feed.

CHAPTER 26

A Strange Gift and an Impulsive Purchase

I took the short ride into town from campus and parked my truck in front of the CVS on Main Street. I walked the short distance up the block to Charles' antique shop and tried to enter the shop. The door was locked, and that was when I noticed two things. The interior lights were off and a sign in the window said "For Sale—call 617-555-5559" I took out my cell phone and dialed the number on the sign. A man answered, "Good morning, Anderson Realty, this is Sal speaking, how can I help you?" "Hello my name is Maximillian VanderCreek and I am calling to inquire about the antique shop on Main Street." "Ah Mr. VanderCreek I have been expecting your call. I have a package for you. If you would meet me at my office I can give it to you and explain things."

"Expecting my call? I'm not sure I follow you Sir. I was calling to see if I could get in touch with Charles, the owner of the antique shop?" I replied. "Yes, well as I said Mr. VanderCreek, perhaps you could come to my office and I can fill you in there." "Where is your office Mr . . . ?" "It's Anderson but please, call me Sal. I am at 320 Market Street, just around the corner from the antique shop. When are you available to stop by?" "I'll be right over if that is convenient for you. I am at the antique shop now." I replied. "Very well then, I shall see you shortly Mr. VanderCreek."

I walked over to 320 Market Street. One end of Market Street has a market as its name implies, along with a coin laundry mat, a walk in clinic, and a shoe repair shop. The rest of Market Street is residential. Several giant old homes have been subdivided into apartments. The Market Street apartments are highly sought after by upperclassmen, within stumbling distance from "Punch Drunk Alley", the name give by the college students to the segment of River Street accessed off of Market. There are 12 drinking establishments along this strip of street but they are not for the uninitiated. This is the "townie" part of town. These bars cater to the hard working men and woman who built this town and they don't welcome the college visitors. These are not college bars. Only a select number of upper classmen dare to drink in any of the dives on Punch Drunk Alley. On most weekends at least one fist fight between a "townie" and a foolish college student erupts out onto the street.

The Oak Leaf Pub is about the closest thing to welcoming, as you will see if you're a college student on Punch Drunk Alley. You won't be asked to leave out right, but order any thing other than a beer or straight shot and you may be thrown out on your ass. They have a Pizza Place on the second floor that is open after the bars close. Many a drunken student will stumble upstairs for a late night snack, before stumbling back home. A sign in the window mockingly states, "Proud sponsor of the freshmen 15", a reference to the average weight gained by a freshmen in their first year of college. Anderson's Realty is at the end of Market Street just before River Street. It looks like any other house at the end of the block, save for the small shingle hanging from its mail post. I entered the door marked office, and was greeted by an older woman whom I assumed was the receptionist. She looked at me through red puffy eyes and gave me a barely audible greeting as I entered. A man in his mid 50's came out from the only other visible office and introduced himself as Sal.

"You must be Mr. VanderCreek, I'm Sal Anderson. My Father Sal senior started this business 35 years ago, I have worked here most of my life and now run the business. I hope you'll forgive my receptionist. It has been a hard day for all of us. Why don't we go into my office to talk?" Once we were settled in his office, Sal continued, "You see Mr. VanderCreek, my family has known Charles forever, it seems. My parents, Charles, and his wife Lilly were close friends. Mr. VanderCreek, I do not know any way to tell you this other than, Charles is dead." Dead. The word hung in the air like vapor, the reason for the receptionists red eyes now evident. "May I ask how?" I inquired gently, for I could now recognize the sadness in Sal's eyes too. "It appears he died in his sleep, however, he was acting rather strangely on Sunday evening when he came in to talk with me."

"On Sunday, I was in his shop buying a Christmas gift for my girlfriend's mother. He seemed fine and in good spirits though I must say he seemed to be talking to his wife as if she were there having a conversation with him. The first time I was in his shop a few months back, I purchased a necklace from him for my girlfriend. As I recall he seemed to talk to her then as well. I thought he was a kind, if not a bit eccentric, gentlemen. I enjoyed talking with him. He had interesting stories to share. When you say he was acting strangely what do you mean, if you don't mind me asking?"

"Well, Mr. VanderCreek, it had been a while, since I had talked with Charles. And as you mentioned he did seem to have conversations with his dead wife, but that is something he has done since her death. What was strange was how excited he seemed. He came storming into my office Sunday evening, around 5:00pm. We were just getting ready to lock up when he came in. He was beaming from ear to ear, saying something about "It's finally done, it's finally done!" When I asked him what was done he waved off my question and said "Sal Junior, we have work to do." When I asked him what was going on he said he had a job for me.

Charles asked me to do three things for him, first he asked that I witness him sign a revised will and have Jackie, my receptionist notarize it for him. He requested I hold onto the will in my office safe for him since he had no living family members. He then told me to list his shop for sale, along with the contents, stating his responsibilities were complete. I am not sure what he meant by that. Lastly, he asked me to hold onto this package for you. And this is the strangest part; he said to tell you "Lilly insisted that you will need these."

After, completing his requests I asked Charles again what was going on. Why did he want to sell his shop so suddenly? What was he going to do? His reply seemed to have a different meaning to me at the time, but hindsight is 20/20 as they say. He told me he "was embarking on a great journey, one he had been waiting to take for a long time." I assumed he was going to travel, and asked him when he was leaving. He told me he would leave that night. It all seemed peculiar to me but Charles seemed so happy and excited I didn't question his actions. I told him that I would do as he asked, that I would put a for sale sign in the window on Monday. I mentioned we could handle the sale of the shop when he returned. He smiled at me and said I have everything I need in the signed and notarized documents, he gave me a hug and went home to the apartment he has over the antique shop.

I went to the shop early this morning to put the sign in the window. I noticed his apartment door was open and I went up to talk to him, and that was when I found him. He was sitting in his easy chair with a picture of Lilly in his hands, a smile on his lips as his vacant eyes continued to stare down at his wife, he was gone. I called the police and they came by there a few hours ago and took him away."

I sat in stunned silence, trying to absorb the reality of what I just heard. One thought continued to cycle through my mind, Charles' whispered words to his Lilly when we left his shop "Good bye my love, until I am at your side again."

Several minutes passed as I processed what Sal just told me. "I am sorry Sal, for the loss of your friend. I only had the pleasure of meeting with him twice, but I enjoyed his company greatly." Sal replied, "Well I guess you made an impression on him, he left this for you." I took the small sealed package from Sal, thanked him, expressed my sincere regrets for his loss once again, and left him. I walked slowly back to my car, analyzing the information that I knew.

Charles was dead. The ominous feeling I had as I left his shop yesterday now seemed prophetic. He seemed at last to be back with his Lilly. I got in my truck and drove home to my farm, the unopened package sitting on the seat beside me. "Lilly insisted that I would need these" was what Sal said Charles had told him. I had a feeling I knew what was in the package. I kept replaying in my head the two encounters that I had with Charles. I had undeniably felt some kind of energy, a presence, when I had been to see him on both occasions. The flickering lights, the sensation of a cold breeze moving around me in the shop, I know I felt something, it was real. Just what it was, has me rethinking my own ideas of a soul perhaps, and what happens when someone dies.

I have wrestled with the concept of a soul for some time and have always believed humans, like all life, must follow the same laws of science. I know matter and energy can not be created or destroyed only changed. Humans are another part of the energy cycle. At death the energy contained in a living thing just doesn't disappear. I have always felt it had to go somewhere. If the soul is the energy of life, as I theorize, could it be possible Lilly's soul stayed close to Charles, for so many years, because of the responsibility of the Evening Star? If not a soul, certainly some type of presence, I felt it myself. It seemed I had a lot more questions than answers.

I got back to my farm and set to task. First, I called the lawyer whom I have used for several real estate deals over the past 35 years. He has arranged for the purchases of several of my homes including the farm. By making purchases through him I am able to stay anonymous throughout the transaction. I dialed his number, a secretary answered, "Stanford and Brown this is Linda. How may I direct your call?" "Hello Linda. This is Maximillian VanderCreek, is Jack in? Yes, I'll hold, Thanks." I was not on hold long when a familiar voice came on the line. "Maximillian, it has been a long time, how are you?" "I'm good Jack, how have you been? It has been over 10 years since I have spoken to you. I hope life has been treating you well." "I have had a busy and fruitful decade Max. I have been married and divorced twice, and have my eye on the future Mrs. Brown as we speak. Thank goodness I'm an excellent lawyer; rock solid pre-nups have saved me a fortune. What can I do for you at this time Max?"

"Jack, I would like you to make another real estate purchase for me. This one requires the contents to be catalogued, assessed for value, and stored. After the purchase I would like you to arrange for the space to be rented. It is a commercial space with an attached apartment above the store front. It's a college town. They could use a nice bookstore, something other than a bar if possible. I will be heading out on a trip and unavailable for a few weeks. I will fax over the details for the purchase. Please make a generous offer; the contents of the shop are important to me. As always Jack I appreciate the work you do for me. I'll talk to you soon." "No problem Max, you pay me very well. I will get on the purchase today and give you a call in a few weeks, have a nice trip."

My first order of business taken care of, I sat down at my kitchen table with Charles' package in hand. As I sit turning the package I am hesitant to open it. There is no logical reason to have trepidations about the contents. It's the meaning of them that I worry about. How has such a random act as buying a necklace for Lily, come to play such a pivotal role in our lives? I slowly open the package. Inside there is a blue velvet jewelry pouch and a hand written letter. The letter, dated Sunday December 13, 2009 is as follows:

Dear Mr. VanderCreek,

I first want to thank you. It was clear from the moment I met you several months back that you understand the depths of love one can feel for his betrothed. By being that man, by being able to open your heart to love your Lily so completely, you have opened a pathway for a powerful force. That was so clearly evident from the first minute you walked into my shop. It was as if you had an aura around you. It was the first time Lilly ever let her presence be felt by anyone other than me, and that told me something. Do you remember the flickering light?

That fateful day you walked into my shop, and it was fate make no mistake of that, it set a course of actions that would irrevocably change three lives. Fate has brought us together. You and Lily will now take up the thread that connects us. Your combined force is exceptionally strong, far more powerful that it was with Lilly and I. Your lives will now be shaped by that power and guided by the Evening Star. I wish I had more time to explain things to you, to learn what is special about both of you and what amplifies the collective strength of your force. But my Lilly has assured me your path is good and that you and your Lily's souls are bound to each other.

We agreed that your next logical step should be to marry the woman of your destiny. By the time you read this letter you would have figured that out. Please accept this gift from us, to you and Lily, we hope you enjoy a long and love filled life together. I am sure you have many questions, answers will come in time. Look to the Evening Star to guide you, and remember how powerful love is. For now, know that you are on the right path, and that together you and Lily will forge a dynamic union. My one fear is for how your

Lily will react to all of this. I fear she will be saddened and confused by my sudden passing, for when you read this I will be gone.

Please know, both of you, that as I sit here writing this to you I am filled with more joy than I have felt in over 30 years. I know that tonight Lilly will come for me, she will guide my passing and we shall be reunited, to spend eternity together at last. Good bye to you both, perhaps we will meet again in the afterlife.

Very sincerely yours,
Charles Adammo

I read the letter through several times, each time I have more questions. One thing I agree on is that Lily will not react well to the news of Charles' passing. For as much as Lily has spent her life exploring the concepts of the fantastical, I know she is having a hard time accepting the power of the Evening Star without a scientific explanation for it. By the time we leave New Zealand her entire world order will be changed.

Contemplating Lily's reaction makes me remember the package, the gift from Charles and Lily. I pick up the velvet pouch and untie the string. I pour the contents onto my palm. It is as I had thought. Two rings tumble out onto my hand. They, like the Evening Star, are beautiful in their simplicity. One for me, a braided band of platinum, and for Lily, I realize that the one ring is actually two. There is a matching platinum braided band whose ends do not meet. At the ends are two flowers with small rubies as the bud at the ends. The space left in the band allows for the second ring to lock together with the first. The second ring also has the same braided band, the braids end by wrapping around a magnificent diamond. The effect is as if the diamond is a flower in bloom, the braided platinum its vine and platinum leaves surround and set the diamond in place. Together the two pieces interlock to form one ring, though I imagine they can be worn separately.

I turn the rings in my fingers marveling at their beauty and craftsmanship. They are perfect, something I myself would have picked out for us. It is an extraordinary gift and I am astounded at Charles' generosity. I am also quite taken aback as to his insight into my feelings for Lily. How is it he should know I would desire rings for Lily and I, when I myself had not discerned my intentions until the early morning hours on Monday, after Charles had already passed on?

Thinking of Charles, his wife Lilly, the Evening Star, Lily and I, and how we have all become intertwined is bewildering. I know that I would have liked to have met his Lilly when she was alive, and despite only having had a brief time shared with Charles, I feel his absence as a significant loss. I would have enjoyed the opportunity to spend more time with him, there are so many questions, so many things I would have liked to discuss with him. I guess I should consider myself fortunate to have had the chance to meet him at all.

"Well Charles and Lilly if you are listening, thank you for your most generous gift, and for the pleasure of being connected to you even briefly. You are right Charles, I have a lot of questions, but I shall do as you said and look to the Evening Star and my own heart to guide me in my quest to find the answers I seek." As I spoke those words I had hoped to feel or see something, a rush of air, a light flicker, something to give me a sense that Charles and Lilly were still connected to me, but there was nothing.

I decided to wait until we returned from New Zealand to tell Lily about Charles, though I will pack his letter and the rings in my carry on, just in case my plans change. After all if Lily accepts me for what I am, perhaps a Christmas engagement would be in order. I am filled with questions and uncertainty. I decide to go for an afternoon trip into the Adirondacks. I will go out to the cave where Lily and I hiked, that area is ripe with prey and I always feel better equipped to handle my problems after a long run and hunt.

CHAPTER 27

Our Connection Grows Stronger

It is presumptuous of me to think that Lily will not sense something. I have not been able to stop thinking about the letter, the rings, or the fact that in a way I envy Charles. If what he believed is true, and I hope it is, then he has been reunited with his beloved, together in the after life for eternity. If not, I imagine he died happy with just the thought of returning to his Lilly. I don't have the luxury of ignorance. I know one thing, even if Lily accepts me, and I want that with all of my being, I will still one day suffer the pain of losing her. Charles was wrong; our souls can't possibly be tied for eternity. Of course, I am sure he thought that I was human, but Lily is a mortal human and some day she will be taken from me by death. I can try and protect her from harm but humans are fragile in both body and mind. She will eventually die. I, on the other hand, will not.

I have the potential to exist indefinitely. If I can't die then our souls cannot meet in the after life. I would be willing to suffer an eternity, with the pain of her loss, if it means I can have Lily even for just her lifetime. To love and to be loved, as I am, it is more than I dared dream possible. Never in the last century, not even as a human, have I ever truly felt that I would someday find love. I have never actively sought it out and yet feel as if somehow, call it fate, luck or an act of my strange biology, Lily and I have found each other. I sense that we belong together and I will do everything in my power to see that we are together for as long as she will have me.

Even a run in the deep woods couldn't stop the torrent of thoughts and emotions swirling through my mind. Charles is dead. I love Lily, and want to spend the rest of her life together. In just one weeks time I will be back in New Zealand confronting the demons of my past and I will tell Lily the truth. As I realized that my cluttered mind would not be easily soothed, I returned to my farm to feed on some of the blood from my Cortland run. After feeding and getting showered I decided to go out into the barn to meditate. I need to quiet my mind before I meet with Lily tonight. I lie in a pile of hay and slowly inhale the scents around me. I conjure images in my mind of time spent sitting atop a hay pile with Genevieve, I can almost smell the fresh baked cookies she would have waiting for me.

Genevieve was an amazing mother. She loved me completely and was always there to help me seek the answers to what ever problem, my adolescent self, had at the time. Even after milk and cookies seemed too juvenile for the grown man I had become, Genevieve would come and sit with me in the barn and talk. She was easy to talk to. Rarely judgmental, with an exceptional knack for listening, Genevieve was the perfect sounding board for me to bounce my ideas off of. She had a way of answering my questions with ones of her own. Helping me find the answers I needed with out really providing them herself. She taught me the tools I needed to be an independent thinker able to eventually solve my own problems.

I miss Genevieve, she died too young, but in a way I am glad she was not alive after I transitioned. I fear what might have happened if I were with her that day instead of my horse. I quickly shake the horrid thought from my already crowded mind. After a time, the magic of the barn works to sooth me. While my mind is no longer frenetically cycling through the problems I face, I slowly bring order and calm to my thoughts.

It's just after 6:00pm as I make my way over to Lily's. I have picked up some Italian food from Two Brothers Italian Eatery on Center Street near Lily's house. I let myself in and greet Pumpkin who gives me a cursory lick on my hand as she waits for me to feed her. She is sniffing the air, undoubtedly smelling the Italian food in the bag. I reach into the bag and take out the small carton on top. It contains one meatball that I cut up and mix with Pumpkins dry food.

I have grown fond of Pumpkin, and like Lily, one way to make her happy is with food. I set the bowl down for the dog and she greedily eats and licks the bowl clean. After a quick pit stop in the back yard, Pumpkin comes back inside, nuzzles my hand appreciatively and curls back up on her bed for a nap. At five past seven Lily walks in looking bleary eyed but happy to see me.

"Hi." I say as we embrace. I love to hold her in my arms, her head pressed against my chest. Her warmth and the way she smells are like nourishment for my soul. Standing together like this feels wonderful. "Hi" she answers back. As she looks up at me I notice a red line running across the right side of Lily's forehead. "Did you scratch yourself on something?" I ask as I gently brush the hair back from Lily's face. Lily just laughed, a tired giggle, and said "This is not a scratch, but a crease mark. I fell asleep at my desk grading the last of the essays. Good thing students don't get back the tests, that last one had a little drool on it. After all of those papers, over six hundred pages of myths, monsters and mysteries, my eyes just wouldn't stay open anymore. At around 4:00pm I fell asleep at my desk. I was out for about 45 minutes. Now I have always been a big fan of napping, I usually feel rejuvenated after a nap. But this one was weird. I had the most vivid and peculiar dreams, which is strange since I was not out that long and I rarely dream during a nap. It wasn't a continuous dream either; it was more like short video clips of weirdness."

"Do you want to tell me about them?" I ask. "Only if you promise not to laugh or read into them, some of what I remember is really crazy. I preface this with a reminder that I had spent the previous six hours straight, reading about an array of fantastical stories. That said, I remember one had something to do with ghosts. There were hundreds of vaporous apparitions gliding through space. It was almost as if they existed in a parallel universe to ours. Like all those who have died were meeting up with long lost loved ones. It gave me a distinct feeling like being in a bus terminal or airport. There were streams of people coming and going, connecting to and letting go of friends or loved ones. I saw my father, he was alone in a corner, waiting, he smiled at me and then was gone in a wisp of smoke. I thought I saw Charles and a woman smile at me before they turned to vapor and were replaced by my old dog from when I was a child, a Shepherd named April. We only had her for 3 years. She was hit by a car a few months before my father died. Her smoky form dissolved as she ran in the direction my father's apparition had gone. I remember something that I think was about New Zealand, it seemed very Hobbit like, and then there was one of you."

"Of me, were you fantasizing about me?" I asked teasingly. Lily laughed another tired giggle and said "You were very young, but the eyes and hair made me think it was you immediately. Remember the story you told me in the barn, of how you and your mother would sit in the hay with cookies solving your problems? Well it was like that at first, the woman sitting with you resembled your description of your mother, but then she became me. You, as an adult, walked into the barn and it seemed like the child was ours. We seemed really happy. Then it got a little strange because when you smiled at me you had fangs, and the baby had fangs, and the cookies were actually a basket of new born kittens and the baby picked one up, and that's when I woke up. It was pretty bizarre. After that, I finished the last paper and put the grades in my computer and here I am. Hey you ok? I told you not to read anything into my weird "napmare". Lots of weird papers, not enough to eat, my own random subconscious thoughts all mingled together. It happens sometimes when you sleep with a lot on your mind, thoughts play out in your dreams, not in any normal way. Everything gets jumbled, real with imaginary. That's never happened to you?"

"It's happened to me I guess. It's just that I do not recall most of my dreams, and if I do, never as vividly as you seem to. I find dreams incredibly interesting, but as you say they tend to be a jumble of things in your life, mixed with your subconscious, not something I spend too much time analyzing." Again, I find myself circumventing the truth. I have never thought of myself with a child. Not as a human and definitely not as a vampire. I have run tests in my lab and every female egg that has been placed with vampire sperm, specifically mine, has been devoured by the sperm, not fertilized. The two are incompatible. I guess those factors, plus the fact that Lily never once mentioned children, made me think she felt as I did, that we would have a life together, just the two of us. It seems at least subconsciously she sees herself as a mother. And as I thought it, I felt it. I felt a maternal yearning in Lily.

I was analyzing. Lily's connection to the Evening Star was growing, even if she did not yet realize it. Her "napmare" was a jumble of my thoughts too, Charles being dead, New Zealand and my demons, Lily and I being together and my telling her the truth about me. These are all thoughts and images I was having as I went out to feed and in the barn, although the part about the child was obviously not mine. The rest of her dreams however, have convinced me, that soon she will realize the truth. Once she discerns the true power of the Evening Star she will see me exactly as I am.

To Lily, I said "You look tired. I picked up some food for you from Two Brothers and I gave Pumpkin a meatball with her dry food. Why don't you eat and we can turn in early. By the way, how did I do on the essay?" "Well, I probably graded your paper the hardest in my effort to be unbiased. I was trying not to give you an A. I was looking for some reason why your work was not worthy of it. I am happy to say I couldn't find any. Your paper was extraordinary. I would love to discuss it with you another night, right now babe I'm almost too tired to even eat." Almost; she quickly devoured the plate of food I placed before her.

Lily eyed the empty plate with a sheepish grin, replying "Who am I kidding, too tired to eat, especially Two Brothers, they are the best Italian take out in town." I said in reply, "You can have the leftovers for breakfast, some good carbs for your marathon grading session." "Tomorrow will be much easier than today. Half the answers are on Scan-tron and the short answer questions will be easy to grade. Much easier than 107, different, three page essays." After dinner we went to bed early. Lily was asleep within minutes of her head hitting the pillow. "Sleep my sweet." I said and I stroked her hair as she slept, her body pressed close against mine.

CHAPTER 28

A Meeting of the Minds

On Tuesday, I dropped Lily off at her office at 9:00am. There she toiled away the hours grading the rest of the exams, putting the grades into her computer, and submitting final semester grades to the registrar's office. When she was through she went home and slept until Wednesday morning. She had one more test to give to her Evolution class on Wednesday. This class was much smaller, only 18 students. The test was at 2:00pm. After the exam Lily spent the afternoon and into the late hours of the evening grading those tests as well as calculating and submitting the final grades.

Wednesday evening was a repeat of Tuesday. Lily went home and straight to bed and slept till Thursday. We had decided on Tuesday morning that since Lily was going to basically be working or sleeping and did not have time for much else, we would meet Thursday around noon. Lily planned a meeting with Ginny Grimes, Bill Treetop and Andrew Johnson for 2:00 at the library, the actual library on campus, not Paul's bar.

I spent Tuesday and Wednesday out on an extended hunt. It was rather spontaneous actually. After I dropped Lily off I realized I had nothing to do until we left for New Zealand on Saturday. With nothing to do I was concerned that I would spend too much time in thought. Too much time thinking about Charles, Victoria, my secrets, all things that if Lily felt them, could derail my plans. As a diversion I took off north to Canada. I love Canada. It is full of remote, inhospitable wilderness. In the winter the terrain is nearly impassable and temperatures can plummet. It is an unforgiving place and few people have the courage or survival skills to venture into the remote locations where I travel. In other words, it's the perfect place for me to go to blow off some steam and let loose for a bit.

Keeping secrets had never really been hard up until now. I never cared enough to let someone know me. I never cared if I hurt someone emotionally. Now that I do care, each secret I keep, each lie I tell, causes a stabbing guilt that tears at my soul. For now I have reached the point where I can't bear to hurt Lily, it physically pains me. Each lie meant to protect her, separately are small transgressions, but collectively they hide a profound deception. The level of which, grows worse with each day I continue to lie to my beloved.

On my little getaway, I tried several times to channel the connection of the Evening Star. To test over what distance our connection held. It was difficult at first to focus on Lily. I sat meditating in a den I had taken from a bear and her two cubs, whose pelts provided a moderate cushion upon which to sit. When I allowed myself to clear my mind of all thoughts but Lily, I found the thread, as Charles called it. And it very much was like a thread stretched between us. Our distance made it feel as thin as filament, fragile and barely tangible, yet it was there.

I suddenly knew that wherever on this planet Lily should go I would be able to find the thread that connected us. Seeing for the first time, the magnitude of the power of the gift we had been given was sobering. I felt fairly certain though, that being a vampire has given me an advantage in my ability to discern so quickly some of the power of the Evening Star. I knew Lily had not yet figured as much out. This soothed my mind. We would be leaving on Saturday. Only a short time now and I will be free of the lies, and ready to face what ever response Lily may have to the truth.

I made my way back to my barn in Franklin by 2:00am Thursday morning. The extended trip was rejuvenating. I felt strong and centered. I practiced clearing my mind of thoughts of Charles' death, of Victoria and of Lily learning my truth. I had devised a plan of how and when I would tell Lily everything. Now that I had a plan, there was no more need to keep running the thoughts through my head. The only thing left to do was wait. For a vampire two days is but a blink in time.

I arrived at Lily's house at 10 am, she was still asleep. I took care of the needs of a very irritated Pumpkin and then made my way into Lily's bedroom. She looked angelic, sleeping so peacefully. The rhythmic rise and fall of her chest and rapid eye movement under her lids suggested she was in deep REM sleep. Dreaming of what, I could only guess at. As I sat on the edge of the bed and reached out to stroke her hair Lily stirred. Her eyes opened and found mine and I was gifted with a radiant smile that lit up her face.

"Good morning sunshine" I said as I leaned in to kiss her, her warm sleepy breath caressing my cheek as I nuzzle the side of her neck. "Hey, good morning, what time is it?" She replied with a voice still scraggy with sleep. "It's after 10:00am" I said. Lily responded as if a fire had been lit under the bed. Jumping up she exclaimed, "After ten? Crap! I had hoped to get up early this morning; I still have so much to do before we leave. I was hoping to run into town before our meeting with the rest of "Team New Zealand". I have some errands to finish up." "Relax my love we have the rest of the day today and all day tomorrow to tie up the loose ends. I am ready to go, so I can help you get ready."

Lily slowed her frantic search for clothes to wear and said "Ok, it's fine, I just never sleep that late and I am a little thrown off my routine." "If you would like I could make you something for breakfast while you are in the shower." With a slight huff, a mischievous smile spread across Lily's lips, and she replied "I have a better idea, since my morning isn't exactly going as I planned, why not make a total mess of it. Care to try to make me late for our meeting?" With that Lily slipped out of her t-shirt and panties and beckoned me to follow her into the bathroom. I certainly had no need for breakfast, but I had other strong desires, and I left a trail of clothes in my wake on my way to join her.

Our tryst was not quite an "afternoon delight" it was more like brunch, but it was far more satisfying than any food could be. We arrived at the campus library at ten after 2:00. When we met up with the others, Ginny gave Lily a smirk, glanced at her watch and commented "You look flushed Bean, afternoon workout?" I expected Lily to playfully brush off the comment. Her response was surprising, not so much for what was said but for how. When Lily looked at Ginny to respond, there was a distinctly alpha female quality to it.

"It's Professor Bean to you Ginny. Don't forget, this is an internship, think of me as your employer and act accordingly." This short sentence was delivered with such uncharacteristic vitriol it stunned the group into silence. But it was Lily's eyes that gave me pause. They reminded me of the look the mother bear gave me when I entered her den and she tried to defend her cubs. And then as fast as it had come, the look was gone. Lily's countenance returned to the decidedly less aggressive and friendly visage we were all accustomed to.

"I called this meeting, so you could all get a chance to meet before we leave, and to go over the ground rules of the trip and my expectations for each of you. Bill and Andrew, I think you know Ginny, this is Max. All of you have signed up for this trip as independent study credits. Ginny, Bill and Andrew will be getting undergrad credit and Max will be getting graduate credits. You three as undergrads will be responsible for gathering data, imputing data into the computer and doing a lot of the grunt work. You each need to bring your laptops with you, and be sure to have the appropriate adaptors and batteries you will need. Max as a grad student, you will be assisting me with the interviews and on site detective work that will hopefully help us in our quest for answers."

It was smart of Lily to lay out the rules for the trip, but with Ginny's remark, Lily's response, was like drawing a line in the sand. She continued, "Your grades will reflect your performance of the tasks you are assigned. We will all be working as a team. You were all given this opportunity, based on your insight and enthusiasm for the study of Vampirism. I want you all to remember that you represent this institution while on this trip. There will be plenty of down time for you to do as you please. I expect you to have your responsibilities to this class as your first priority, and behave in a manor that is consistent with the ethical code of the college. I feel like we are on the verge of an amazing discovery and anticipate an exciting adventure. I look forward to working with all of you, in our quest for proof of the existence of vampires."

After Lily's opening remarks the rest of the meeting was spent going over the logistics of the trip. Lily explained, "Our journey begins with several flights. First we fly out of local Hills Airport, to JFK International airport in New York on the 19th. From N.Y. we have an 11:30am flight on American Airlines to Los Angeles International Airport. We have a seven hour lay over after which we take a flight on Air New Zealand to Auckland, New Zealand and catch a connector to Christchurch. The total trip takes about 29 hours and with the time difference we arrive on Monday the 21st at 8:20am. Our return trip is set for the 28th of December arriving home on the 30th. You all signed up for this trip knowing it occurs over the week of Christmas and I assume you understand we will not be taking time out of our schedule to celebrate. We have a lot to do in a short amount of time and I want to ensure the effort is rewarded with a good product at the end. Does anyone have any questions?"

Lily answered several questions and I formally introduced myself to Bill and Andrew. Ginny had mentioned they were a couple and they seemed to be a happy one. When I went to introduce myself, Andrew said "It is nice to finally meet you. Bill and I have been admiring you from afar in class all semester." Bill chimed in "Yeah, you kind of stand out. You're much better dressed than a typical college student, and let's face it; you are beautiful to look at. Your eyes are riveting. The color defies anything I have seen before, a bluish, grayish almost lavender color. Stunning with your black hair and . . ."

Andrew interrupted "Ok Bill, if you keep it up I'm going to get jealous." Bill returned, "Oh, sorry Drew, you know I only have eyes for you. Anyway Max, it's nice to meet you." "It's nice to meet the both of you. And thank you for the compliment. I'm sure I will enjoy working with you both." We finished up the meeting around 4:00pm and after a quick stop by Lily's office for a few last minute things, we drove back to her house.

On the ride back home Lily spoke animatedly about the trip and the success of the meeting. "I think that went well. I wanted to make sure everyone understood the division of labor and my general expectations. Ginny was a little quiet, but she had to be reminded of the boundaries, a situation like that can easily get out of hand, with her, her quips seem less like friendly banter and more like a personal stab. My "chick" instincts tell me to keep an eye on her and definitely keep her in check."

To hear Lily's opinion, on her response to Ginny's remark, made her response seem more appropriate. Very, alpha female defending her turf, that's my Lily. "Max, I realize that we have talked very little about what I expect from you on this trip. I want you to know it's because I see you as an equal. You have shown such knowledge and depth of insight into all the topics we have discussed I sometimes feel as if you should be the teacher. I may have set this whole trip up, but I hope you're up to working together on this. I really value your ideas and opinions and look forward to seeing what we can discover together."

I looked over to Lily, my love for her filling me, and answered her with complete honesty when I said "Lily, since I signed up for this class, I have always thought of it as our personal quest for answers, for truth. I anticipate there will be many uncovered, both answers and truths. I am also sure, as you probably already know, even with answers, one often has more questions. I will be there with you as a fellow investigator, but more importantly I will be there as the man who loves you, to help you not just seek the truth, but cope with the truths we uncover. Sometimes Lily, the truth can make one wish for the ignorance of a lie. You have invested so much of yourself, in this journey that started long before we met. Whatever you learn, it is important for you to remember how you feel right now. I feel your love for me, it radiates from you. It's like being wrapped in your warm embrace. And Lily, you know the depth of my love, you can feel it. I have felt a connection to you from the first day I laid eyes on you, even before the Evening Star. And the first time your lips kissed my cheek after I helped you down the cow path, you felt it. It was almost as if our bodies knew before our brains that we were meant to be together. I hope you always remember that." "Max, I have already learned the only truth I need to know and that is that you love me. Anything else we discover, as long as we are together, I'm sure we will handle."

I tried not to be cryptic with Lily. So close to learning the truth, one might ask why not just tell her now. But, I know in my soul, the way for Lily to accept me is through Victoria. It cannot be coincidence that my past and present are about to come face to face. Some greater force is at work, and it has been so, possibly for far longer than I have expected. But I am convinced that Victoria is the key to my salvation.

CHAPTER 29

One Truth Uncovered

It is Friday, the 18th of December. I watch Lily as she stirs in her sleep, she will be getting up soon, ready to tackle the last minute list of things to do before we leave tomorrow, but now she is in the midst of a dream. Her eyes dart rapidly under her lids as if she were watching a tennis match. As I sit and contemplate the beauty and graceful curves of her sleeping form, I run through the trip itinerary that Lily and I discussed last night. We leave tomorrow morning on an 8:00am commuter flight to JFK from Hills Airport. Our flight out of JFK is at 11:30am, we have two stops along the way in Los Angeles and Auckland. The total trip time is approximately 29 hours but with the time difference we end up in New Zealand on Monday morning.

Lily has set up a meeting with Victoria for 3:00 pm on Monday afternoon. We will interview Victoria together and on Tuesday we will interview the witness at noon. Lily has set aside time on Wednesday and Thursday for second interviews with Victoria and the witness, depending on what she learns, she has the rest of the week open to do research in town and at the local hall of records. I am not sure as of yet, exactly how I will tell Lily. I hope the situation will present itself after we interview Victoria.

From the look on Lily's face it seems her dream has become troublesome. She wakes with a start. A shouted "No!" pierces the quiet of the bedroom. "Lily, it's ok, it was just a dream." I say soothingly. When Lily looks at me I see she has a sleepy confused look about her. "Oh, Max, what time is it?" "It's just seven, were you having a bad dream?" "I guess, it was dark, I was alone. It's all too fuzzy to remember any details. Sorry if my shout woke you." "It didn't, I have been up for a while, just thinking about the itinerary we discussed last night." "Well, I'm glad were up early, I have a lot of last minute things to do before we leave in the morning."

After a quick bite for Lily, we decided to go to town to hit CVS one more time. Lily insisted she needed more batteries and film. Along with those, she picked up a few more impulse items, things for the plane, gum, candy and lip balm. When she seemed to have all she needed we paid for the purchases and head out down the street. It was still early, not all of the stores that occupied the strip were open. I was hoping that Lily would not want to go down by Charles' Antique shop. I didn't want to tell her yet, about the letter or the rings. While they were a gift presumably from both Lilly and Charles, it had been my intention that day, when I went and found the for sale sign, to purchase rings for Lily and I. How Charles or his dead wife Lilly would know before I had decided, that rings are what I sought, still picks at my mind. Regardless, I am not ready to address that now.

Just as I thought we would make it safely out of town Lily said, "I just have to go to the cash machine. I have traveler's checks but I want to have a few hundred on me when we travel, just in case." "Just in case what?" I asked, trying to draw her attention away from the stores and towards me. "In case, you know, travel to a far away land, in quest of vampires . . . in case any number of things occur. At the very least there are sure to be grifters along the way. It seems when one seeks to find information, it can be especially helpful to grease the wheels, so to speak." "You watch too many spy shows." I said with a smile.

Lily crossed the street in a diagonal, a few stores before Charles'. She never paused to glance back in the direction of the antique shop. We went into the bank and Lily made her transaction, as we made our way to the door she said over her shoulder, "Lets see if Charles is open yet, I would like to say hello and wish him a merry Christmas." She was a few steps ahead of me, when, turning in the direction of Charles' store, she gasped. What we saw surprised us both. The store front window had been covered with a coming soon sign. "Mia's Marvelous Café and Book Store", was being heralded. All I could think of was that Jack worked fast; he certainly earned his enormous fees.

"What the hell?" Lily exclaimed. I answered honestly, "I'm as surprised as you", although we were surprised about entirely different things. "I have to go ask Sal, over at Anderson's Realty. Nothing gets bought or sold in this town without him being involved. He will know why Charles's shop is closed. It's just on Market Street, do you mind if we go?" I wanted to be with Lily to comfort her as she received the news of Charles' death, but if Sal saw me with her he would wonder why I had not told her myself. I tried evasive maneuvers. "You want to go now? Don't you think this can wait until after we get back from our trip, you still have a lot of things on that to do list?"

She would not be deterred. One more lie, I hoped it would be my last to Lily. "Would you mind if I met you there? I forgot I need shaving cream for the trip. I will be right behind you." Lily countered with, "Why don't you get the car after you are finished at CVS and meet me out front at Anderson's. The address is 320 Market. Do you know how to get to Market?" "I know where it is, it's near the Oak Leaf Pub. I'll be by in a few minutes." I left Lily, alone, to learn the news of Charles' death. I am ashamed, but do not know of another way that still lets me maintain the secrecy of the letter and the rings.

I know she feels strongly for him and I can feel her worry as she walks to Market Street.

"I went to CVS and bought some shaving cream to keep up the lie and slowly drove over to Anderson's. As I approached, I felt it, Lily engulfed in sorrow and confusion. I pulled up in time to see her walking dazedly out of Anderson's. Thankfully Sal remained in his office, and did not see me. I got out of the car, helped Lily in and got back inside and drove slowly away from Anderson's. Keeping up the charade I asked the question, for which I already knew the answer.

"Lily what's wrong?" "It's Charles. Max, Charles is dead." And then she wept quietly. After a few minutes Lily reiterated the story Sal had told her. She had no knowledge of the package left to me by Charles, and I was not worried about her finding out that I had bought the store and all of its' contents. Not only was Jack fast but he did an excellent job at keeping me anonymous.

Lily talked about her feelings for Charles. "Even though I only had that one time to meet him, I feel as if I lost a loved one. Something about him, the necklace . . ." Lily trailed off. "I guess I thought I would have more time to talk to him, to learn more from him about the Evening Star. He seemed like such an interesting gentleman. I will miss him." "Lily, Charles led a long and interesting life, from what I learned from him. I am sure he is happy to finally be reunited with his Lilly. He told me he believed he would see her again and that their souls were bound to each other. I hope she was in his thoughts as he passed."

We drove the rest of the way home with Lily in silent contemplation. The rest of the afternoon was spent helping Lily pack and getting Pumpkin ready for her stay with Paul. I drove Lily and Pumpkin to Paul's Library Pub, and agreed we would meet back at her house later. I had to go out to my farm, get my things and close up the house for when we would be away. I also wanted to feed one last time. I have four bags left of AB+, from Cortland, they won't stay fresh for another two weeks, so I will drink them all and be well fueled. I will have to go without sleep for a while, I am not comfortable sleeping with Lily yet. If she were to watch me while I was in a deep restorative sleep, even for a few minutes, she would think I was dead.

When a vampire sleeps it is strictly for restorative purposes. It gives the cells an opportunity to divert energy away from unnecessary tasks such as breathing and beating one's heart and focuses on repair and replacement of damaged cells. It is an opportunity to remove those dead cells and the metabolic waste from the body. The wastes diffuse to the surface, leaving the skin with a white patina. I could pass for a corpse very easily. Thankfully I am fit. I have been feeding often leading up to this trip, and this large meal of blood I will enjoy, it will be enough to sustain me for a while. I know there are sheep and other game where we are going, not that I should need it, so sleep is not a priority. After I complete my short to do list, I head back to Lily's for our last night in town, we head out at dawn for a journey that is sure to be life changing for us both.

CHAPTER 30

The Adventure Begins

For a typical human the trip to New Zealand from the east coast is arduous at best. The 29 hour plus journey could be made more or less bearable, depending largely on the fate of the seating arrangements. I wanted to make sure Lily was comfortable, and, give us some private time before "team New Zealand" got under way when we landed. I would have gladly paid outright for two first class round trip tickets, however since the trip was arranged through the university, it was not an option. I opted to circumvent the rules a bit. At the airport, I managed to suggest to two first class ticket holders, that they would be extremely interested in switching tickets with us for a large financial profit. Together the other party and I spoke to the airline employee at the boarding gate. The agent, who is already primed to try and please the customer, was easily coaxed into making the switch. I would say it was fortuitous that Lily was in the restroom while this entire transaction took place, but actually I may have suggested she had to use the restroom. A gentle persuasion for the greater good is how I tried to sugar coat my deceptions. "Just a short time longer", these words became my mantra.

To hide my deception from Lily, Ginny, Bill and Drew, I would say that I was able to upgrade my and Lily's tickets with frequent flier points. I have told Lily I travel a lot so I was hoping they would all just buy it. When the flight boarded, Lily and I were in first class, the other three from our group were in coach. For me the trip would not be arduous, I could sit in one position for days at a time with no muscle cramps or comfort issues. I have traveled in the bowels of rat infested freight ships over roiling seas. No, this trip will be simple. I would try to make it as comfortable for Lily as I was able, and eagerly wait for the true journey to begin, the journey seeking truth, acceptance, and possibly forgiveness.

While my last trip to New Zealand was like my rebirth, this journey is more like my baptismal. I hope to be forgiven for my sins, to Victoria and her family and the hundreds of lives I directly or indirectly ruined in the first ten years after I transitioned, and from Lily for the lies and omissions I told her over the last several months of our courtship. Mostly I hope for acceptance. I long to be embraced by Lily, knowing she accepts and loves me, as the creature I am.

The trip for Lily and I was rather enjoyable. We had a chance to talk about an array of topics from music to art, politics and religion. We found we shared similar ideals in most key areas. We took turns reading passages from the various books on crystals, magic and witch craft that we obtained from Odd Ball Gifts. It was a time for easy, leisurely discussions, and frequent cuddling while Lily napped, or slept. As the last leg of our flight neared its completion, I could not help but feel slight trepidation at returning to this place that held such mixed emotions for me. I hoped I would be able to mask my feelings enough, until the right moment when I would finally share my truth with Lily.

When we finally arrived at the small inn where we would be staying, on Banks Peninsula in Little River, New Zealand, it was after 10:00am local time on Monday the 21st of December. We left a cold and snowy winter in New York and entered a lush green oasis. The weather was warm. I could see an almost instantaneous change occur to Lily's hair, skin and overall demeanor when we stepped out into the warm magnificence of our new surroundings. Lily absently put her hair in a knot and rolled up her sleeves. She had a grin from ear to ear as she looked out at the panoramic view of the lush New Zealand country side. As the sun kissed her cheeks her skin seemed radiant and flawless.

"You look incredibly happy" I said to her as I slipped my arm around her waist. "I can't believe I'm here. This is like a dream come true. So much of my life I have spent reading my great grandfathers journal, doing research, following leads, but to come here, halfway around the world, is just beyond exciting. Of all the places my great grandfather wrote of, this was, for me, the most mysterious and alluring place he'd ever been. I don't know why this one place intrigued me so much, possibly because the facts of what purportedly occurred here have been a mystery for so long, or because New Zealand always seemed like such a remote and magical distant land. It does feel magical, like anything could happen here. I think if a tree suddenly bent down a branch to hand me an apple, it would seem appropriate, in surroundings such as this. Looking at the pure primeval richness of the lands makes one almost believe in the likes of Fangorn Forest and the Ents of the Tolkein books."

I leaned in and kissed her neck and said "Looking at how incredibly delighted and radiant you are at this moment, seems pretty magical to me. We have a few hours until we meet with Victoria, how would you like to spend it? You don't seem tired." Lily beamed at me her beautiful, slightly crooked smile, "I am too excited to be tired, besides, like I told the others we should try to stay up late so we adjust to the time change. Try to fall into the local routine as quickly as possible. I told them to settle in to their rooms, set up their work stations and meet us for supper and a debriefing of our meeting with Victoria at 7:00pm. It is early enough if you want to try our luck at the local county clerk's office? We can look into the history of the Thomas family, and the family of the witness. We can do some historical review in their archives." "That sounds like a solid plan", I replied. With that we were on our way to one of the smallest clerk's office I have ever seen and I have seen a lot. They can come in handy when looking into potential places to live, finding areas where I can remain anonymous.

The county clerk's office was one room in a small building that housed the local sheriff's department and two holding cells along with offices for the department of public works, parks and recreation, and tourism. The young clerk who greeted us as we entered informed us that all records of public knowledge were housed in the basement archives. We were shown the way to the archive room and left to research the records at our leisure. The clerk informed us that the office closed at 4:00, and we were free to stay until then. He reminded us that these were public records. They were not to be removed or altered and to please carefully re-file any records we researched. We spent nearly two hours in that glorified storage closet.

We researched Victoria Thomas' family history, the ownership of her farm, how long her family lived there before they were killed, and any relatives she had. We found the records for Jed Carpenter. He was the then nine year old witness to the massacre. He has lived on the farm near the Thomas' place all his life. His farm and the Thomas' land have been in his family since the region was settled. Young John Thomas and his new bride Victoria first bought a small parcel of land from the Carpenter family, after they married. They slowly, over several years, bought connecting parcels. John and Victoria had three children, John junior, Michael, and little Victoria. When they died they owned over 20 acres and the small farm house. It seemed that after they died, the Carpenter's re-sold off all but the farm and about two acres of land. The elder Carpenter, put the land and money in trust for Victoria, and when she turned 18 she moved back home. She has stayed there her entire life. For awhile the farm was registered as a Bed and Breakfast, but several years ago it went back to resident status.

We left the stale, cramped archives room at a little before two. Coming out into the warm lushness of the late afternoon sun seemed to revive Lily. We went back to the inn and freshened up for our meeting with Victoria Thomas. At ten of three we arrived at the farm. I had thought about this moment for months. I was worried about the type of reaction seeing the farm again might trigger. But as we approached, all I could think was how quaint and charming it seemed. As we walked up the cobblestone path to the door, Lily said, "Well, here we are, the moment of truth has arrived at last." Her words resonated in my head, the moment of truth, the moment of truth. As Lily knocked to announce our presence she gave my hand an excited squeeze. I prayed that whatever lay behind that door would lead to my salvation.

The door was opened by an oversized man in his 50's, his frame so large it nearly took up the entire doorway. Lily introduced us. "Hello, my name is Lillian Bean and this is Maximillian VanderCreek. We are here to interview Ms. Thomas." The giant introduced himself as Jack Carpenter. He said he was the youngest son of Jed Carpenter whom we were scheduled to meet with tomorrow at noon. Before stepping aside to let us enter, Jack, after giving us both the once over said, "You two seem at least outwardly to be of a slightly different breed then most of the side show seekers that have come knocking in the past. But all the same, I want you to know that the woman in there practically raised my brothers and sisters and I, after my mum passed. We're family. She has seen more years than the two of you combined, I expect you will treat her with the dignity and respect she deserves." With that Jack the giant stepped aside and ushered us into the quaint farm house.

I had braced myself for a violent flash back or an overpowering sensation of pain and guilt as I re-entered the room where the demons of my past lay waiting for me. Instead, as I looked around, all I saw was a modest home, kept impeccably clean and tidy, yet still possessing a welcoming lived in feel. The rooms were bright, and the décor tastefully done. We passed the kitchen, and living room, with its huge stone fireplace. The fireplace was the first recognizable feature from my memories. As I looked at the fire place I started to remember the lay out of the interior nearly a century ago. My memories didn't come crashing back in a violent torrent, but slowly, in snap shots, the gore and destruction omitted. We entered the living room. Seated in a cozy arm chair, beside a low coffee table laden with tea and pastry, was a tiny old woman. Her clear, blue eyes sparkled and her long silver hair cascaded over her shoulders. As we approached, Jack the giant introduced us.

"Victoria, Ms. Lillian Bean and Mr. Maximillian VanderCreek are here to see you." Victoria stood and walked gracefully over to us. She turned toward Jack and replied "Thank you Jack. Why don't you head on over to see your father. We will be fine, and I will give you a call if I need anything." "Very well, Ms. Bean, Mr. VanderCreek, I guess I shall see you tomorrow when you will visit with my dad. Have a pleasant evening." Victoria said, "Jack is a good boy, he's like a son to me. He likes to be here when I meet with researchers such as you. He worries about me." Victoria reached out to shake Lily's hand and said, "Lily it is so nice to finally meet you. Your letters were so interesting, all the research you have done, I feel terrible I have little to add to what you already know, but I certainly enjoy meeting new and interesting people." Victoria turned to me, her piercing blue eyes, remarkably clear for a woman her age, looked as if she could peer into my soul. She extended her hand to shake mine. The moment my hand closed around Victoria's I felt a feeling similar to the one when Lily and I first touched. It was not quite the electric jolt I felt with Lily, more like a tingle. It left me with the feeling of being reunited with a lost piece of myself. The feeling was subtle, but as I stared back into Victoria's eyes, and watched them go wide and her pupils dilate, I knew she felt it too. She looked almost as if she were suddenly recognizing me, though I knew that was not possible.

Victoria spoke first. "How intriguing, Mr. VanderCreek, how did you come about getting involved in this research?" "Please, call me Max." "Very well, Max. What is it that brought you here?" I couldn't help but sense an underlying meaning to her question. "Well Madam" Victoria interrupted, "Please call me Victoria." "Well Victoria, you see it was quite by accident I should find myself here before you. I had decided to take a few courses at the University, and found Professor Bean's work extremely interesting. She had mentioned an opportunity for an independent research project and I signed up for it. It wasn't until just a few weeks ago that I found out we would be visiting this town and you specifically." "I would not call that an accident Max, I call it fate."

Victoria led us to the seating area and offered us tea and pastries. She sat with her tea in her lap and looked between Lily and me and smiled. "I get a strong feeling there is more to your relationship then teacher and student." Lily looked momentarily uncomfortable. Victoria quickly added as she looked to Lily "Please, don't think me too forward when I say that, I am not passing judgment. It is just that the two of you seem to radiate this connectedness. I hope you don't mind, but I like to get to know a bit about the people who come to see me. I feel I know so much about you Lily from your letters, but you Max, are a mystery. You see, as I'm sure you could imagine, people interested in my story range from the morbidly curious to the down right nutty. Of course there are some who are genuinely interested in researching the facts but I like to get a feel for the people I choose to share my life with."

Victoria looked toward me, and with a most serious expression asked, "Do you intend to share your life with this woman?" The question took Lily by surprise. She could scarcely hide a shocked look in response to such a personal question from a virtual stranger. But I just looked Victoria directly in her piercing blue eyes and replied, "Yes. I want to share my life with Lily. My greatest desire is that she loves me for the man I am, for the rest of her life." Victoria responded, "Very well then, we are going to need something a little stronger then tea for this discussion."

CHAPTER 31

My Truth Revealed

Lily turned to me with a questioning look. I sensed the confusion she was feeling. I could almost hear her saying, "What the hell?" as she looked from me to Victoria, who was returning from the kitchen with three glasses and a bottle of Brandy. Victoria poured the amber liquid into two glasses and handed one to Lily. Lily said "What about Max?" Victoria replied, "Oh, he is welcome to it, but I don't suppose he needs it as much as you and I will." She toasted Lily's glass and drank till hers was empty.

"I apologize Lily, your look of utter confusion, and possibly concern for my sanity, is written all over your face. You see I have had many people over the years, come to see me. Many had been seeking the sort of side show Jack mentioned when you arrived. I usually entertain them for a short visit and try and impart a little bit of New Zealand charm on them as my guests. They come and go and never learn much, as I have never told to anyone the truth I shall tell you tonight."

Victoria refilled her glass and took a sip before continuing. "On August 14, 1923, my father, mother and two brothers were slaughtered. My father was found in the field along with several dozen sheep in our flock. My mother and brothers were found dead in bed. I was found abandoned, wrapped in blood soaked bed sheets completely unharmed, on the front porch of the Carpenter's farm. Everything I just told you is of public record. Also of public record is the fact that Jed's mother and father Mr. and Mrs. Albert Carpenter took me in and raised me as their own. That is the only real information any researcher has ever been told, until today."

Lily stared at Victoria, waiting for her to go on. "Jed became my big brother. He had a special way with animals and nature and taught me all about sheep and farm work. He watched over me. As close as we were though, there always seemed to be a pain in his eyes when he looked at me. As I got older I thought he pitied me. That made me angry and one day I told him I didn't need to be pitied, and stormed off from him. When I got back home he was waiting on the porch. I sat next to him and he confessed to me, what no one else ever would, he told me the true story of how my family died and how he had witnessed the attack of the sheep. I pressured him to give me the details, not of the murder, but of what he saw kill our sheep. It was the description of the killer's eyes that made me certain there was more to my recurring dream then I had thought." Victoria paused in her story; her gaze was penetrating as she searched my eyes.

"Jed mentioned that in the moonlight he could see a man-like creature. His eyes wide, like a mad man, their color struck him as something almost unnatural. I was young. Jed was trying to protect me, but what he didn't know and I have never told him, or anyone else, is the story of the dream I have had all throughout my life. You will talk to Jed tomorrow. He will tell you what he saw, the recollections of a scared nine year old, clouded by nearly a century of time past. I cannot tell you what happened that day. I was just an infant, barely nine months old. But I can tell you of my dream. It only made sense to me after Jed reveled to me what he had seen, and then it took some years for me to truly accept what subconsciously I had known all along."

Lily took a long pull of her drink and poured Victoria another shot. Victoria sipped her drink slowly, seeming to gather the courage to reveal a secret she has hidden from everyone for her entire life. She continued, "As I mentioned, since I could remember I have had a recurring dream which began long before Jed or anyone ever mentioned the true details of my families' deaths. In my dream I first see an infant cradled in the arms of a raven haired man. Then I am the infant, and see things from the vantage point of being cradled in the man's arms. The man of my dream has the most remarkable color eyes, not quite blue, or even grey, but a color closer to the bluish purple of a lilac or lavender." This time as Victoria spoke, her eyes never left Lily's and Lily seemed to hang on ever word.

"The magnificence of those eyes, still shone brightly, as tears of anguish fell from them, sprinkling my cheeks and lips. I would often wake after having the dream, with the salty taste of his tears lingering on my tongue. In this dream I reach out with one chubby finger and stroke his cheek. The man looks at me then, almost as if he has awakened from a trance. My finger slides from his cheek to his mouth, where I feel the smoothness of one of his elongated canine like fangs. I am staring into the face of a vampire."

Lily spoke, "Oh how terrible for you to have to carry the burden of such troubling dreams all these years alone." Victoria's responded, "On the contrary Lily, I have felt from the first time I remember having the dream, a deep sense of sorrow, almost pity for the raven haired man. The look in his eyes was as if he had been tortured to the point of losing himself, losing his humanity. But when my finger touches his cheek and he looks at me with those eyes, something changes. The cloud of grief and confusion lifts, almost as if they were a veil. The clarity with which he looked down on me seemed to be filled with wonder and hope.

After Jed told me the truth of what he saw I realized the raven haired man was my family's killer. Jed's description of a wild eyed mad man seemed so incongruous to the look of hope and humanity in the strangely beautiful eyes that peered down at me in my dream. I knew somehow they were the same person, but at the same time I knew they were not the same. The man Jed witnessed killing our sheep was a mad man, driven by a powerful force beyond his control to commit such lethal attacks on an innocent, decent family. I have thought for decades about this dream and what it tells me. I cannot be sure why, but I believe something happened as the vampire killed my family because the man in my dream, while physically the same being who presumably just wreaked such violent destruction, was not the same man.

Jed will describe the thing he saw as a vicious wild animal in the body of a human. His form was human but no trace of humanity was evident. I on the contrary, saw a man in my dream so achingly human, consumed by grief and remorse, lost from himself, from the world. Only a man deeply connected to his humanity could feel such emotion. It was as if he was brought back from the brink of a soulless existence, by what I only guess at, but he seemed to search my eyes with a look of repentance."

I broke the silence that was so complete it was as if the world around us stood still, holding its collective breath. "It was the purity, the goodness, the transcendent nature of you and your family that saved him." It was almost as if the two women had forgotten I was present. When they looked at me, as I spoke, it was as if I had broken some thread that connected them. "When the blood of your pure, virtuous family filled his veins, it was as if he were reborn . . . as if I was reborn."

Victoria looked at me with tears streaming down her cheeks, the same look of compassion in her eyes. Lily sat, struck momentarily mute, as she tried to process what I just said. To Victoria I said, "I have spent nearly a century trying to atone for the sins of my past. The day I cradled you in my arms, when you touched my cheek, my fangs, you looked at me with such a soulful smile, I did repent, I vowed to never let myself become the soulless monster that gripped me for nearly 10 years. That day I regained the humanity that had been lost when I transitioned into a vampire. I cannot undo the destruction that I caused, not just to my victims, but to the loved ones left to deal with the aftermath. I can only tell you that because of you, and the sacrifice of your family, I was saved from an eternity of depraved merciless indifference to life. I was saved as were the countless number of innocents from a brutal and vicious death. I'm sorry Victoria, for how I irrevocably changed the course of your life. I didn't choose the life I have; it is the existence which I was given. I don't expect your forgiveness, but I ask for it. I have tried every day since I placed you on that porch, hiding in the trees, watching until you were safely brought inside, to take a morally correct path. I have given every effort to aid others in need, trying to repay my tremendous debt to humanity."

Lily looked from me to Victoria and back again, shaking her head in disbelief. I said to her "Lily it is true. I am the creature who came here nearly a century ago, and destroyed a family, but I am, as Victoria said, not that creature. I am the same person who loves you and who you love, the same person who days ago you told, "together we can handle anything that comes our way". Lily . . ." as I reached out to touch her arm, the woman I love with all my being pulled away, recoiled, like one would from a cobra. "I'm sorry Victoria, I have to go . . . I . . . I . . . Please forgive me." And with a pained look in my direction, Lily hastily left the farm house.

I sat there momentarily too overwhelmed by an array of powerful emotions, mine and Lily's combined by the power of the Evening Star. I knew Lily needed to process what she had just learned. A lifetime of studying what was thought to be just myth has come to be the truth. Not only is she coping with the realization that vampires exist, but knowing now that the man she loved, gave her heart to, is actually a vampire and has kept a secret such as this for so long. I was anguished, knowing I caused her this depth of pain and confusion. I wanted to run after her, to tell her I was still the person she loved.

EVILUTION

If she would only listen to her heart and the Evening Star, sense her connection to me, feel how much I love her, she would know I am not the monster that killed Victoria's family.

As if sensing my thoughts Victoria spoke, "You are not a monster Max. She will see that, give her time. Unlike me, she has not had years to accept the reality of your existence. While she may have hoped as a scientist that it be true, the reality for her is now all too real, too personal. Your connection to Lily is strong she will come back around. Now, this has been an emotional day for me as well. I am not as young or fit as the two of you, and I feel I must retire to my room for a rest. I would like to meet with you again Max. I have so many questions I would like to ask. If you wouldn't mind, I ask you not to personally visit with Jed. He is older than I, and frail of body. His mind is sharp as a tack, but the shock of seeing you might be more than his heart could take. To him you are a monster. Your face is the subject of nightmares and guilty torment that he did nothing to stop what he saw happening. Perhaps you could come by tomorrow, alone. We have so much to discuss. I am glad fate has brought you here Max. I want you to know I forgive you, for I know it was not of your choice to do as you did."

I found it difficult to express my gratitude for the unbelievable kindness she showed by giving me her forgiveness. My only response, "Victoria, I am forever in your debt." "Well now Max, we will talk again tomorrow. I must ask that you go now so that I may rest."

I left the farm house. I walked out into the radiance of a stunning sunset, I felt buoyed, lighter then I have for nearly a century. Victoria's act of compassion, her forgiveness, relieved me of a burden I had carried with me every day for so long. I knew if Lily would find it in her heart to accept me, to forgive me for the lies and deception, it would be possible to have the life I dreamed with her. If not, if she could not accept me, then I would go. Off to some remote land to spend my existence alone, with just the memories of the blissful time

I shared with her to sustain me. I walked slowly back to the inn and went up to our room. I found a note from Lily that read,

Max,

> *I do not have the words to express how I feel right now, perhaps a little like Alice after she fell through the rabbit hole. The events of this afternoon have left my world turned upside down. Please give me some time alone. I will tell the others you are away researching something for me. I don't think it wise for you come to interview Jed. Give me a few days to sort things through and then we will talk.*

Lily

I grabbed a few items from my suitcase tossed them in my back pack, and left the inn. I left no note, for what could I say in a note? I left hoping that Lily would call me back to her accepting embrace. I realized, I may never hold her in my arms again, never again feel the warmth of her body pressed against mine, never again hear the words, I love you uttered from her beautiful lips. My buoyed state deflated, I sunk into an abyss of loneliness and loss. I said I would suffer an eternity of loss and it would be worth it for the chance to love Lily. I still believe that to be true, but I had hoped for an opportunity to love her for much longer. And when I thought of losing her, it was in death, not rejection.

I walked away from the inn and headed out to find a place where I could go and be alone. I needed to meditate, like I had done in the bear den. Lily felt my emotions then, even if she didn't realize it. Perhaps I could focus on the thread that connects us, send out my love to Lily. Perhaps she will finally feel the connection we share through the Evening Star. If she listens to it, I hope it leads her back to me. For now, I will go away. Tomorrow, while Lily meets with Jed, I will have another visit with Victoria.

CHAPTER 32

A World Upside Down

I spent the night contemplating the simple letter Lily had written. I could understand her feeling as if her world were turned upside down. In minutes she went from contemplating the existence of vampires, with all her theories and ideas of what a vampire might be like, to being faced with the reality that not only do they exist, but she was currently in love with one. I imagine she feels betrayed by me for keeping the truth from her for so long, but it was now a question if she feared me. I can still feel the emotional sting of when she recoiled from my touch earlier. I didn't sense fear in her now, but there was confusion and unease, anger, sadness and a lingering distrust. It remains to be seen how she will respond after hearing what Jed has to say, I only hope he saw very little and forgot a great deal.

I walked the lush hill side, looking for a secluded place to pass the evening. I suppose I could have gotten a room at another location, but being out in the elements is more aligned with my nature. Besides, when I am outside I feel much more in tune with myself. That is what I was trying to do as I sat under a Miro tree, a local type of evergreen, and slowly worked to clear my thoughts. Now that my secret is out, I have nothing to hide from Lily. I can open myself completely to her, let her feel me, the true me, for who, and what I am. It is actually quite liberating, freed from maintaining a false identity, not the very least having to pretend to eat food. I was finally free to let myself commit fully to loving her without the guilt of always having to lie, about something. I let the feeling of relief wash over me. I was determined to keep my emotions focused on the positive, focused on the love and concern I have for Lily. I wanted her to find the thread as I have. I believe if she does, she will see we are meant to be together. I know this in my soul, we are meant to be together, I kept repeating the line in my mind, we are meant to be together . . .

I sat nearly motionless for hours sending out a beacon of love to Lily, desperate for her to find the thread of our connection. Shortly before dawn I moved for the first time. I wanted to let Lily feel the real me. Well, the real me, can experience some very thrilling things. I always feel so amazing when I let myself go, unleash the man not bound by physical limitations, and explore the world around me as only a vampire can. It is still exhilarating climbing hundreds of feet up an ancient redwood to view the world from that vantage point or to run with a heard of deer or to find some new way to enjoy the wonders of the natural world using whatever special abilities I may have by virtue of being a vampire. Every day is an opportunity for adventure. The only thing I need to make it the adventure of a lifetime is to spend it with Lily for her lifetime.

I can't be sure of what she may or may not have felt as I projected my positive energy toward her. I decided to walk into town to the local coffee shop. I would freshen up in their washroom before going to see Victoria. I may even sit and pretend to drink coffee and read the local paper. Reading the local paper and listening in on the local chatter can be very insightful, when one is trying to learn about an area. It seemed that the "presence of researchers" visiting the Carpenter and Thomas homes did not go unnoticed. Many a raised eyebrow and whispered voice referred to me or Lily. I caught several furtive glances cast my way as the locals gossiped about our visit. From my eavesdropping I learned that while not public record, it seemed that the locals if not outright believers in the story of a vampire attack, were at least open to discussing it as an alternate theory to the public record of animal attack.

After turning down a refill twice, I left the waitress a five dollar tip on a one dollar check, and went to meet with Victoria. We never set on a time to meet, but it was after 10:00 and I was anxious to do something. Waiting around was getting me nowhere, I was just getting restless. Besides, I didn't want to run into Lily going in or out of Jed's house. I wanted to give her the space she requested. I also wanted to avoid being seen by Jed or his giant son. I didn't want to take the chance of anyone connecting the dots, so to speak.

When I walked up to Victoria's house she was sitting on the porch. In a million years I would never have expected to find her out on the rocker smoking a joint. But there she was toking away, like she had done it often. My sly smile as I approached caused Victoria to acknowledge with a nod toward the joint in her hand as she exhaled a cloud of fragrant smoke. "It's medicinal" she declared as she took another toke. It was then that I noticed how thin her frame truly was. If I looked closely I could imagine how much healthier she would look with a few pounds on her. On further observation I noticed a sallow tone to her skin. She was not well. Today Victoria looked more tired and frail than the vibrant historian she appeared to be yesterday. I imagine the experience was quite draining for her, finally knowing the truth of her past.

"Good morning Victoria." I said as I came up the steps. "Good morning Max" she answered as she tapped out the joint, half smoked. I wanted to ask her, medicinal for what, but instead I waited for her to start the conversation. I felt certain if she wanted to tell me, she would, in her own time. "Has Lily talked to you yet?" she inquired gently. "She left a note. She wanted to be alone for a while to sort things out" I told her. As Victoria waved me over to a seat next to her she said, "I see, she will come around, give her some time." I answered sincerely, "I am a little concerned about what she will think after she speaks to Jed. I don't know what or how much he saw, but I am sure it wasn't good. I am worried she will fear me. I would rather suffer the very fires of hell then harm Lily, I hope she recognizes that."

Victoria and I talked for a while out on the porch, but as noon approached, she invited me in for tea. Knowing I had no need to drink it, the invitation was merely a way to get me inside so as not to see Lily or Jed. I had spent the morning answering a myriad of questions about life as a vampire. Victoria seemed to have an endless number of questions. Shortly after noon I was overcome by a powerful feeling of revulsion and fear. I could sense the sickening feeling of bile coming up Lily's esophagus, of the physical nausea she was experiencing. I had to collect myself for a moment, the raw emotions so visceral, I felt as if I might actually vomit. Lily was afraid. How could I salvage what was us, if she feared me?

Victoria saw my reaction and asked "Is everything alright?" I replied "No, it's Lily. What ever Jed has told her, has left her repulsed and fearful, I can feel it. I can never have a life with her if she is afraid of me. I don't know how I could possibly change her opinion of me. We have been so close these past few months, if she hasn't seen in that time that I would never hurt her, I don't know what else would change her mind."

Victoria thought about what I just said and after a few moments replied, "I had hoped Max that my being able to forgive and accept you, would be enough for Lily to accept you. I meant it when I said you both seem very connected. I felt and still do that the strength of your bond will overcome this. It is also why I asked such a personal question as to your intentions to share your life with her. If you would have answered me differently, Lily would have returned to New York, without the truth, and I suspect I would have been killed." "What do you mean?" My shock at her cavalier remarks of me killing her, were evident in my tone. "Well, I just thought that if you would tell her the truth, then you must want to try and live on the path of goodness and light, if you chose to hide the truth from her then you must not want her to know the true you. That would be deception and lead down the path of evil and darkness, which for a vampire, usually involves feeding from and killing someone. Since I obviously knew immediately who and what you are, and I knew you were aware of that fact, then I figured you wouldn't let me live."

"How can you talk like that, so casually?" I asked in amazement. "You know the answer to that question. You figured it out on the porch, am I right?" I responded somberly, "I surmised you are not well. Having only just met you it is hard to know how sick, but I imagine now you are terminal. That is why you were not worried about the outcome, you are already dying. Am I right?"

"I have an inoperable brain tumor. It is growing rapidly. I get blinding headaches, severe nausea and my vision is becoming diminished. I have been given six months at best. However, the pain will worsen, and I will go blind and as the pressure builds and more areas of brain are compromised, I will deteriorate rapidly and soon die. Oh, please don't look at me like that, I never could stand pity." "It is not with pity that I look at you Victoria. It is more like wonder. Why have you forgiven me? How can you sit talking to me, as if we were two old friends having tea, when you know what I did to your family?"

I couldn't fathom how Lily, who has felt the depths of my love, could fear me while Victoria, who had every reason to fear and loathe me, could accept me and forgive me. I added, "Victoria, when I first found out about the specifics of this trip, I was afraid of facing the demons of my past. I had never dreamed of seeing you again, let alone being forgiven by you and accepted. But once I found out it was you that Lily was coming to interview, I felt as if I had to follow the path laid before me, whatever the consequences. I never dreamed I would fall in love with a mortal woman or ever have a chance to feel the love of another. When that happened it was under the guise of being human. I wanted our love to be pure. I knew I had to reveal the truth. I felt that somehow you were the answer to my salvation and to Lily being able to accept me. I thought Lily of all people, who likes to be open to the possibilities of the fantastical, who has researched vampires since she was a child, who believed they were misunderstood, I thought she would understand me."

"Have you told her that?" Victoria asked. "Go to her. Tell her what you told me. She will see you, as I do. A vampire yes, but not the soulless creature detached from all humanity that destroyed my family, the real you, intelligent, thoughtful and deeply connected to your humanity. It is as if, you have undergone an evolutionary change. Becoming a more efficient organism than humans, with a deeper connection to nature and the world you live in, combined with the humanity and goodness of your previous human self. I have no doubt Max that you are on the path of goodness and light. Go find Lily, talk to her. Tell her what you have told me. What ever happens, I would like to see you both at least one more time before you leave. Good luck Max. If you're honest and open, she will see it. She will feel it and know it is right for you two to be together."

I thanked Victoria again for all the kindness she has shown me and as I walked to the door she said "Max, if you could leave out the part of my dying, I would appreciate it." "Of course Victoria, I will see you again soon." I stepped outside into the waning daylight and started to walk back to the inn to find Lily. I hoped Victoria was right. If Lily would just let me explain everything, she would see the overwhelming love I have for her. I hoped it would be enough.

CHAPTER 33

Acceptance at Last

I walked back to the inn and saw Ginny, Bill and Drew all having lunch in the small reception area. They had their laptops out and between breaks to eat, they were working. I wonder what Lily has told them, certainly not the truth, not all of it. Ginny nodded a greeting, Bill and Drew waved and smiled cheerily. I acknowledged them with a nod and walked somberly up to the room Lily and I had got to share, but have yet to be in together. I opened the door and saw Lily crying softly on the bed. From the doorway I asked, "Lily, can I come in? We need to talk." Lily lifted her tear stained face to look at me. Some say the eyes are the window to the soul. Looking at Lily now, her soul seems tortured. Gone was the look of joy and happiness that usually greeted me. Instead, pain, confusion and a new wariness met my gaze.

After a moment Lily spoke, "It's true then." Without moving closer I answered, "If by true you mean vampires exist and that I am a vampire, then yes. But Lily the most important truth is the fact that I am the same person you fell in love with. I am not the monster Jed told you about. I haven't been that person since I held Victoria in my arms nearly a century ago." "Some researcher I am. After all this time, how could I not know?" "Lily, I have worked very hard to keep

211

it from you. But you saw it. Think back and put the pieces in place. To be frank, I was worried you would figure it out before I got a chance to explain. Even without the Evening Star you would have figured it out soon." Not seeming placated Lily asked, "How old are you?" As I looked back into her unwavering, penetrating gaze I said, "My body stopped aging when I transitioned at twenty six. I was born April 6th 1887. I have existed on this earth for 122 years."

It was my turn to ask the next question, the answer on which hinged my future. "Lily, are you afraid of me?" I held my breath for long minutes awaiting her response. Slowly she answered, "I haven't slept for nearly two days as I have contemplated that very question. My rational mind tells me I should be; especially after the very detailed recounting of the Thomas family slaying which Jed shared with me. To be truthful, my emotions are all over the place, but I am not afraid of you." I wanted to sweep her into my arms and never let her go. Instead I slowly closed the distance between us and sat near her on the bed. We sat in silence for several minutes, Lily looking at me as if seeing me for the first time. I could feel her emotional turmoil as her conscious mind wrestled with her new found knowledge. After what seemed like an eternity, Lily put her arms around me and said, "Max, tell me everything is going to be ok. Tell me we can get through this."

The moment of that embrace will be etched into my mind for eternity. For in that moment, as Lily's arms wrapped around me, her head resting on my chest, I felt the one thing in my existence I longed for the most, love and acceptance for who and what I am. I wept with joy, so overcome with emotion. I tried to give Lily the assurance she needed. Whispering in her ear as I held her close, "Everything is going to be ok. We are going to be ok. I love you." We sat like that for some time, neither of us able nor wanting to release the embrace. After several minutes I turned Lily's tear stained face to mine and said, "I'm sorry. Sorry for keeping secrets from you. I never meant to hurt you. All the lies and omissions, I told myself it was for your benefit. From the moment I laid eyes on you and even before, it seems, I have been drawn to you. As we became friends, I felt that in time I might be able to share my truth with you. I was afraid to lose you, but once I fell in love with you, I knew I had to tell you the entire story if we were to ever have a chance at a life together. When you told me of this trip and Victoria, I felt certain the connections had to be more than coincidence. I felt fate, or some other force, was bringing us together. I hoped, when you did hear the truth, you would find a way to accept me."

As Lily wiped away the wetness from her cheeks she replied, "I'm sorry for pulling away from you, I know it was hurtful. I was so overcome by the truth and all that it means, I temporarily lost sight of the depth of my feelings for you, and how you feel for me." "Lily I thought I lost you. After you left Jed's I felt your revulsion, it made you physically sick" She looked deep into my eyes and said, "To be honest, I did feel revolted from Jed's description. His memories were so vivid and detailed. He has felt guilt all these years. He thinks somehow he could have stopped you from killing the family. He was only nine Max, and he's carried that burden ever since."

I answered honestly, "There is nothing he could have done except die with the rest of my victims. As it is he is still a victim. I stole his innocence, and I obviously stole his peace. Your reaction to his recollection was palpable, strong enough to cause you to be sick." "Max, I wasn't feeling well before I had gone to see Jed. His story didn't make me sick. I think I ate something that didn't agree with me, although I'm sure the story didn't help. Before you came in, I had been sitting here trying to understand my new reality, struggling to sort out my emotions, when I was suddenly engulfed in yours. Max, I found the thread. When I did, I felt the flood of your love mixed with the pain of my rejecting you. I felt the power of your remarkable form, so wondrous. It was as if your soul was reaching out for my understanding and acceptance. I could feel your desperate yearning for my love. I love you Max, you, the extraordinary being that you are; a vampire."

We embraced again, I savored the moment. I felt as if we could almost fuse into one, so perfect was our fit. I tentatively kissed her; still unable to fully believe her fear of me was abated. Her response was clear. Lily pulled me down onto the bed. We lay together kissing and talking. I laid bare the story of my existence. Later that night our passion was rekindled. The experience was transcendent, the strength of our bond so powerful, the thread, more like a rope binding our souls. The truth I so feared to share did set me free, free to truly love and be loved by this remarkable woman.

We stayed up into the early morning hours; we had so much to say to each other. Lily had many questions; her thirst for scientific knowledge is one of her traits I admire so much. We talked until sleep finally over took her. As Lily slept wrapped in my embrace I sat pondering the magnitude of my good fortune. The woman I have pledged my heart to, loves me for me; and the woman who has the most reason to despise me, has forgiven me. And then I slept.

I awoke the next morning, to find Lily still curled up in my arms, sleeping peacefully. I gently kissed her temple, her cheek, her neck and her shoulder. When Lily stirred awake I said, "Good morning my love, would you like some breakfast? I can be back in five minutes with pancakes and syrup. I think I even detect the smell of bacon and coffee." "Mmm", Lily replied as she leaned in to kiss me. "That sounds delicious, but I think I need to cut back on the carbs, my pants have gotten a little snug." "I think you look perfect. I also know an excellent way to burn off a few calories." I jokingly replied as I kissed her passionately. We made love again, after which, we showered together, tenderly bathing each other. Again I reflected on my incredible fortune to find such a remarkable woman. We decided to spend the next few days together in the forests of New Zealand. I wanted to show Lily the world as I explore it, give her a taste of my abilities.

Lily devised a plan to keep Ginny, Bill and Drew busy. The four met for breakfast. For the first time in our relationship, I didn't have to pretend to eat. Lily told me to meet her out front in an hour. At breakfast, Ginny was acting strange. When Lily asked her what was wrong she said in short clipped sentences, "I'm fine. I just finished transcribing your notes from your interview with Jed Carpenter. The recollection was a little tough to take and something in the retelling gives me a sense of deja-vu. I can't put my finger on it, but I am left with a feeling like I am missing something, something important."

Lily tried to recall what could be in her notes that got Ginny's interest piqued. She seemed sure her notes were vague enough, but before she could come up with anything, Ginny got up to leave. Lily quickly told the three that she and I would be extending our trip. She said that she felt we had exhausted all the research opportunities here and decided to visit some other towns and churches to see if we could find any more information. Lily gave out the final assignment for the three of them. She told them to e-mail their work to her when it was complete. When they were finished they were free to enjoy New Zealand as they wished. They agreed to all meet up out front on the morning of their departure where we would escort them to the airport. After thanking them for their efforts and ensuring them they were all on track to receive A's if they completed the last assignment, she wished them a happy holiday. According to Lily, Bill and Drew seemed happy at the prospect of an easy A and extra leisure time in New Zealand, Ginny on the other hand seemed less then enthusiastic.

After the breakfast meeting adjourned we set out on our trek, unhurried and relaxed. Now that Lily has learned the truth, we have no more need to interview anyone or do further research. We decide to spend the time leisurely. I was letting Lily into my world, and we were enjoying being together in the beautiful and pristine landscape of the New Zealand countryside.

At the end of the third day spent exploring the wonders of our surroundings, and Lily learning the scope of my vampire abilities, I had one more secret I wanted to share with her. Deep in the ancient woods we discovered a magnificent waterfall. Amidst the sound of the crashing water, and the earthy aromas of the surrounding landscape, I got down on my knee and asked Lily to marry me. I took out the ring Charles and Lilly had given me and as the words "yes" lovingly left her lips, I placed the ring on her finger. Lily's smile was radiant, she seemed to glow from within, and then I saw, it was the Evening Star. It sparkled with an inner brilliance, more profound than it had been previously. The power of our love is what brought the Evening Star to us, and as our love has grown stronger it is reflected in the brilliance of the Evening Star's light.

CHAPTER 34

A Nobel Act and a Parting Gift

It is December 28th and today we will escort Ginny, Bill and Andrew to the airport. The last several days have been incredible; Lily like a giddy school girl, as she marvels at each newly learned fact of my abilities and riding the emotional high our engagement has caused. Lily and I are going to extend our stay in New Zealand for another week. She doesn't have to be back to work until January 13th and classes don't start until the 18th. We will leave here tomorrow to explore some more of New Zealand's beautiful sights. We have decided to visit Victoria this evening, to share with her the news of our happiness. I know she wanted to see us both again before we left.

We spent last night in our room at the inn. After cleaning up we went down to the front to meet our group and take them to the airport. When we arrived, we found Bill and Drew ready to go out front. A van was waiting and their bags were already stowed in the back. We approached the two and after some small talk about how they spent their last few days Lily asked, "Where is Ginny? We have to get moving if you are going to catch your flight."

Lily and I agreed that we would not share my secret with the others or the world just yet. In fact it was Lily's suggestion. One evening in

217

the woods Lily confessed, "Max, when I did all that research it was for me, not for the world. I wanted to satisfy my own curiosity. Now that I know the truth, I selfishly want to keep it hidden for now. I can only imagine the media circus that would erupt if the truth became public knowledge. The truth, if you do want to share it with the world, would need to be presented the right way to avoid widespread panic. Sadly, not everyone would welcome a vampire with open arms." I knew she was right. And I was relieved actually. I wanted to share the truth with Lily because I loved her, and knew I needed to be honest with her if we were ever to share a life. But I was not looking to be the poster child for Vampirism.

After five more minutes Lily decided to go up to Ginny's room to get her moving. In the hallway, in front of Ginny's door, was the chamber maid cart. The door to Ginny's room was open and a young girl was making up the bed. Lily knocked at the door to ask the girl if she saw Ginny leave. The chamber maid said the room was empty when she arrived but said there was a note left on the dresser. The girl handed Lily the note that was addressed to her.

Dear Professor Bean,

I have decided to extend my trip for a few days. There are some questions I have that I want to look into. I e-mailed my paper to you, and I called my folks to let them know of my plans. I hope to see you next semester. Be careful professor.

Ginny

After Lily read the note she was left with an uneasy feeling. What did Ginny mean she had questions of her own, and why the, "Be careful" warning? Had she figured out some of the truth? Lily returned to the van, as she approached I could tell something was wrong. She told everyone to get in the van. Once inside she told us that Ginny left a note saying she was extending her stay and we were leaving without her. From her demeanor I could tell there was more to it than that. I would have to wait until Bill and Drew were gone to talk about it with her. After dropping off Bill and Drew the van driver brought us back to the inn. We decided to walk the mile to Victoria's house. It would give us time to sort out Ginny's note.

As we walked we traded thoughts of what the note might mean. "Max, she knows something, the questions and the warning to be careful, what could she know and how? "Lily lets not jump to conclusions. While I agree it seems Ginny knows something, we really can't know the extent of it until we talk to her. I think we wait and see what happens. If it is something big I'm sure she will contact you about it. Now let's forget about it for a while. Remember we are on our way to share the news of our happiness with Victoria, so be happy."

Lily smiled and chuckled, resigned to forget about Ginny for awhile. We walked hand in hand enjoying the spectacular countryside, when Lily stumbled. I easily caught her and swept her up in my arms. I expected Lily to comment on her "glass ankle" as the reason for her stumble, but when I looked at her, I knew something was wrong, and then I felt it, pain; incredible searing pain.

"Aghh! Max, something's wrong. It hurts, oh God, please make it stop!" Lily was overcome with pain, and she was writhing in my arms. Her screams became incoherent sobs, before eventually dying off as she mercifully passed out. We were near Victoria's farm house and I quickly brought her there, not caring of the risk of being seen traveling at vamp speed. Something was wrong with Lily. Just as I approached the porch to Victoria's I felt the hair on the back of my neck stand up and was suddenly hit, like a punch to the gut, by a menacingly familiar scent. It was the same one I had smelled back in the woods with Pumpkin on our camping trip and by the cave with

Lily. And suddenly, standing between me and Victoria's house stood the creature responsible.

In an instant I was fully transformed into the feral animal I can become, my thoughts consumed with protecting Lily. The only other creature a vampire fears is another vampire. I would be torn limb from limb before I would let this one near her. I bared my fangs and just as I was about to try to shuttle Lily to safety, he spoke.

"Please don't run Maximillian. I would never dream of harming my great granddaughter, or her betrothed. Besides we need to get her inside, and we are going to need something to feed her." "Who are you?!" I growled. My rage just barely contained. "Take it easy young man; if I meant to hurt either of you I would have months ago. My name is Augustine Angelone. I am Lily's great grandfather." "But you are a vampire!" I hissed, and then my rage waned as realization settled in.

"Why have you been tracking me?" "Yes Max, I am a vampire. I have not been tracking you, at least not in the beginning. I have been tracking Lily. I only started tracking you after I saw you in the woods with the deer." Just then Lily groaned. "Listen Max, I can explain all that later. Right now we need to get Lily inside and get her some thing to feed from. Because you see, young man, your bride to be, is transitioning."

As he said the word it was like a veil had been lifted, suddenly all the signs were clear. The ravenous hunger as the body fuels up for the transition, strengthening the body in preparation for the arduous and painful process. Lily's ankle miraculously healing after possibly being broken from the slip in the shower was a result of the coordinating efforts of the cells as they prepare for transition. The nausea and vomiting as the body is starting to reject that type of food as sustenance. That is why we were so drawn to each other, and why Charles said our souls would be together for eternity, not because he thought I was human, but because he or more likely Lilly knew she would become a vampire.

I quickly made my way up the steps and knocked at Victoria's door. When she saw Lily in my arms she ushered us inside without hesitation. After hastily introducing Augustine, he explained what was happening. I will have to obtain a substantial amount of blood for Lily to feed from after the transition is complete. I turn to Victoria and ask, "Do you know where the nearest hospitals are? I need to get Lily some blood." Victoria gave me the location of two of the closest hospitals and Augustine agreed to go in search of the blood.

Victoria turned toward Augustine, "I remember you. Years ago, when I was a young girl you came, researching vampires. You wanted to know my story." "Augustine's dark eyes locked with Victoria's. "Yes Ms. Thomas, that was before I turned. It seems you were not entirely truthful about your recollections with me." Victoria stood bravely staring back at Augustine. Ignoring his remark she said, "Would you give me your word Mr. Angelone, that you will not harm anyone for their blood?" Victoria sensed immediately that Augustine was different than I. I understood her concern for the community and her friends.

Augustine smiled at Victoria; it was not a pleasant grin. With fangs protruding menacingly, a malicious smile on his lips, Augustine replied, "Ms. Thomas, if I wanted to expose myself and my family, I would take great pleasure in ripping out the throats of every living being in this dismal little town. But as luck for you and your town folk would have it I am trying to keep a low profile. I haven't killed a human in six months. I have snacked, just a taste, never enough to kill. You are all so easy to manipulate, practically walking vampire vending machines." To me he said, "I will be back shortly, keep Lily calm and away from her, if you want her to stay safe."

Moving as fast as secrecy allowed, Augustine made his way to the first and closest hospital. They had no blood bank and due to a string of surgeries were out of any stores. Signs posted all around the entrance pleaded for donors to replenish the supply. He traveled next to the second and last opportunity to find what we needed. As misfortune would have it, a bar brawl gone bad, would leave two men bleeding to death in the emergency room. Every spare pint was being used to try to save the lives of the two injured men. The smell of all that spilled blood made it difficult for Augustine to maintain his control, he raced back to Victoria's.

While Augustine was gone, I stayed by Lily's side. I felt helpless, unable to relieve her pain, forced to listen to the agonized screams as the transition process painfully progressed. When Augustine returned he entered the home, a dead sheep hanging limp at his side, blood coloring a spot at its throat. "There was no blood to be had, without killing someone. Is there somewhere else I could go?" Looking at Augustine with the dead sheep, Victoria had suggested she had a dozen more sheep grazing up at Jed's. I explained that a newly transitioned vampire requires human blood, without it they will go mad as they slowly lose their humanity.

Augustine spoke "I will go out again and bring back a donor." Victoria stopped him. "You will not harm a soul here Sir, do you understand?" To me she asked "Max, would my condition prevent me from being a donor?" Augustine threw the sheep on the floor and looked from me to Victoria. I replied vehemently, "Absolutely not Victoria, I will not entertain the thought of you giving Lily your blood." "What's wrong with you?" Augustine asked coldly. "Brain tumor." answered Victoria, very matter of fact. Augustine replied, "That would not make a difference as far as your blood being a viable choice for her." "Then its settled." declared Victoria. "No! Victoria, you do not understand. This is not like donating a pint, we would need all of your blood, you would die." I exclaimed, trying to impart the severity of her suggestion.

"I am already dying. What's the difference if it's now or in six months? If I could save Lily as my family did you, what nobler way to die? Besides, she would be saving me as well. I do not want to endure the pain any longer, and it is going to get much worse. I will be blind and slowly die with out my independence or dignity. Besides, it is not your choice."

Just then Lily screamed out in agony. I cradled her in my arms as her cells slowly died. Each cell inside her body was undergoing a dramatic evolution, entering a state of suspended animation as the transition cascades outward from her organs to her skeleton, to her skin and remaining tissues. The transitioned cells quickly convert all the blood in the body to food to reanimate their functions. As a newly transitioned vampire, Lily will wake with a hunger so painful it causes madness. Just as Lily began to open her eyes, Victoria took a knife from the tea set and drew it across her throat. As she slipped to the ground small beads of red became a bright crimson line that slowly started to seep down her neck. With blinding speed, Lily leapt out of my arms and sunk her newly formed fangs into the spot where blood had started to flow. I stood momentarily stunned by the turn of events, and watched Victoria smile as the light slowly left her eyes.

THE END OF BOOK ONE.